W9-BHW-798

Rumspringa's Hope is a story of true love. A story of finding your purpose in life. A story of following God's will. When Emma is reunited with Caleb, her world is no longer as simple as she thought it was. She must now figure out what her purpose is and who God intends for her to marry. Delightful and thought provoking. I definitely recommend it.

—Cynthia Hickey
Author of *Cooking Up Love* and *Taming the Sheriff*

The heart of any Amish story lies in the struggle of the Plain People to deal with the world outside the confines of their simple life—a world that threatens to crush them with its fast pace and contradictory values. In *Rumspringa's Hope* Beth Shriver puts her finger on this conflict, and with deft storytelling brings it out into the open for the reader first to see and then to understand. Woven into this delightful story is an unresolved romance, unexpected adventure, and a heartwarming conclusion, and when you come to the end of *Rumspringa's Hope*, you will have a deeper grasp of the Amish way. Well done, Beth.

—Patrick E. Craig
Author of *A Quilt for Jenna*, *The Road Home*, and *Jenny's Choice*

The SPIRIT of the AMISH
BOOK ONE

Rumspringa's Hope

BETH SHRIVER

REALMS

Most Charisma House Book Group products are available at special quantity discounts for bulk purchase for sales promotions, premiums, fund-raising, and educational needs. For details, write Charisma House Book Group, 600 Rinehart Road, Lake Mary, Florida 32746, or telephone (407) 333-0600.

Rumspringa's Hope by Beth Shriver
Published by Realms
Charisma Media/Charisma House Book Group
600 Rinehart Road
Lake Mary, Florida 32746
www.charismahouse.com

This book or parts thereof may not be reproduced in any form, stored in a retrieval system, or transmitted in any form by any means—electronic, mechanical, photocopy, recording, or otherwise—without prior written permission of the publisher, except as provided by United States of America copyright law.

Scripture quotations are from the King James Version of the Bible and the Holy Bible, New International Version. Copyright © 1973, 1978, 1984, International Bible Society. Used by permission.

Although this story is depicted from the town of Lititz, Pennsylvania, and the surrounding area, the characters created are fictitious. The traditions are similar to the Amish ways, but because all groups are different with dialogue, rules, and culture, they may vary from what your conception may be.

Copyright © 2014 by Beth Shriver
All rights reserved

Cover design by Bill Johnson

Visit the author's website at www.BethShriverWriter.com.

Library of Congress Cataloging-in-Publication Data:
An application to register this book for cataloging has been submitted to the Library of Congress.
International Standard Book Number: 978-1-62136-599-0
E-book ISBN: 978-1-62136-600-3

First edition

14 15 16 17 18—987654321
Printed in the United States of America

To Ty, my husband, for encouraging me to do what I love to do.

The person who sows seeds of kindness
will have a perpetual harvest.
—Amish Proverb

Chapter One

Emma stood at the foot of the ladder looking up at her brother. "If you don't get down from there I'm coming up after you."

"There's no use trying to talk me out of it." Mark stopped and tucked in his chin so he could stare down at her. "You're too scared of heights to climb a single step." He grinned and again turned his attention to the window above him as he climbed a few more steps. The farm *haus* and the ladder belonged to their neighbor, Roy, whose daughter had caught Mark's eye. Roy was known for his bad temper.

Emma cringed, knowing what would happen if Roy caught wind of Mark's latest escapade. She stamped her foot. "Mark, now! Get down."

Her brother didn't bother to acknowledge her words. He'd almost reached the top of the ladder, and his focus was entirely on the window above him.

The cold February night air froze her bones, and the anxiety made her chest tighten. She longed to walk away from their neighbor's farm to the warmth of their own *haus*. There maybe she could breathe easier.

But somebody had to watch over her errant little brother to keep him in check. It seemed just about everyone else had given up on him. Even their *daed,* Ivan, and their *mamm,* Rebecca, seemed not to know what to do.

"Come down this instant," she whispered, her voice hoarse.

He peered at her from the top of the ladder, his head almost even with the window sill, and shot her a look of triumph.

"You're going to get it." She tried to squeeze more air into her lungs to get more words out, but they caught in her throat.

Just then Roy's daughter let out a scream.

Mark scampered down the ladder, nearly falling from the last few rungs. He ran past Emma and headed for home, leaving her alone in the dark. She heard voices inside the house, then all was quiet.

"Slow down..." She could barely squeeze out the words. She doubled over and into a coughing spell.

By the time she made it home, Mark had disappeared into his bedroom. All the others were asleep.

Emma was too exhausted to deal with him anyway, but come tomorrow there would be a penance to pay.

Chapter Two

The following morning the bleak Pennsylvania sky hung dark and low with a threat of snow. Emma sat up in bed and listened to the commotion downstairs. Roy's voice was loud enough to bring her *daed* stomping into the kitchen.

Emma pushed off her warm quilt and climbed out of bed. She dressed quickly and took slow steps down the stairs. Mark was in her line of vision. His smirk made her want to smack him for all the trouble he caused. Roy was to his side, though apparently looking at her father and mother.

"I'm a *gut* neighbor," Roy bellowed, "but I've had enough of your son. He's getting worse as he's getting older."

"So, what have I done?" Mark shrugged and grinned.

Mamm gave Mark an exasperated look. "Let loose a herd of thirty milk cows, stayed out all night, and believe me, I could go on," *Mamm* said.

The veins in Roy's neck pulsed with anger. "Just two days ago I caught Mark throwing rocks at Naomi's window. And then last night…the ladder…" he sputtered, his face turning purple. "…her window. You were climbing…"

"Is that true, son?" Their *daed*'s voice was taut.

Emma stepped into the kitchen and joined in. "And getting caught with a beer." She shook her head.

"Sis, not you too." Mark tilted his head in that way the girls loved. His charm might work on others, but it didn't for Emma. She'd seen it too many times.

Emma held up a hand. "I don't want to hear it." She'd had

her fill of him and the way he'd been chasing after Roy's daughter. Chores sounded better than listening to what was sure to be an explosion once Roy got started.

"And he still owes me some time to pay for the window he broke," Roy said.

Emma's eyes shifted to Mark's. "You didn't even finish working it off?"

That must have given him too much time with Naomi. For whatever reason she seemed to be enamored with him now. He was a handsome one and charming in his own way, but a pain in Emma's side. Her patience was worn as thin as Roy's.

Not wanting to hear another word of the argument, she slipped out of the kitchen and then out of the house to breathe in some fresh air. She was about to return to the house and start the first batch of laundry when the sound of boots scuffling in the pebbled dirt made her pause.

She knew the sound of Zeb Bowman's gait as he walked closer. Even buried in a warm, heavy coat, his tall, skinny frame couldn't be missed, like a scarecrow in a cornfield. It wasn't exactly a welcome sound or sight.

He gave her a smile.

"*Hallo*, Zeb. What brings you here so early?" It wasn't early for an Amish, but it was just too early to see him.

Emma was past the age most women married, but much younger than Zeb's thirty-three years. Her *mamm* was set on finding her a suitor and seemed to think the widower would be suitable. Emma had no interest in anyone—except for one. And he was no longer part of the community.

"It's a beautiful morning. And I have news to share with you…and something to ask." Zeb's customary greeting made her realize what a stressful day it had already been. The sun hadn't reached the middle of the sky yet. And now she had to give him her attention.

"Actually it isn't so beautiful."

He took one large step into the house with Emma, standing within inches in front of her, looking down at her with his dark blue eyes. "Your *bruder* again?"

"*Jah*, but that's nothing new." She didn't feel like small talk, and there wasn't anything new to tell.

He nodded but said nothing more about her *bruder.* "I can't stay long. Do you have a minute?" Zeb had a way of conversing that made it difficult for others to disagree. He was kind enough and soft on the eyes, but she wasn't ready to say yes just yet. Others had vied for his attention when his wife died. Amish women didn't remarry. The men most always did. For whatever reason, Zeb continued in his attempts to court her.

Before he could even get another word out, her throat constricted. She tried to breathe but her lungs were working as hard as they could with no relief. Zeb held her shoulders as her forehead started to sweat.

"It seems to be getting worse. Maybe you should go see Doc." His stare confused her, and then she realized how bad her coughing must sound to him. She didn't want anyone to make a fuss. She shrugged him off and went to the house. He followed a few feet behind.

The large white clapboard home had sparse furniture except in the kitchen where eight seats filled the large room. The fire in the family room warmed the cozy area. Multicolored rag rugs warmed the wood floors in every room. Four bedrooms were just enough to accommodate her family, with a washroom to share and outhouse out back.

She slipped off her coat and took Zeb's. He sat on the couch close to the fire and rubbed his hands together.

"You said you wanted to ask me something?" Emma plopped a wicker basket down on the family room floor.

"*Jah*, you know how well my dairy farm is doing. I've got fifty Holstein cattle now. Doubled the number over the last year." He hesitated, staring at his hands, then looked up, his eyes seeking hers. "Well, I think it's time to settle down."

Emma froze.

Zeb had a large, sprawling farm, but used most of it for grazing and used only a small area for growing crops. She questioned whether that was one reason her *mamm* was so adamant that she spend time with him. He would provide a secure life for whomever he married.

Mamm poked her head into the room and smiled. "Well, Zeb, I didn't know you were here. Would you like some coffee to warm ya a little?" She wrung her weathered hands, waiting for his response.

Zeb kept his gaze on Emma. "This isn't such a good time. I'll save my question for later." Then he looked to *Mamm* and smiled. "No coffee, but *danke*."

The sounds of her sisters' baking lessons carried from the kitchen, which was a relief for Emma. The smell of something burning and the squeals and laughter were a welcome distraction.

Emma couldn't help but grin, although she was sure her *mamm* didn't find it humorous at all. "What is it this time?"

"Cheese bread," Maria sang out. She appeared behind Martha in the doorway. They both had strawberry-blonde hair like their *mamm*. People always remarked that they looked so much alike, despite the gap in their ages.

"*Ach*, my favorite." Emma squeezed Zeb's hand and genuinely smiled for the first time that day. "I should go in and help."

He chuckled. "I wish you would accept my help every now and then." One side of his mouth lifted.

She nodded, having heard the words too many times. She knew he wanted to be around her family, but why? The more they knew him, the more she felt obligated to consider him. And he knew that. "Thanks for stopping by."

He buttoned up his jacket then tipped his hat, like he did every time they parted, and turned to leave. "You're welcome to come over for dinner, if you like."

She hesitated. Her *haus* was her refuge, and she took every opportunity to be there. She didn't always feel comfortable sharing a meal with Zeb's family. He had built his *mamm*, *daed*, and younger brother Merv their own *haus* attached to his, which was common, but premature due to his wife's passing.

He looked so hopeful, she couldn't refuse. "I'll be there in time to help with dinner."

"All right, then." He took a moment to catch her eye and lifted a hand to say good-bye.

The smell of spices filled the air as Emma strolled into the kitchen. *Mamm*'s herbal tea was brewing on the stove. She heard Maria talking with her in the kitchen. Martha was off fetching eggs. The room was warm with humidity from pots boiling on the stove. *Mamm* stood over them sprinkling in some salt, and Maria cut up sausages. Emma walked to the large window over the sink that opened to the corn field.

"This is the first time I've been asked to go to singing." Maria twisted a straggling lock of her reddish hair and sat down at the large wooden table. Maria's tight lips drawn together told

Emma what she needed to know to catch up with the conversation. Emma and Maria shared most everything, from their hearts to their hairpins. There was only one other person in whom Emma had ever confided in the same way.

"I understand, but you need a chaperone." Strands of gray hair had come loose from *Mamm*'s tied-back hair and seemed to float around her plump face as she went to the sink. She washed her hands and looked over at Emma. "You've been working harder than usual this morning."

"*Jah*, I'll help with the noon meal." Emma nodded, and gathered the silverware, not wanting to draw attention to her work well done, partly so as not to appear prideful.

"Emma, will you chaperone me to singing on Sunday?" Maria twisted her hands, waiting for Emma's answer.

Emma wasn't sure what to say. She didn't want to get in the middle of the obvious tension between Maria and *Mamm*. She took extra time in answering, hoping one of them would intervene before she had to. "*Jah*, if *Mamm* approves," she finally said.

Maria beamed at Emma for only a moment until *Mamm* lifted a hand to speak again.

"Your brother can chaperone." *Mamm* had her back to them, cleaning up the kitchen from the breakfast meal.

"*Nee*, *Mamm*. He'd ruin it somehow."

Her sister was probably right, but what else could her parents do? They had tried everything they could think of, but nothing had improved his behavior. *Mamm* seemed to be weakening; it had been apparent for some time now that reasoning with him time and again was wearing her down.

"It would be nice for Mark to be with you, Maria. Let Emma spend time with her friends." *Mamm* never met her gaze, avoiding conflict that might arise with her answer.

Maria's shoulders slumped, and Emma knew she had disappointed her. "I'll ask him to be on his best behavior." She wanted to do more than that, but it did no good to dwell on the issue. Emma questioned why her brother had changed so much when he became an adolescent. He'd always had a lot of energy, but this was different.

Maria huffed out a breath and went back to the counter where she was preparing the meat for Stromboli. "Some are talking about *rumspringa*."

She didn't look up, just kept working as if she'd said nothing at all. Although it was considered a rite of passage, *rumspringa* was still frowned upon by most parents. Emma understood you couldn't condone such a custom unless it was something you'd grown up knowing about and accepted by most of the Amish communities.

"Why now? Spring planting isn't for a few more months." *Mamm* continued with her work, adding ingredients. She stirred the mix together with more force than usual. Talk of *rumspringa* clearly upset her.

"A lot say they're going." Maria sighed. "They're going to talk about it after singing." She twined her fingers together as if sorry she'd said the words out loud.

Emma frowned. "I've heard that many say they are going this year, but most don't actually go." Emma didn't know what this group would do, but she hoped they would go to the city. She had always wanted to see what was out there, not to live, but to serve.

Emma went about slicing the salami and cheese while *Mamm* cut up the onion. As *Mamm* waited for the water to boil she glanced over at Maria. "It's early to be thinking about something that's happening in the spring.

"*Jah*, but there's been a lot of talk lately for some reason."

Maria's words spoke volumes. Emma couldn't imagine she truly wanted to go. Maria was a gentle soul who seemed very content on the farm. She wouldn't know what to do in the city, but then most Amish didn't.

Mamm's face tightened. Her cheeks were taut and eyes dark. "I see." When *Mamm* was upset, she held her tongue, lest she say something that she couldn't take back. She didn't have the patience to talk through the issue.

Emma waited to see what she would do at the moment.

"Emma, let's go make the soap." *Mamm* wiped her hands on her apron as she walked through the mudroom. They both watched her go.

"I should have expected that. I shouldn't even talk about it." Maria grunted, and then gestured toward the door. "Go ahead. I'll finish this."

"*Danke*, Maria. But you know she's only upset because she doesn't want to lose any of us. And you would never go. She knows that."

And at that moment she felt for her *mamm*. The talk about *rumspringa* clearly upset her, and it was something Mark might actually do. *Mamm*'s denial and her *daed's* ignoring the problem only made things worse.

She sighed. "*Jah*, I just wish she would do something about Mark. He's too hard to deal with anymore."

"I know how you feel, but I think there's more of a reason for his bad choices. I don't think he can control himself like we can."

"Like what?" Maria's eyebrows furrowed, and she crossed her arms across her chest, clearly ready to reject whatever reason Emma presented to forgive their brother.

"I don't know, for sure. But sometimes I see him struggling with whatever it is." Emma was going on a hunch. She didn't know how to explain it and admitted to herself that she'd lost patience with him as much as Maria had.

Maria frowned, and then went back to the misty pot that was rumbling with a strong boiling hum.

Emma grabbed her coat and followed behind her *mamm*, who was walking too quickly to catch up with. *Mamm*'s arms swung back and forth as her short legs kept stride. The thought of having time with her and making the soap had lost its appeal. *Mamm* would remain tight-lipped until she could get this off her chest by talking with *Daed*.

As Emma stepped into the old, red barn, she thought about better times, before the problems had begun. "*Mamm*, what started Mark's outbursts and such?" It struck Emma that they had started about the time her coughing fits got worse.

As she watched *Mamm* gather the necessary supplies, her heart ached for her—for all of them. Mark was not easy to live with.

"He's just hard headed. He'll come out of it soon enough." She paused and glanced at Emma. "A lot of the burden has gone to you. He tends to lean on you a bit more than the others."

"I don't know if I want that responsibility."

"It's already done, it's not your choice."

The cold wind moaned through the slits in the wooden sides of the barn. Emma lit a couple of gas lanterns and placed the glass chimneys over the flames. They would give light and a little warmth.

Mamm grabbed a handful of lard from a metal bucket. "Take as much as you can carry."

Emma had wanted her *mamm* to show her how to make soap, but until today Maria had always gotten to it before she did. Being the oldest, Emma's duties were greater and more demanding. She took on the role well, but sometimes wished for the small pleasure of something different to do—something an opportunity like this provided.

She pulled up her apron and loaded it full of the lard until it was too heavy to hold. Following her *mamm,* she dumped the lard in a large kettle in the barnyard. "How much do we need?"

Mamm's mood lightened, and they both started enjoying the project at hand.

"Six pounds of lard, two-and-a-half pints of water, and one pound of lye will make plenty to last awhile. We'll have enough to sell at the Weaver's store too."

Zeb's parents owned a small store and had a produce stand by the road. Emma often offered to help when he took his turn selling the goods they grew and raised.

Emma heated the kettle, and when it started to boil, stirred the mixture. Once it melted, they weighed it.

"Now we let it cool, put the lye in with the water, and then let it set."

While they waited, Emma watched the fluffy clouds glide by and thought about Zeb. He was good to her—never raised his voice—and worked hard for his aging parents. There was no reason to discount him. She needed to stop thinking of wanting something—or someone—different.

Her *mamm* sat down next to her. "What's on your mind?"

"Nothing, really." She could hear what her mother would say and her own rebuttal, so what was the point of talking about her choice in a husband?

"Are you happy with Zeb?"

"*Jah*, sure." Their marriage would tie Zeb's and her *daed*'s land together, making the largest farm in the community. It wasn't something she could protest even if she wanted to. She could be happy there.

"*Gut*. You will be glad you have it all behind and settle in." *Mamm* turned away and went to check the lard.

Emma put a hand on her chest. Her throat constricted. She fought for air.

"*Shhh*." *Mamm* stroked her back, shushing Emma.

Emma lifted a hand, stopping her *mamm*. "I'm better," she croaked.

"Doesn't sound like it. You should go see the doc. It's getting worse."

"*Jah*," she said just to appease her *mamm*. It would pass. It always had so far anyway.

They went about cleaning up while they waited. "Ready?" Emma took the lye over to the kettle with the lard.

"*Jah*, just stir until it's thick and coats the paddle in sheets." *Mamm* prepared the table to put the soap on to cut into bars. She laid a frame of squares they would fill with the melted soap, and then stood back to admire their work. "You're good at this, Emma."

"Adding some color to them would be nice. Like sky blue, green as the corn stalks, or yellow like the sun." Emma pictured the various hues she could add into the white soap.

Mamm nodded enthusiastically and wrapped her arm around Emma's waist. "*Jah*, you need to enjoy what makes you happy, Emma, not what you feel obliged to do." She smiled, still admiring the soap. "There are a lot of colors out there, pick your favorite."

Chapter Three

Three bonfires blazed against the dark night. Emma buttoned up her coat and moved closer to keep warm, mesmerized by the yellow licks of fire that spun up into the air above her. The chatter of what sounded like a hundred voices spread throughout the field, close to Abram Esh's barn. It would be seeded with corn, come spring, but tonight it was a place of revelry, socializing, and connecting for teens in the small town of Lititz. Most of the faces she knew, but some were strangers, coming from nearby townships for special occasions such as Sunday singing.

"Spring planting will be here sooner than we think," Zeb said to Abram, but his eyes followed Emma. She came up next to him, comforted that Abram was between them. They stood next to *die eltern*, who were preparing food and gathering drinks.

"If the weather cooperates, we should have a good cash crop this year," Abram said. He and Zeb talked more about crops while the teenagers chased each other hollering, telling jokes, and teasing one another. Emma felt a little annoyed, but then, she had been told she was an old soul, and what she considered misconduct was playfulness to others. She wrapped her arms around her coat for warmth and walked over to Maria, Mark, and his friend Andy Lapp. She'd heard enough about the weather.

Maria's hair was pinned up, but auburn wisps always escaped, and her *kapp* was disheveled. "I didn't know there were so many our ages." She turned her gaze toward Mark. "Did you?"

Emma straightened the *kapp* over Maria's head.

Mark had a nervous itch, and he seemed to always scratch his head when he was talking about something important. "*Nee*, I bet the Eshes are wishing they hadn't volunteered their place for the get-together." Mark answered Maria, and then glanced at Andy. It was true, they had never had this many show up for singing.

"Where did they all come from?" Mark took a swig of soda. Emma reached over, took it from him, read the label, and handed it back. He held back his anger well, but she saw the annoyance in his eyes. She couldn't help but monitor him. He seemed drawn to life on the wild side. He didn't understand he was too young to act that way without serious consequences.

"All around Lancaster." She should mingle, but she didn't have much desire. She was older and felt every one of her twenty-three years. It seemed everyone around her was barely sixteen, the youngest age to take part in *rumspringa*.

Andy ran a hand over his red hair, which matched the freckles across his nose. "Everybody seems to know each other."

Maria pointed ahead a few feet. "Not everyone." A group similar to theirs huddled together, observing the mass of young adults. A few others clustered around, as well. "The rowdy ones are just more noticeable." One dumped his plastic cup of beer on an unsuspecting partyer's head. The two chased each other around as the others watched laughing.

"And the ones having fun," Mark chimed in. "Right, Emma?" He grinned. He was one of the youngsters who would take advantage of every minute of freedom.

"You worry me silly, without any thought for anyone's concerns."

"Lighten up, sis." When she didn't respond, he took two steps and grabbed her by the arm. "Did Andy tell you Caleb is here?"

Emma caught her breath. Her throat went dry. She took a moment before she turned to Andy, Caleb's brother.

"Sorry. I didn't know if you'd want to see him." Andy shrugged as his neck turned scarlet. He knew about his brother's relationship with Emma and that it was a touchy subject.

Finding out this way that Caleb Lapp was there didn't help matters. Emma tried not to show her annoyance. "Why didn't you say something?"

Mark stared back at her with large, dark eyes and scratched his head. He quickly took her hand and dragged her away. "I figured Andy would, with his big mouth."

As they walked through the mass of teens and a few young adults, Emma stopped and did a double-take. Even though she'd been told Caleb was there, seeing him was still a shock. Old memories she'd stuffed away came back to her. She looked away and concentrated on breathing. She couldn't do this. It was too hard and had taken her so long to forget about him and court another. She didn't want to remember everything all over again. She tried to turn to head back toward the fire.

"Mark, I'm not—"

"*Nee*, he wants to see you."

"You told him I'm here?" She shook her head as tingles spread up her arms.

Caleb had a gentle way about him, which was why it surprised many in her community when he not only left, but also helped others when they left for *rumspringa,* as well.

The deacons and minister had been frustrated that such a fine young man would be a part of such disappointing conduct. When the bishop noticed what was happening, he told Caleb there would be no communication, not even with his own family. He wasn't baptized, so it was a touchy situation. It seemed harsh at the time, but he'd created a hole in the dike so large, it drained their community. Most came back eventually, but it had taken more time than usual.

"Actually, he asked about you. I thought you'd want to know." Mark wiggled his eyebrows at her. It bothered her—this whole situation did. She turned back to find Zeb, hoping he wasn't watching her. She didn't want to feel guilty about seeing Caleb, but a growing part of her wanted to talk to him.

"I'm not sure about that." She glanced at Mark to see whether she could tell if he was telling the truth, but couldn't see if his eyes were calm or wild. Either way, she would say *hallo*.

"What ever happened to him?" Maria said, she and Andy having caught up with them. Maria was probably as curious as Emma was, and it was better that she ask the question.

"Who knows, since the deacons won't let him talk to anybody." Mark always knew the gossip, but also thought a lot of Caleb so would hopefully be kind in his words.

"Maybe because he started taking the *rumspringa* groups to the city," Maria said.

Maria briefly looked at Emma. She knew how hard it was for Emma to hear it all over again.

As Emma approached Caleb, he stopped midsentence and stared at her until she was standing in front of him. He stuck his hands in his pockets as his smile tipped to the side. His brown locks were tinted with gold, and when he turned to her, she tried not to admire his strong jaw.

"Caleb, I'm surprised you're here."

He grunted a laugh, and Emma noticed how her comment sounded. It probably wasn't the first time he'd been told that tonight. "I heard there was going to be a big get-together and thought it would be a good time to see everyone again."

"Do you miss being here?"

He gave her a crooked smile and then looked down as if he wanted to say *jah*, but couldn't. "Yeah, I do."

"No Pennsylvania-Dutch anymore?" She grinned, and he did too. Emma missed his Pennsylvania-Dutch, but he seemed to be more comfortable using plain English.

"Guess I've gotten out of the habit. It sounds pretty silly in Philly."

Her eyebrows shot up, and she took a step back. The big city was only an hour and a half away, but the opposite of the life she led. She couldn't imagine softhearted Caleb living there. "That's where you live now?"

"*Jah.*" He grinned and watched her closely. "I didn't plan to, but that's how it's worked out. At least for now."

She laughed at his choice of words, remembering how much she'd missed him. "I can't imagine you there."

He'd left with the promise to return and make things right. She hadn't seen him again and had sulked for days when she accepted that he wasn't coming back

He rubbed his hands together. "It's very different, but I feel called to be there."

"I can't imagine what that must be like. What do you do there?"

"We take in the homeless, runaways, substance abusers... the list goes on." He couldn't hide his smile. He obviously loved what he did. She wondered how many people here knew who he really was.

"That sounds tough and a little scary."

"Yeah, it can be." He looked at the farm and watched the teens around them. "But what I do the most is evangelize."

Her head went back, showing her astonishment. "Really?" She wanted to say more, ask more questions. She couldn't get over the feeling she wanted to do exactly those things he was doing. She could envision him helping others, showing them God's love through his actions, but not in a city like Philadelphia. There was too much of…everything. She wanted to go, see what he did, and how. But in Philadelphia?

"I feel a calling to be there, help these kids out when they go there on *rumspringa*. Hopefully keep them from making bad choices."

"I didn't know that's what you were doing there." She stopped, overwhelmed by this information. Once it started to sink in, she could see how Caleb's soft heart and straightforward personality would be a good mix for this type of work. "Where do you live?"

"When I first got there, I went to a Mennonite church." He paused, probably waiting for Emma to say what she was thinking. Most Amish and Mennonites didn't mingle, having broken off into their own sects long ago.

"I still attend there. Good people. They support my mission, so I can at least have a place to lay my head and get a hot meal." His smile touched something inside her. He was living out a scripture that sprang to mind.

"Matthew 6:25: 'Do not worry about your life, what you will eat or drink…'" She whispered the rest, with growing admiration for this young man of whom she had thought poorly for so long.

"Finish it." He grinned. "Your memory of the Scripture is still better than mine."

She didn't want to be prideful. But this was Caleb. "'Do not worry about your life, what you will eat or drink; or about your body, what you will wear. Is not life more important than food, and the body more important than clothes?'" She didn't know if this was the life he lived. If so, she felt even more admiration for him than she already had. "Is this what you try to follow?"

Caleb nodded. "*Try* is the key word." He grinned, and then let out a breath and gave her a sad smile as he looked her over. "You're a beautiful young lady, Emma. Even more so than when I left. But then I always knew that about you."

She squirmed a little, lifting one foot and then the other. The way he looked at her made her uncomfortable, but he was just discovering her again, the girl he'd known now a woman.

He held up a hand. "I'm sorry. I didn't mean to be so blunt. I've forgotten myself being in Amish land again."

"*Danke* for saying so. It didn't sound like something you'd say." And then she saw how different their cultures were now and how it had changed him in such a short time.

"You're analyzing me now, aren't you?" He smiled again, showing off his dimple. "Wondering how I can live in a city filled with evil. You think I've become like them, sinful and full of lust." He leaned closer, his big, blue eyes staring into hers. "I'm still the same guy, Emma. I just live in a different place."

She knew her eyes were as wide as a baby deer's, but she couldn't get over seeing the old Caleb through this amazing man. "I hadn't thought of it like that. But you have changed, Caleb." She noticed the difference in him, and cared about him enough to worry that he might yet stumble.

"So have you." He said it straight-faced, capturing her gaze with intensity. She wondered what he meant and was about to ask him when Mark showed up.

"I knew you two would have a lot to talk about."

So the *charming* Mark was here tonight. Emma hated to be cynical, but she never knew what to expect from him.

"It's good to see you together again," Mark said.

"Hey, Mark, I need to talk to your sister a little longer. Do you mind?" Caleb was good with Mark, talking to him with the respect not often shown by those who were enduring his behavior on a daily basis. And Mark responded well to Caleb.

"Sure, sure. I'm glad you're back." He slapped Caleb on the shoulder and winked at Emma. It irritated her, but she did her best to look the other way.

When she turned back to Caleb, his expression had changed. "Is there something wrong?"

"That would depend on you. Even more so, your folks." He turned his head to watch Mark stop and talk with an unfamiliar group. Emma wavered as to how well he'd be received.

"What is it?"

"Has Mark talked about his plans to you or your parents?" Caleb tilted his head slightly, waiting.

"*Nee*, what is this about, Caleb?" As much as she wanted to know, part of her didn't. Anything involving her brother seemed to lead to problems.

"Well, I never thought I'd see you here." Zeb strode up behind Emma and took her hand in his. Caleb glanced down at their fingers twined together and smirked.

"Hello, Zeb. How've you been?"

"We're doing great. How about you?" He couldn't make it more obvious that they were a couple. Why he felt the need to do so, Emma didn't know. Zeb wasn't one to feel intimidated by anyone. Maybe Caleb was the first.

"I was just telling Emma about my move to Philly." Caleb waited. He seemed to know what to expect as far as the judgment and head shaking that went on when he shared the information. Just like Emma had done.

"What keeps you up there?" Zeb's question seemed neutral. He was good at that—prying for information in a nonchalant way. But he was Old Order through and through. Some asked for leniency, but not him. He considered it weak to indulge in any ways of the world.

"It's really very interesting, Zeb, now that I understand everything Caleb does."

"I have a ministry there at one of the churches." Caleb was being cordial too. But she expected that from him. Zeb could get a person going at times. He did have certain demands on him. The deacons, bishops, and minister would expect his involvement in the community when his time came.

"Really? What church?"

"Mennonite." Caleb placed the bait. The nicest guy would win, but Emma wasn't sure at the moment which one it would be. Caleb seemed bolder now than he had been before.

Zeb grunted. "Switched to the other side, eh?"

"Different church. Same Savior."

Zeb lifted his eyebrows. "Can't argue with that." He held out his hand. "I hope it goes well for you."

"Thanks, Zeb." They did a one-pump shake.

He paused and tightened his forehead. "For what?"

Caleb kept his eyes on Zeb's, taking his time to answer. "For not giving me a hard time."

He looked over at Emma, and then back to Caleb. "Gotta pick your battles."

Emma's jaw dropped, and Caleb grinned. "I'll stop by tomorrow, Emma." He nodded to Zeb, and Emma readied herself for an earful of questions from Zeb as to why Caleb would be coming over.

The thing about it was, she didn't know.

Chapter Four

Emma put the last container of milk in the cooler and finished tidying up before heading to the barn to find her *daed*.

How will Mamm and Daed feel about Caleb coming for a visit? she wondered. Her parents were likely to be leery about him being around. A soft whistle carried throughout the barn, and as it grew louder, she realized she'd soon find out. "Mornin', *Daed*."

She stamped her boots on the ground to keep warm. "Ahh, I didn't see you there." Her *daed* nodded toward the pasteurizer and tipped his straw hat back over his thinning gray hair. "Your brother do the milking?"

Emma hated being in the middle. If she told her *daed* Mark hadn't finished the job, her brother would cause her trouble. But if she didn't tell *Daed* the truth, he would find out eventually. "*Jah*, but not without a battle." She kept her eyes downcast and busied herself rearranging the glass milk bottles in the cooler, willing the gas-powered machine to separate the milk faster so she'd be done before Caleb got there.

She glanced up at her father as he yanked a rope into a knot and walked over to a barrel full of water. As he lifted the lid, he spoke calmly to her. "Save the battles for me."

"Confronting him doesn't do any good. I just want the chores done."

"It's best that you don't. I'll deal with what comes your way."

Emma knew that wouldn't work. She was the only one

Mark listened to. *Daed* was a close second, but he was getting too old and tired to bother with him. As soon as *Daed* confronted Mark, he would know she'd told *Daed,* and he'd have a fit. It was better if she just handled him herself.

Daed stuck the rope through a hole in the lid of the barrel. Then he knotted the other end, which had a flat, round piece of cork floating on top of the water. "This should help to see when the water's getting low."

Any animals in the barn needed fresh water daily. Mark had slacked off once, which was more than *Daed* would tolerate. Now the job left to Maria and Mark was mucking stalls. *Daed* seemed to be the only one who could give Mark consequences that he followed through with. But it wasn't enough for *Daed* to be the only one Mark listened to in a family of six. Emma heard the sound of boots scuffing the ground and peeked outside to see if it was Caleb. He stood tall, his brown hair hung just over his collar—an unacceptable length for an Amish man—but was he still Amish?

"We have a visitor," Emma told her *daed*.

Daed stretched his neck to see who she was looking at, and frowned when he saw Caleb. "What's he doing here?"

"He wants to talk to me about Mark. They seem to have gotten reacquainted at the bonfire last night."

Daed shook his head. "I'm glad you and Maria aren't interested in that nonsense. *Rumspringa* has gone from get-togethers in the community to leaving and doing who knows what out there." He hiked a thumb over his shoulder—ironically in the direction of the big city. But Emma agreed with him—and with the majority of those who weren't enamored with the outside world.

"I should tend to Caleb."

Her *daed* was a gentle man, but strict. Each one of her

family members would get a reprimand from the deacons if Caleb continued to spend time with Mark. Her *daed* grunted and said, "If he's doing anything that will help your brother, I suppose I'll allow it."

"*Danke, Daed.*" With that she left the barn, leaving him to finish separating the milk, something she would never do in ordinary circumstances. As she approached Caleb, he slowed his walk and waited for her. His broad shoulders and strong physique were pleasing to look at.

"Mornin'," she greeted him.

When he smiled, memories of when they were together flooded her mind—even the ones she tried to hold back. He was a handsome one, which was the first attraction, but he also had a missionary's heart. She admired that about him. At times she dreamed of going to other countries or perhaps in the United States to help others, but Amish didn't do missionary work. It was an impossible dream.

"It's good to see you." His smile told her he was happy to see her. There was a contentment about him that relaxed her even though they were near her *daed's* listening ears.

She felt a sudden smile take over her face.

His grin widened. "What are you thinking?" He stuffed his hands into his coat pockets. "For a moment it felt like you hadn't ever left." How many times had he walked down the lane to their *haus* and greeted her, full of excitement as he told her his plans. Now here he was after living in the city and evangelizing. A piece of her heart tightened as she imagined doing the same.

"Not that much time has passed since I lived here." He offered his arm, and she hooked hers through. He led her to the dormant corn field that would soon be tilled and seeded, and then to the porch in back of the *haus*. They sat down and looked back out over the field. The dark Pennsylvania soil was rich with nutrients to yield a good crop and seemed to go on forever. "Can't see where the field ends, even without stalks of corn hiding it," Caleb said, breaking the short silence.

She sat across from him on wooden chairs Mark and her *daed* had made. "Do you miss it here?"

He nodded. "But I'm where I'm supposed to be." He turned to look over at her. "Are you?"

Emma wasn't sure. If that were true, why did the twist in her heart tell her differently? "I suppose."

Caleb turned to her. "Why do you hesitate?"

She shrugged. "I admire you spreading the Word, especially in a place like Philadelphia." She lifted her eyes to his, hoping he may have an answer to feed her hungry heart.

"Well, there would be no point in doing it here." He grinned.

She let it go. There was no reason to continue pining over it. If it was meant to be, she would have an answer. She quickly changed the subject. "Why did you want to talk about Mark?"

Caleb took a moment before answering. "Mark wants to go on *rumspringa*."

Emma put a hand on her chest and stared. "Did he tell you this?"

Caleb nodded. "He wants me to be the one to tell you and your parents. I told him that he would need to do that—that it was part of showing maturity. I'm telling you this now to give you time to sort things out."

"He can't go, Caleb." She almost scoffed, but as she looked deeper into Caleb's eyes, she knew this could be a real possibility. "Can he?"

"I don't know how you can stop him; he's sixteen now. But I wanted to make sure he told all of you. I worried he might just take off when the time came."

"*Danke*, Caleb. I'll let my parents know."

"Let us know what?" *Daed* went up from the side of the porch and stood in front of them, looking over the field, creating a quiet tension between them. "Caleb, I heard you were back making a visit."

"I thought it would be a good time to see everyone and spend some time here."

"The deacons give you their blessing?" He still hadn't looked Caleb in the eyes but seemed to be very interested in what he was doing around their farm. Rightly so if the deacons were to get involved.

"They know I'm here. Your field will soon be ripe for seeding."

"*Jah*, should be a good crop." He turned toward Caleb. "So what's this about?"

Caleb looked to Emma as if to see how she wanted to proceed, but she hoped he'd be the one to tell *Daed*. She didn't even want to be standing next to him when he heard, let alone be the one giving him the news.

Caleb looked straight at her *daed*. "Mark is interested in *rumspringa*."

Daed grunted. "I'm sure he's curious."

Caleb nodded, and then turned to face Emma's *daed*. "He wants to participate."

Daed didn't respond, just kept looking over the dirt field. "You encourage him to do this?"

"*Daed*." Emma frowned at him, but Caleb touched her shoulder before she could say anything more.

"I wouldn't do that, Mr. Miller. I didn't do it before. Everyone made their own choice. Just like Mark is now." *Daed* cleared his throat. It sounded closer to a growl. "You expect me to believe that?"

Caleb shook his head. "It doesn't matter. This is about your son, not me. I just thought you should know." He turned to Emma. "It's always good to see you."

She looked from *Daed* to Caleb, not sure what to say or to whom. "I'll walk with you, Caleb."

"*Nee*, you stay right here." *Daed* refused to look at Caleb as he walked back down the path, and then he turned and rambled away.

When her *daed* was out of sight, Emma caught up with Caleb. The run warmed her up and took her breath away by the time she got to him. "I'm sorry, Caleb."

"Slow down, are you all right?" He cupped her cheek and frowned. "Don't apologize for what someone else did," he said, clearly but gently.

"But he shouldn't treat you that way."

"Your *daed* has a right to how he feels. Besides, it wasn't an ideal situation with me being the one to tell him."

"I should have told him, not you." She thought back to the moment Caleb paused long enough for her to step in. She didn't, not only because she knew how much her *daed* would be against this, but also because she knew Caleb would say it the best way possible.

"Stop worrying."

His selfless responses made her feel petty and like she was complaining.

"So, now it's up to my parents to deal with this?" She found herself finding ways to keep him there. His bright eyes, confident stride, and hair brushing against his collar invigorated her senses. And he was living out the appointment *Gott* gave him.

Did I receive the same message but miss it somewhere along the way?

"No, it's Mark's. *Rumspringa* is a rite of passage. No one

should make Mark stay while the others go. Not that I agree, but it's part of the Amish ways."

As much as Caleb was right, she still didn't want to believe him. As difficult as it could be here for him in the community, she couldn't imagine him surrounded by the fast-paced city. "I suppose you're right."

"There will always be those who are curious and need to find out for themselves." Caleb let out a heavy breath, as if the world had landed on his shoulders.

Emma turned to him and took in Caleb's familiar blue eyes. "If Mark does go, will you keep an eye on him?"

"You know I'll try. But I can't promise anything. They're all on their own. Not like here."

Emma's breathing increased as she stared down the dirt path. It was difficult to hold back her persistent cough. Caleb would not accept what she tried to pass off to others as a common cold. "Why did you come to the bonfire last night, Caleb?"

He gave her a sharp look, but took his time to respond. "I hoped to see what I'm in for when these teens hit the city."

Searching his eyes, she saw something more. "You're not recruiting, you're discouraging them."

Caleb stuck his hands in his pockets. "No one would believe that now, would they?"

If only everyone knew how misunderstood Caleb was, they might finally let go of the past. He was in the city to serve, not encourage teens to leave their homes. But she wouldn't count on people understanding—not unless they learned what he did and how he did it. Watching over a group of teens in a foreign place had to be incredibly stressful. Yet, they surrounded him as if he were one of them. Surprising because he was older, and "old" was the last person an adolescent wanted to be around on *rumspringa*.

"*Danke* for coming by, Caleb. Will I see you again?"

"I might stick around for a while. It's good to see you, Emma."

Emma would see him the next day. She'd make sure of it.

Chapter Five

Zeb watched Caleb walk down the dirt road away from Emma's farm. He pushed back the heat that sprung up inside him, but he couldn't take his eyes off of Caleb, so the burn spread. The plans he'd made needed to kick into motion sooner than he'd anticipated. He had some arrangements to make. He'd been waiting too long not to do everything just as he intended.

Once Caleb was out of sight, Zeb continued walking to the Millers' *haus*, hoping Ivan would be there for him to talk with. The Millers had prime farmland, something he lacked now that so much of his land was devoted to grazing. Merging the two families would benefit them both, he was sure.

He knew he didn't have to talk with Ivan at this point in a courtship, but he wanted to win him over as much as Emma. He had a big surprise in mind for Emma. They'd been together long enough, and this would be so special, she wouldn't be able to say no to him.

As he walked up to the *haus,* he took in some deep breaths. He couldn't appear bothered by Caleb's visit. He knew from experience that the insecurity of a jealous person is less attractive, so he would make sure his emotions were intact. Emma and Caleb had a short but intense relationship before Caleb left—one Zeb had helped her get over. He didn't want to go through that again, even if there was only the slightest chance of losing her.

Before he could knock on the door, Mark stepped out. "Hey, Zeb." Mark pumped his hand.

He took advantage of Mark's jovial mood. "Where are you headed in such a hurry?"

"I heard Caleb was here and wanted to say *hallo*." Mark scanned the barnyard, and then stopped on Zeb.

"He just left." Zeb nodded toward the gravel lane.

Mark's shoulders slumped slightly. "*Ach*, I was hoping to find out about the trip."

"What trip is that?" Then it clicked. "*Rumspringa*?"

Mark nodded with vigor.

"You sure you're up for that?" Zeb was blunt with Mark at times and thought his family should be more so as well. There didn't seem to be any rhyme or reason as to what set him off, and right at this moment, he seemed happier than Zeb had ever seen him.

Mark frowned at Zeb with frosty eyes. "Why wouldn't I?"

Zeb was familiar with the boy's moods. He ignored the change in temperament, figuring he had received some opposition about going. "I went when I was about your age, had an interesting experience. But then you come home to our world again."

Mark tilted his head with interest. "If you liked it, why did you come back? Why do they all come back?"

Zeb thought of a number of reasons but settled on one to keep it simple. "We don't belong there, Mark."

He frowned. "Maybe I do."

He put a hand on Mark's shoulder and grunted a laugh. "You haven't even been there yet."

Mark took in a breath and pushed away Zeb's hand with force. He was tall and lanky but as strong as a workhorse. "But

I know I will." He balled his fist and headed toward the lane to the main road.

"Your folks know you're leaving?" Zeb called after him.

Mark waved a hand as if to brush away the words. He almost let him go but didn't want there to be anything that would make it difficult to talk with Ivan. He jogged up to the boy and stopped in front of him. "I'll go with you. I need to talk with your *daed*."

Mark scowled at him. "He doesn't know I'm going. Don't tell him."

Zeb didn't like this situation at all. He wanted Ivan's full attention concerning Emma, not to deal with *rumspringa,* of all things. "I'll make a deal with you. You come in while I talk to your *daed,* and I'll help you find Caleb."

Mark hesitated, and then narrowed his eyes.

"I'm talking to him about Emma, not you." Zeb grinned, which made Mark smile as well.

"But I don't want to miss Caleb."

Zeb was tired of hearing Caleb's name. Caleb had been here for only two days, and Zeb had heard enough about him already.

"*Jah*, me too." He led the way to the *haus*, taking in the smell of cinnamon rolls and fresh coffee. Emma stood at the sink next to Rebecca and Maria, who was collecting the dirty plates. "It smells mighty good in here."

"Zeb!" Emma looked surprised. Zeb thought maybe her visit with Caleb would work to his advantage. He smiled and took three strides toward her.

"That coffee smells good." He nodded once toward the pot on the potbelly stove.

"Would you like some?" She reached for a mug sitting on the Formica counter.

"*Jah*, to warm up. It's chilly out there." He looked around the kitchen but there was no sign of Ivan. "Is your *daed* around?"

"He's in the barn." Zeb could tell from her tight smile that she knew he'd likely seen Caleb leaving, and that it made her uneasy. But Zeb knew she wouldn't do anything to upset him. He treated her too well. She had to know he had plans for them to have a life together.

"I'll go out and help him." He tapped Emma under the chin with a finger, and Rebecca handed him a cup of coffee as he left the kitchen. He stepped onto the porch to take a sip and looked over the Millers' farm. Theirs was one of the biggest in the community, with fields both in front and behind the house that went on farther than the eye could see. Ivan was well-respected, giving wise advice when others had problems with their crops. He was a serious man, strict and a rule follower, showing little emotion.

Zeb blew on the hot coffee, letting the aroma fill his nostrils. He thought about *rumspringa* and how the last couple of years hadn't been such a production. Ever since the incident with Caleb a while back it seemed to slow down a bit. But this year a larger group planned to go. Caleb's presence seemed to generate greater interest. The deacons had to be concerned with him here again. Zeb should know. His *daed* was one of them.

When he walked into the barn, Ivan was sitting on a three-legged milking stool, his arms and legs crossed. "Zeb, take a seat," he said without looking up.

Zeb grabbed a steel bucket, turned it over, and sat next to him. "What's on your mind?"

"It's you that has something to say."

"How'd you know?"

"You're an ambitious young man. Ambitious people always have something to say." Ivan slowly lifted his head, finally looking Zeb in the eyes. Ivan's face didn't change expression, making it even harder to tell what he was thinking. Ivan spoke his mind, but Zeb had learned not to take what he said personally. "A couple of things, actually."

Ivan made a rumbling sound in his throat and lifted his eyes to Zeb.

"Spring will be here before we know it, so I want to get started building another *haus*. My *mamm* and *daed* can move into the old one, and there would be one for Merv when he's ready to wed."

Ivan nodded slightly.

"There's a five-acre parcel I've got my eye on. Close to here but far enough for some privacy." Zeb felt the approval of his choice of land before Ivan said a word.

"Is there a reason you're telling me this?" His chin was tucked down, and his eyes rose to look straight at him. He was an intense man, so Zeb didn't think much of his intimating mannerisms.

"Just don't want anything to get in the way is all."

Ivan knew exactly what he meant. Zeb's *haus* would be for him and Emma.

"Is that all you want?" Ivan had tipped his head down when a rush of cold air surged through the barn.

"*Jah*..." He couldn't help but meet his eyes. As much as Ivan appeared not to notice what went on, he always seemed to know more than people realized.

"*Gut*, because that's all you'll get." He didn't move or even blink.

Zeb wasn't sure what Ivan meant by the remark. It didn't sit well with him that Ivan gave such a vague response. Ivan was even more mysterious than usual. But it came down to Emma, and her *mamm* wanted her married as much as Zeb wanted to marry her. He stood and hung the bucket back up on a nail. "Need any help in here?" He looked around, trying to figure out what Ivan was doing.

"*Nee*. Thanks for the offer, just the same." He tightened his arms around his chest, and remained like a statue, so Zeb turned to leave.

"You do right by her."

Zeb stopped midway in his attempt to turn around and looked back at Ivan. "Of course I will." If Zeb didn't know Ivan's ways, he might be offended, but his request wasn't all that surprising. He waited to see whether Ivan had anything else to say, but the man only stared, unmoving. "Is there anything else?" Zeb finally asked.

"*Nee*." Ivan's lips didn't move, but Zeb heard the word.

As Zeb strode away, he decided to chalk it up to a *daed* losing his oldest child to start a life on her own. Although it was what every parent wanted, it had to be difficult to let go. In thinking back, he noticed this conversation probably wasn't much different than any others he'd had with the man.

Zeb walked by the house to see Emma before going home for chores but didn't see any sign of her. He was about to go inside when he noticed an unattended laundry basket and a few scattered items of clothes on the line. As he peered around the corner of the *haus*, he saw Emma sitting on a concrete step with her eyes closed, moving back and forth for warmth.

"Aren't you cold out here?" Zeb asked.

She started at the sound of his voice, her brown eyes now wide open. "I'm okay." She moved over so he could sit next to her. "What were you and *Daed* talking about?"

"The weather." He grinned to let her know it was all good without giving anything away. "Were you resting or praying?"

"Both."

"A prayer of thanksgiving or a heavy heart?"

She looked up at the blue sky with a few billowy clouds floating by. "It's Mark."

He nodded. "*Rumspringa*?"

She turned to him. "He told you?"

"*Jah*, he wants to see Caleb. I told him to wait to talk to Ivan. He's probably forgotten about it by now."

She pushed brown ringlets of hair away from her eyes. "He's going. No matter what my parents do or say. He's set on it." Emma dropped her hands between her knees.

"He probably just wants to be like all the others who are going." He let out a long breath. "Planting season will be coming around soon. Your folks would miss him helping out."

"*Jah*, I've thought about that too. But if it comes down to him really leaving, there's only one thing left to do."

He couldn't think of a good solution and figured they'd have to leave it up to Caleb as to what to do. "What's that?"

"I'll go with him."

Chapter Six

Emma reclaimed the abandoned laundry basket and sat back down on the porch, giving Zeb time to soak in what she'd said. She knew he wouldn't like her idea. No one would. But ever since Caleb had come back, her desire to evangelize had begun to grow.

Zeb looked at her and frowned. "For a minute there I thought you were serious."

Emma kept her hands busy folding clothes.

"I am serious." She looked away, not wanting to see his expression.

Zeb shook his head. "This is getting out of hand. Too many are going."

That might be true, but she felt responsible for Mark, who seemed so unpredictable. Going with Mark would also give her a chance to see what Caleb's world was like and meet some of the people he helped.

She felt warmth on her arm. "You look so worried." Zeb moved his hand up toward her shoulder. When he began to finger the curls that had escaped her bun, she moved away.

He pursed his lips in the same gesture he made every time she shied away. "I wish I could help you with this, Emma. But it makes no sense to me that you would go. You're needed here as well."

Who did he think needed her—her *mamm* and *daed* or him? "I wish Mark would get it out of his system."

He scoffed. "It might be good for him to go. The culture

shock alone might bring him home a changed young man." His nostrils flared, and he turned away.

This was bothering him more than Emma expected. She was uncomfortable with him knowing these things about her family, but he needed to understand why she felt the way she did, and what she was up against. He didn't have to deal with a raging adolescent young man.

"I hope so." She glanced at her *daed* coming out of the barn. She shouldn't have told Zeb about this. She didn't want him involved.

"I'm glad you talked with me about it. There is no need to worry. Things will settle down, and when it's time for Caleb, he'll probably stay put." Zeb grinned.

As she stared into his eyes, she wondered whether he was more worried about Caleb than her family. But then she might feel the same if he was going away with an old flame. "You're probably right."

"You worry too much." He draped his arm over her shoulders and steered her toward the *haus*.

"I have more burdens to bear than you do." When she heard herself say the words, she bit her tongue. "I don't mean to complain. There are many with more to deal with than me."

"*Jah*, you do. You have your coughing spells. I'm sure your parents and Doc would be surprised to find out they've been coming so often lately."

"What?" Her head started swimming. She didn't know why she had so many coughing fits when she was around him. But Zeb knew she wouldn't want to worry her *mamm* and *daed*. Would he be so bold as to make them think she was sick and shouldn't leave?

"You're frustrated and concerned. That's understandable." He drew her in close to his chest, but she didn't find comfort in his arms. He pacified her like a child. "It'll all work out. You'll see."

She pulled away. "*Jah*, I suppose you're right. I'll see you later, then."

As he turned to walk down the dirt road leading away from her *haus,* she watched him go, a slight swagger radiating confidence. She wanted time alone to finish her chores early so she would have the entire afternoon to work on the quilt she wanted to sell at the festival.

As she entered the *haus,* the sound of her *mamm* humming drifted from the kitchen. It was a rare thing to hear, but as Emma turned the corner, her *mamm* fell silent. Emma studied her *mamm*'s gentle smile. "*Mamm*?"

Her *mamm* moved closer and put a hand to Emma's cheek. "Do you have something to share with me?" *Mamm* asked.

"*Nee*, why?"

"Your *daed* said Zeb had a talk with him," *Mamm* said.

Emma thought her *mamm* had given up on her marrying. But looking at her now, Emma could see she hadn't.

"*Ach*, did I speak too soon?" *Mamm* put a hand to her chest and let out a laugh. "Your *daed* would be so excited."

Emma couldn't imagine that *excited* was the best word to describe what her *daed* felt. But she was sure he would be grateful to have her off on her own. "*Jah*, there is nothing to tell."

"I was mistaken then." Her cheeks were light pink, and Emma felt a tinge of guilt that she as wasn't as excited as her *mamm.*

Emma was curious as to what *exactly* Zeb had said to her *daed.* When she looked into her *mamm*'s face, Emma wished she could have told her something more. "I'm sorry, *Mamm.*"

Mamm patted her cheek again and sighed. "Don't wait too long."

The back door slammed shut, causing *Mamm* to jump. Mark came bounding into the room and looked around. "Where's Zeb?" His eyes were dark and wild, narrowing in on Emma.

"He already left." Emma lifted up her palms to show him as well as tell him that was all the information she had.

"Why would he do that?" He pointed at *Mamm*. "Did you tell him to leave?" His voice rose to an annoying level.

Mamm shook her head. "*Nee*, son." Emma's first instinct was to tell him to calm down, but *Mamm* thought of another idea. "If you go now, you could still catch him."

Emma didn't know why *Mamm* was encouraging him, other than the fact that she didn't want a fuss.

Mark closed his eyes, his demeanor changing by the moment. "If he wanted me to come with him, he would have waited." The emotional whiplash from outbursts drained him. But at the moment he seemed more sad than angry. When he sulked, it was even more stressful than the expressive outbursts. Emma went from loathing his behavior to feeling sorry for him.

"Did you remember about the festival?" *Mamm* said. Distracting Mark sometimes worked. He was diffusing and switching gears. Emma could almost see the transformation. The festival was only once a year and they all looked forward to it. It was sure to lift his spirits if they talked about it.

"*Jah*, but now I started thinking about this."

"Let's talk about the festival," *Mamm* said.

"Will Zeb be there?"

"I wouldn't think he would miss the festival," Emma answered with a soft tone.

Mark nodded. "He missed *me*." He turned away, walking toward the stairs.

"Not on purpose, son." *Mamm*'s voice seemed to calm him a little. "Why don't you finish up the table you've been making? Then you can sell it at the festival."

He paused and turned around. "Maybe later."

As upset as Emma got with him, she could understand why he was so rebellious. Mark couldn't rationalize his emotions or anyone else's. There were other young men who were trying their families' patience, so they weren't alone. She tried to remember that, but it wasn't always easy.

Mark balled his hands into fists and marched upstairs. The pounding of each foot resonated in Emma's ears. Maybe that was best. Let him settle down alone for a while. He wouldn't listen to reason when he got into his solitary moods, so some down time might be good for him.

Emma went into the kitchen. Not that there was a meal to make. She just needed to do something to keep busy. When the back door squeaked open, Emma looked over the island in the middle of the kitchen to find out who it was, but all she could see was a little white *kapp* with blonde wisps sticking out. "Maria?"

"*Nee?*"

"Martha?"

"*Jah*. You're not supposed to see me." Two little blue eyes barely peeked over the top of the counter.

"Why is that?" Emma looked away but could still feel the two little eyes staring at her.

"I dirtied my dress." Martha's soft voice could barely be heard.

"Well, take it off and put it in the laundry." Emma was curious as to how badly it was soiled, so she went over to look at it. The dress was covered with dripping mud. The trail started at the mudroom and continued on into the kitchen where Martha stood.

"What in heaven's name were you doing?" Emma asked as she guided Martha back to the mud room. After Martha took off the filthy dress, Emma took it out the back door to hose it down. Martha stood at the door watching her sister rinse off her dress, baffled as to how she could make such a mess of herself.

After Emma finished and came back inside, she wrapped Martha up in a towel and had her sit by the fire in the living room until she warmed up. Emma sat on the hearth and looked at her sister. "Tell me again what you were doing."

Martha looked at *Mamm*, who glanced at Emma and then spoke. "Mark told me about hog wrestling."

Emma's eyebrows went up, guessing the rest of the story. "*Ach, nee.* You didn't."

Martha giggled, and then Emma started in. Maria tried to stifle her laughter, but soon she was laughing too.

"*Jah*, but when I got into Molly's pen, she looked too big, so I tried to catch the littler ones. But they were too fast." Martha brought the story to an end. "So I decided to wait until spring when the babies come out."

Emma shook her head and then couldn't help but laugh as she imagined the scene...until she realized that it wasn't just mud she had cleaned off Martha's dress.

Chapter Seven

Caleb hated to be in the middle of family affairs, but the position *Gott* had placed him in called for exactly that. He'd left the community on *rumspringa* and had not come back, not because he wanted to live the English life, but because he wanted to guide teenagers when they were in the big city.

So many had aspirations to experience Philadelphia, others wanted to live there, but Caleb had learned the hard way that Philly wasn't what the Amish expected it to be. It could trick and consume a person. He'd seen many fall into harm's way. Some floundered. Most made it back home, but others didn't fare as well. They'd fallen into what he called Satan's playground.

Someone near and dear to him had gotten caught in the evil one's trickery, and Caleb would never forgive himself for not doing more to prevent it. If he ever did accept forgiveness, he might finally go home again. If they'd take him back.

But the situation with the Millers was personal. He'd spent too much time there growing up not to have a strong bias toward the family. He'd always had a soft spot for Mark. But then he was easier to manage as a kid. His demeanor was changing as he got older.

Ivan and Rebecca were older parents and figured time would balance things out. From what Caleb had seen in the city, he thought maybe Mark had some mental health issues—something a doctor could help with—but the Amish were leery about using medication for such matters.

"Caleb." Maria's ragged voice came up from behind him as she ran down the road toward his family's farm.

His head jerked up. "Mornin', Maria."

"I've been looking for you." Her weak smile told him something was bothering her. She pushed back the long strands of hair that dangled against her shoulder and caught her breath.

"What's on your mind?" He tilted his head to study her. She had grown up since he saw her last. Not the gangly little girl nipping at Emma's feet. He'd never thought of her as pretty, but now she had a certain plain yet beautiful face.

"I'm glad you're here, Caleb." She twisted to the side, looking down the main road through the community. Her eyes stopped at her family's farm. "I'm torn."

"About *rumspringa*?" He didn't wait for the answer. "Why do you want to go?"

"How did you know?"

"I just do. But everyone's reason is different."

She shrugged. "I'm not sure." She finally looked him in the eye. "Why did you?"

He smiled. He'd always liked Maria's manner. She had a strong way about her that created a complexity he appreciated. But he didn't believe she was asking for herself. She was asking for Mark. Maria would never leave home.

Caleb answered her question, "My brother had it in his head that he wanted to go. My parents wanted me to go with him."

"But he was older than you, wasn't he?" A slight wind tugged at her *kapp,* and she reached up to pull it down.

Caleb chuckled at the familiar gesture.

He nodded. Most knew not to ask about his brother, but this was Emma's sister, so he'd be patient with her. "And he had a wild side to him. My parents thought for sure he wouldn't come back if I wasn't there to bring him home."

He paused and watched her eyes flicker back and forth. She was listening intently. "But he never did."

Caleb sucked in some air and slowly released it.

"I'm sorry. I shouldn't have brought it up." She was one of the few whose remorse seemed genuine. But even this time he knew she wanted the rest of the story.

"He's still in Philly," was his patent answer. No one needed any more information than that. Not even his parents knew what had really happened. He didn't want to worry them. As far as they knew, he had lost touch with his brother. Caleb wished he had. If it wasn't for him, Caleb would be back here, growing a family and crop. But until it was finished with Abe, he couldn't leave Philly.

"It's not a bad thing to do, if kept within reason. For most it confirms their choice to come back to their home, their families, and live the Amish life."

"And for others?"

"Most of them have a hard time adjusting to the English ways. It's so different from what we've grown up with." He watched her eyes drop to the pebbled dirt under her boots. "What are you running away from?"

Her head popped up, and her eyes opened wide. "Why do you ask?"

"I've heard and seen just about everything over the years, including the answer you're about to give me." He grinned to let her know it was all right, that her secret would be his to keep. He had so many bottled up inside, he'd started keeping a journal in his head. Each one came with a face and prayer for discernment.

"Sometimes I think I'd like to get away." She paused and

turned to him. "Do you see people in the city who act like Mark?"

The look of hope in her eyes grieved him. She so desperately wanted to find answers about Mark, and she held on to so much guilt. "There is every kind of person in the city, the same as here. Only we wear hats and *kapps*." He grinned, and she did too. "He just wants his independence."

She tightened her lips. "That's why I'm going. My *mamm* and *daed* have more than one child, but sometimes it seems as if they've forgotten that."

Caleb understood her concern and frustration with her brother. He'd gone through a lot of the same things with his own brother. It was difficult to determine how much was ordinary, family differences and how much was something more. "Sometimes things get swallowed up, and no one knows where it all went or what happened. Give yourself a little more time."

To his surprise, she moved quickly forward and hugged him. "*Danke*, Caleb.

"That's what I'm here for." He moved away.

"It is your calling now, isn't it?" Her eyes softened.

"Unbeknownst to me, it is." Caleb still wondered from time to time why he was chosen for this task. But in any case it wasn't his place to question, only to do his best for the glory of God.

"Bless you, Caleb." Maria's words brought him back.

"And you." He watched her go down the path he'd just came from. The Millers had much to work out, but Caleb felt they would. Maybe with one of them gone for a while, it would give Ivan and Rebecca a chance to see what the problems were and how to solve them. A break might be good for all of them. He had to admit deep down in his heart, he wished Emma would come, just long enough to see his world. But with Zeb so prominent in her life, he knew that would never happen.

There was something about Zeb that didn't sit right with Caleb. It wasn't fair of him to judge something he didn't even know for sure was there, but it didn't feel right in his gut. Zeb seemed to care about Emma, but there was a void big and wide. So why couldn't Caleb see what it was? Maybe it was so obvious he was missing it. When it came right down to it, Caleb was probably just jealous.

He was deep in thought when he ran into Deacon Reuben. "Deacon Reuben, how are you?"

"Caleb." He stopped in front of him and looked him in the eye. "I heard you'd been around the community. What brings you here?" He was a heavy man, and the words came out in a huff. He leaned on a walking stick as he waited for Caleb to answer.

"Just came back to visit for a while." Caleb didn't smile or even act cordial. He was defensive, waiting for the questions: What was he doing? Was he still a believer? Had he renounced the devil from that sinful place?

"Have you reconciled with your *mamm* and *daed*?" Reuben leaned forward, putting more weight on his stick.

"I'm staying with the Chupps while I'm here. I hope to see them before I leave."

"I don't know if that's wise. Your own *daed* doesn't let you stay in his *haus*, *jah*?"

So that's what this was about—the regular checkup to catch him breaking the rules of being shunned. Most didn't care; they accepted him and knew he was there for a short while and would leave as quickly as he came. But not Reuben. He was the deacon who followed the law to a T. There was no way around it. In Reuben's eyes he was a sinner through and through.

Caleb had asked for forgiveness for breaking the laws of the Amish, but he wondered whether God really cared. They weren't God's laws, they were man's. "No, I don't stay at my father's home, because I don't want to make them have to answer to you or any of the other deacons."

Reuben grunted and moved back as if he'd been shot. "Harsh words to a servant to the community. And from a bitter young man."

Caleb shook his head. "You don't serve the community, you break it down." Caleb looked up then and met his eyes. "But you might be right about being bitter."

He could go into detail, explain what he meant. But it didn't matter. Reuben would take what he wanted from this meeting and throw away the rest. Caleb couldn't do anything right in the man's eyes, so he stopped trying. The bitterness came from not being accepted. Reuben had no idea how much he longed to be working the farm with his family. "See ya, Reuben."

"*Ach*!" Reuben turned and strolled away.

Caleb walked down the main road, the one that went by all of the farms in the community. It would take a while to get to the house he wanted, but his feet took him there, regardless. It was as if his body took over his mind because he was on damage control.

He felt like an outcast here. Ironic that he would feel the worst around people who were supposed to be the most accepting and Christlike. But instead, the drunks, homeless, and lost in the city were the people who tried so hard to get their lives together, and they accepted him unconditionally because that's how he accepted them.

He saw the white silo first, and after passing the hill, the red barn. The farm was picture-perfect, as always. Chickens roamed about, pecking the ground, and the milk cows mooed their protest as milking time approached. He'd lost track of time, engrossed in his self-pity. He snapped out of it and walked to the house. As he got closer, he noticed his youngest brother, now old enough to carry a bale of hay to the barn. He sighed, remembering everything he'd missed—seeing his brothers grow up and his grandfather before he died.

He didn't think, just kept going and wouldn't let himself stop until he got to the door. His oldest brother stopped with pitchfork in hand and watched him approach. It would be awkward at first, but he was sure soon enough, they'd be telling tales and reminiscing about the stunts they did as kids. *Mamm* would cover her cheeks or suck in a breath like she'd never heard them, and his *daed* would smile and shake his head. His family loved him, and he loved them. He had missed them more than he could say.

But the person he had missed the most was Emma.

Chapter Eight

The afternoon snow slowly began to fall, which drew many to the frozen pond. Snowmen popped up and some imaginative prankster gave one a cane and a *kapp* likely snatched from his own *mamm*. The large drifts and white fields sparkled from the intense rays, shimmering like diamonds.

The farmers buzzed with conversation after church service, looking forward to planting season. Emma watched, listening to their excitement, and realized she hadn't thought about what a conversation piece planting was. She thought of it as work—tilling the soil, and then going back over the fields with seed—but for them, discussion of fertilizers and what type of seed was best was a form of entertainment.

A lot of things had taken on different meanings since she had started thinking about what it would be like to be in the city. Emma was content where she was, yet curious as to what was out there. She looked forward to planting season. It meant the end of winter and the springing of new life, Easter and lilies, and her vegetable garden. Now she associated it with something new—a change in where she lived, what she would do, what she would eat, and living around people she didn't know.

Isn't there an easier way to share the gospel?

"You're distracted." Zeb's voice cut into her thoughts "I called your name three times before you knew I was here." He squinted into the sun with a smile.

"I'm sorry. I have a lot on my mind these days." She looked

out over the shimmering snowy field, wishing she could avoid telling him she was leaving but knowing she'd have to so he could be prepared.

"*Jah*, I've noticed. I wish you'd stop worrying yourself over nothing. Mark will be fine, and your *mamm* will be glad to have you here while he's gone." He linked their arms together and walked alongside Bishop Atlee's dormant corn field.

"It's not that simple, Zeb." She didn't know whether he wasn't taking it seriously or whether it just wasn't important to him. Either answer bothered her. Maybe he was right that she shouldn't be involved in this trip. But something bigger than her was wooing her forward, and anything that powerful could only come from *Gott*.

"It's only complicated if you make it that way." He stopped and took both her hands in his. "Is there anything else I should know?"

She couldn't look at him or she wouldn't be able to tell him what she needed to. She would leave with Mark, with Zeb's permission or not. The bright sun hitting the white snow hurt her eyes, so she looked down at her black boots. Feeling his warm breath, Emma noticed how close he was. Then she heard the footfalls of someone rambling over the frozen corn husks left in the field. She turned to the side to see Deacon Reuben approaching.

"Afternoon."

The relief she felt was obvious when the air left her lungs. She could see Zeb out of the corner of her eye, still staring at her with jaw clenched. She had a distinct feeling he knew exactly what she was going to say, and he wasn't happy about not having an opportunity to give his opinion. "The weather is changing," Emma said.

"*Jah*, good for the earth and the soul," Reuben said as he eyed Zeb.

"Supposed to be an early spring." Zeb squinted, maybe from the bright snow or trying to predict what Reuben was really there to say.

"Tell me, Zeb, how are you getting along with the additional Holsteins?"

Zeb frowned, seemingly unsure of what Reuben's question was leading to. Emma was curious as well. It was obvious he was making some sort of point. "Selling a lot of milk," he answered. His usual courteous demeanor had disappeared the minute Reuben mentioned his extra milk cows. Emma glanced over at him, wondering what she was missing. He grinned away his scowl.

"*Ach*, good. I've wondered what it would be like having so many cows and so little crop," Reuben replied.

Reuben's questions piqued Emma's curiosity even more. There must be something amiss for him to ask Zeb about a way of farming that was fairly common. Granted, there was more land for grazing than for crops, but it seemed to work well for him and his family.

"I wonder, myself, some days." Zeb's tone was direct, but his face lost the tense lines between his brows. Emma hadn't the slightest idea what the sudden concern was about. Maybe it was just sheer curiosity.

"Let us know what the outcome is; I'd be interested to know." Reuben gave him a lazy wink.

"I'll do that."

When Reuben walked away, Emma studied his face to see if she should ask. The stern look slowly faded as he led her to his buggy. "Are we going somewhere?"

"*Mamm* forgot her corn casserole. I told her I'd go back to the *haus* and get it for her. Want to come along?" He asked with a cordial smile.

"*Jah*, I should tell my *daed*, though." She felt like a child, telling him she had to ask permission. She'd never been completely alone with him and didn't feel right doing so now. She had questioned at times whether she would ever feel that desire and worried that maybe something was wrong with her.

Caleb's face flashed in her mind, and she sucked in air. Remembering her attraction toward him, Emma felt her cheeks heat up. She turned away to find her family.

"Hop in; I'll take you to them." Zeb held out a hand, and she climbed into the buggy. His was one of the nicer buggies. Soft, red material on the seats made for a comfortable ride. The fringe around the top had been debated by the deacons, who decided it was acceptable if the color was black. The minister requested it be taken off when Zeb drove to church.

As they approached her *mamm*, Emma explained the situation.

"Hurry back so you don't miss my shoo fly pie." *Mamm* leaned forward to see him. "Your favorite, Zeb."

As they rode down the lane to his farm, Emma became uneasy. She'd hoped her *mamm* would say they needed a chaperone, but it was a short trip to his *haus*, so she dismissed it.

As they neared Zeb's house, the Holstein started popping up one by one and then in herds. After a while Emma gave up trying to count. "I wonder why Reuben was so curious about your dairy farm."

"Probably checking to see if I was breaking any rules." Zeb didn't seem bothered by it any longer, so she decided she wouldn't be either. Their community hadn't adapted to many of the worldly ways. They were a conservative group with little room for bending any rules.

"*Jah*, you're probably right." When they arrived at Zeb's house, she stayed put while he hopped out of the buggy and went around to her side.

"Come in with me." He held out a hand, and she accepted. As she followed him, she admired how perfectly groomed their farm was, even more than most. And it was just the two brothers and his *mamm* and *daed*, a small family for an Amish household.

She followed him into the kitchen and took the casserole from the oven. "Smells *gut*."

He took it from her and set it on the counter. Then he stood in front of her with his arms on either side of her, his hands on the counter. He looked into her eyes, his face inches from hers. "I want you to be my wife, Emma." He moved closer, his breath heated.

She knew he was going to kiss her. A casual peck on the cheek was the norm for them. This was not. She looked down and started to move her foot forward.

He moved closer, blocking her from moving away.

Her heart beat double-time as she lifted her head. His eyes were wide and dark.

"Don't be shy." He leaned forward and brushed his lips against hers, and then kissed her.

A strange sensation came over her that she wasn't ready for—one that was only meant to happen between a husband and wife. She shamed herself for the emotion and physical reaction she felt. Did this mean she had deeper feelings for Zeb than she thought? Or was it just a natural response? She didn't see how you could feel that way unless you cared for the person. And she did love him. Caleb had just distracted her.

"What's wrong, Emma?"

"I'm sorry, Zeb. I'm not used to being this affectionate." She reached for the casserole, as if it were her protection.

He leaned back against the counter and laid his arms over his chest. "You're so bold in any other situation, but this…" He grinned as if entertained by her change in behavior.

Emma didn't find it amusing. Her body was still tingling with unfamiliar sensations.

"We should go." She turned on her heel and made her way back to the buggy.

A mix of irritation and anger slid into her mind as she waited for him. He pulled himself up and into the buggy, and sat there looking out over the acres of Holstein grazing on cane and roots that were buried under the snow.

"It's fine, Emma. I know you're shy about these things." He turned his head toward her. "It will pass." Then he smiled and patted her hand.

She took in a breath, frustrated that he couldn't see her discomfort. She would feel better once they were married. She knew other girls her age who experimented with this kind of behavior. Why didn't she?

Is something wrong with me?

It wasn't talked about, so how would she know?

"I'm sorry, Zeb. But I'm not comfortable. Not yet." She looked out the buggy window and the never ending black-and-white cows with their heads down rooting for food.

"I understand. I can wait." He clucked at the horse and trotted along to get there before they missed the meal.

She felt he thought he was doing her a favor, when in her mind she was making the right decision. She glanced over at him. He was older than her. That might be part of his way of thinking. Maybe the patience went both ways.

When Emma stepped out of the buggy, Caleb rambled over

as Zeb took the casserole to his *mamm*. She'd barely touched her foot on the ground when he was suddenly in front of her. "Where have you been?"

His eyes captured hers. "Just went to get some food for the meal. Why?" Caleb cocked his head and looked over at Zeb. He pursed his lips and shook his head. "I didn't see anyone with you. I make for a good chaperone." He softened and smiled. She knew he wasn't concerned about the rules on chaperoning. Because he wasn't considered Amish, he got away with more when he was there.

"That would have been an interesting ride." She appreciated Caleb's sense of humor. Even in the worst of situations, he could find the absurdity that went with it. "It's fine, Caleb. *Danke*."

"Whatever you say." He shrugged. "Hungry?" He walked with her into the meetinghouse that was hosting church, and then over to the tables filled with food. Sliced beef and chicken with potatoes and gravy took up one table. The side dishes of pickled vegetables sat on another, and the desserts were plentiful. Pies and cakes of many flavors, along with an assortment of cookies, were the little ones' favorites.

Emma prepared a plate of food and walked over to talk with a small group of people. Caleb popped over and mingled periodically. It was just enough not to be obvious, but Emma knew he was trying to be with her without being conspicuous. Zeb talked with the men, and specifically with Reuben. And she wondered whether it was about the Holsteins or Zeb's wedding plans.

Chapter Nine

The snow overnight chilled the *haus*. Heat from the coal-oil stove warmed the kitchen as the Millers prepared the noon meal. *Mamm*'s cast iron pot boiled, steaming hot, ready to firm the dough into noodles. Emma kneaded the flour into the mixture to make the egg noodles. *Mamm* was cutting up bits of chicken while Maria peeled potatoes. They worked together harmoniously, one of them passing along whatever was needed even before another had to ask for it.

Emma divided the dough into two portions and rolled each into thin strips, and then she covered it with a cloth. She'd begun to clean up her work area when the faint sound of bells drew her away. "Do you hear that?"

Mamm tilted her head to the side to listen. Her brows went up, and she wiped her hands on her apron. "What is it?"

Maria flew to the front window and pulled back the curtain. "Emma, come look!"

Emma walked over while wiping her hands with a towel. A Belgian horse pulled a red sleigh through what was left of the snow. "Who is it?" She whispered.

"I bet it's Caleb." Maria moved closer to the window.

"*Nee*, it's Zeb." *Mamm* corrected Maria, and then put her fists on her hips. She glanced over at Emma.

Emma felt a shot of guilt pass through her mind when she heard it wasn't Caleb. It seemed like something he would do, not Zeb. Then she thought about all the time she and Caleb had spent together before he left. It added up to be quite a bit.

Her family hadn't always known, except Maria, but even she didn't realize how often they'd been together.

Her parents were more lax with the rules when she was with Caleb, which didn't really make sense to Emma. But maybe they thought differently about him—or about her spending time with him—because he was no longer considered Amish.

"It *is* Zeb." Maria turned to Emma in surprise.

Mamm frowned. "Of course it's Zeb."

"*Mamm*, you know how close Emma is with Caleb. It could have been him."

A small grunt came from *Mamm* and her frown grew.

"But he'll be leaving soon enough, I'm sure," Maria added.

They heard Zeb kick his boots to loosen the snow, and he was about to knock when Maria opened the door.

"*Hallo*, Maria. Is Emma around?"

"*Jah*, I am." Emma peeked around the door. "What are you doing?" Emma's gaze lifted to the apple-red sleigh.

"Taking you for a sleigh ride."

"Where did you get that sleigh?" Maria, like the rest of the family, hadn't seen many sleighs and hadn't ever ridden in one. The new order groups used them to give tourists sleigh rides, but in their community it wasn't so commonly done.

"I've been refurbishing it for a while now." He turned around and admired his work. "Ready for a ride?" He smiled at Emma.

"Give me a minute. I need to find some warm clothes." Emma took the stairs two at a time up to her room to put on some long johns and two pairs of socks. Then she went to the mud room, pulled on her warmest coat, and grabbed a scarf and mittens. Her work boots weren't pretty, but would keep her toes from freezing. She may have overdressed with the weather letting up a bit, but she preferred to err on the side of being too warm.

Maria watched them go, and *Mamm* waved as Zeb led her through the winter wonderland. Her family's fields were transformed into a sparkling white adventure. A frosting of the shimmering flakes cast over the tall trees, dusting the fence posts and equipment not used in the winter months. The snow kicked back under the horse's hooves as they trotted along, and Emma swayed with the beat.

"This is wonderful *gut*, Zeb." She sat in the cozy seat with both hands in her lap watching the beautiful winter scenery.

He smiled and turned to her. "I thought you'd enjoy this."

"It's beautiful out here." She'd been avoiding the outdoors, tired of the frosty temperatures, but this was worth the tingling in her cheeks and nose.

"Want to go to the river?" His blue eyes sparkled in the sun that peeked from behind some clouds. The weather was brisk, but not nearly as cold as it had been.

"I'd love to." She stared at him, squinting her eyes. "Why didn't you tell me about this?"

"I wanted it to be a surprise. I could tell by your face that it was." He clucked at the broad, bay horse and kept his smile. He turned around and glanced at the *haus*.

"What are you looking for?" Emma turned to see the view of her *haus* and the barn.

"I don't want to get out of sight from your *haus*. I know how uncomfortable you were the other day. I don't ever want to do anything that upsets you, Emma."

Emma's heart panged against her chest. The gesture was more than she could have imagined. Wanting to be close to her wasn't as out of line as she made it out to be. Confusing thoughts flew through her mind. Emma had made it clear that she had chosen him, not so much with words, but with time spent together. It was an unspoken agreement between them, and spending time with him now reminded her of that.

"That's *gut* of you, Zeb. I'm not that fragile, I promise you." She smiled contentedly, and when he looked at her, she could see his worry disappearing. Their moment together seemed to have bothered him as much as it had her.

When they got to the old wooden bridge, he tapped the horse with the leather reins to encourage him to the middle, and then leaned back in the seat. "Are you cold?" He rubbed her hands with his.

This outing took her back to the first time he came to court her. Her *daed* had been concerned that he was older, and her *mamm* was thrilled because he could take care of her. She had become distracted since Caleb had returned, and now felt remorse for what she'd put Zeb through. She didn't have a future with Caleb. She did with Zeb.

"I'm sorry if I made you feel badly, Zeb."

He took a moment and then thoughtfully looked her way. "I know you still have feelings for Caleb."

She let out a breath and waited. It was obvious. She knew that now. But she wouldn't take it back and had to admit she didn't want to. She would never be with Caleb. He wasn't a threat to their relationship. "We've been close ever since I can remember."

"And you had plans together at one time." His tone was gentle, nonthreatening, but that made her feel more guilt than if he were chastising her. And his words brought back the hurt she'd felt when Caleb left.

"*Jah*, we did. But that was a long time ago."

"A year isn't that long, Emma."

It seemed long to her, missing him and longing to see him. Realistically it was best that he was out of sight, gone from the community, easier to get over. She thought so, anyway. "Maybe it was longer."

He kept his gaze forward, thinking. "Caleb's name seems to come up a lot. I'm sure that will change once he leaves."

"Of course." She readily agreed. "Just as when anyone comes for a time and then goes back to where they came from."

He stared at her now. "But Caleb is from here. Any chance he might stay?"

"*Nee*, he has found his niche in the city." She paused and looked away from his sharp eyes. "I have to say I'm a bit jealous."

He leaned closer. "About what?"

"Caleb, evangelizing in the city." She met his eyes. He was trying to stay impartial, but she could see the jealousy in them. This conversation needed to end before she said something she shouldn't.

"The city is no place for us, no matter what the cause." He stood and clenched his hands. His firm, unwavering voice said it all.

"But it's what I want to do, need to do, not just for me but also my brother." He wouldn't understand her calling. That was clear.

"You're in a faraway place." He gazed at her intently.

She took in a frosty breath. "I want us to always be honest with each other."

"I agree." When he smiled, his handsome face brightened. Her thought-out plans came to a halt. She was being dishonest already, having already made plans, and their relationship had barely had a chance to blossom.

He clucked at the horse and went down the rest of the way across the bridge. She glanced at him, glad he didn't know her thoughts, but felt guilty at the same time. *Gott* surely didn't want her to forge a path to His calling by being dishonest. She shut her eyes tight, and tried to find the words.

Thud!

Her eyes flashed open. "What was that?"

Zeb gave her a defeated look. "The sleigh is stuck." He pointed to a layer of dirt. "Those warm days melted the snow. Now I'm stuck in the mud." He shook his head slowly. "Didn't think to bring a shovel." He glanced around, climbed out, went over to a mound of snow, and packed it in front and behind the runners. "Emma, will you grab the reins and give Beulah a tap?"

Emma took the reins and slid over to Zeb's side of the sleigh before touching the horse's hide with leather. The sleigh jumped forward and onto a snowy field ahead of them. "Thank goodness. I didn't feel like walking to the *haus*."

"Good work." He climbed into the right side of the sleigh, leaving Emma with the reins. He spread his arms out on either side of him and relaxed.

"Aren't you going to drive?"

He shook his head and sank down farther in the seat. "Take us home or wherever you like."

She couldn't help but grin. She'd never ridden in a sleigh, let alone driven one. "This is a bit of an adventure." The burly horse led them through the field, with Emma alert to any dry spots.

"Were you telling me something?" He looked over at her, but she couldn't face him. She'd been hoping he'd forgotten she had something to say. Emma shook her head and shrugged, garnering her courage. They rode silently, listening to the runners cut through the crystallized snow.

"You drive this sleigh well." He leaned back and grinned.

"You have things under control." As the sun hit his blue eyes, she studied his clean-shaven face and pleasant smile.

She had no control as long as he was involved. But she was determined she would find the courage in her own way in her own time.

Chapter Ten

Gott sent the sun to make the outdoor chores bearable. Emma's basket was almost full of eggs, with only one ornery chicken left to contend with. The hen set her eyes on Emma and gave her a low *cluck*.

"My, oh my. Why do you have to give me so much trouble?"

As soon as she took a step closer, the chicken perched at the end of her nest, flapping her wings. Emma stood tall and marched toward her. The hen squawked loudly, piercing Emma's eardrums.

In one quick motion Emma swiped up one of two eggs and plopped it in her basket.

"She giving you a hard time?" Emma started when she heard the voice and whirled around. Caleb leaned on the doorjamb of the hen house. The morning sun was behind him, so she could only see his silhouette. One shoulder touched the wooden frame, and one knee bent forward. She could picture every detail of him without the light.

Emma stared at the chicken. "I don't know why she doesn't like me."

"You take her eggs away." He chuckled and went over, and then looked in the basket. "How many did she give you?"

"One. There's another in there, but it's not worth getting pecked."

"Wear gloves." He pulled off his own and handed them to her, and then took the basket so she could put them on.

Emma pulled the soft leather glove over her fingers and

tugged it up to her wrist, feeling the warmth from his hands. They were too big, but if they would keep her from getting beat up by a chicken, she'd make them work. She took a deep breath, tucked her hand into the nest, and grabbed the egg out from under the hen. She proudly lifted the egg for him to see.

"Well done." He held out the basket, and she set the egg in with the rest. He looked over at the chicken, now hunkered down back in her nest. "She is a tough old bird."

"Her name is Hilda." Emma pulled off one of the gloves.

"You named her?" He grinned, watching her remove the other glove. "Keep them if you'd like." She handed him the gloves. "I lost my work pair, and I don't want to get these dirty." She pulled out a brightly colored set of mittens. "So I save them for after my work is done or for special occasions."

"They're pretty. Did you make them?"

She hesitated. "Zeb's *mamm* made them for me."

He was silent while he put his gloves back on. "Do you and Zeb have plans?" They left the hen house and started strolling, nowhere specific. He looked straight ahead, waiting for her answer.

"Not officially, *nee*."

They were silent as the snow crunched under their feet. "Do you love him?"

She almost stopped but didn't want to meet his eyes. It was just like Caleb to ask direct questions, but with this one she was stumped. She had feelings for Zeb and felt he would make a good husband, but the way she felt for him didn't compare to what she used to feel for Caleb. She didn't even try to explain.

"He's a good man and is kind to me." It wasn't the answer he was looking for, but it was all she wanted to say. They continued walking quietly together, passing by the neighbor's farm. He was one of a few people with whom she felt comfortable enough to be quiet.

Then a thought went through her head. "Are you with anyone in Philly?"

"No, not now."

She glanced over at him, surprised. But she didn't know why. He'd been gone for a while now and was sure to have met a number of young women there. But it brought up a strange feeling inside. They had been only with each other for so many years. It didn't seem right for either of them to ever be with anyone else.

Splat!

Cold, wet, snow clung to the side of her cheek and slid down her chin. She looked over at Caleb, who held his side, laughing so hard there was no noise coming from his mouth. She bent over and grabbed a mitten full of snow. When Caleb saw her snowy mitten, he grabbed her arm, but she threw the flakes at him before he could make her drop it.

Caleb reached forward, ready to retaliate, when another flying ball of snow hit him smack in the stomach. "We need to get these guys."

Emma looked over to see a group, children on up to teenagers, spread out all around a nearby frozen-over pond. Some were building snowmen. Others skated over the icy pond. But Caleb had his eye on the group with the frozen artillery.

There wasn't a chance she wanted to get in the middle of a snowball fight. "Caleb, don't. We're outnumbered."

His eyes squinted, and his snowball in hand told her it was a lost cause. "I never back down from a fight." He began packing snowballs. "You make 'em. I'll throw 'em."

He pulled her to her knees before she could protest, and she began packing snow together in balls so large that Caleb could barely hold them. They made a huge impact when he hit his target. Emma laughed as they pummeled one another with the white, frozen snow, until she got hit again. Then she was grabbing from the stash she'd made, leaving Caleb high and dry.

"We're almost out of ammo. Let's charge." He was so serious, she almost laughed. But she followed his orders, and they each grabbed the remaining four snowballs. She followed Caleb as he ran to the pond, dodging snowballs along the way. When they reached the opposing group, Caleb tackled the main thrower, and Emma waved her arms in surrender.

After asking the builder if she could rest on her creation, she plopped down against a wall of snow that was being made into a fort. "Don't let Caleb smash it," the little blonde girl told Emma.

He came over and lay on his back, breathing heavily. "Hey, I wouldn't smash this cool-looking fort."

"What's *cool* mean?" the blue-eyed doll asked.

Caleb looked at Emma with wide eyes as he remembered it wasn't a common word for most little Amish girls. "It means good."

"You've been in the English world too long," Emma teased.

"And not with you enough." He sat up, draping his hands over his knees, and looked around at all of the activity. "Reminds me of when we were young, horsing around like these kids are. Good memories."

"You talk like you want to be back here."

Emma chided herself. She shouldn't keep meddling. It wasn't her business to say things that wouldn't be answered the way she hoped they would be. He was content with his life, and she had to accept that.

"I do sometimes. But I can't leave what God has asked me to do, even if it doesn't always feel right sometimes."

"You mean you're not sure if you should be in the city?" Emma's stomach lurched again. She forced herself to squelch the selfish excitement she felt hearing him question his calling. This community wasn't home for him anymore, so she needed to let go of any thoughts that it would be again.

"I get confused when I come back here." He looked down at her mittens. "But it wouldn't be the same if I came to stay."

She kept her eyes on him until he looked up at her. "I never pictured you with Zeb. I figured you'd be with someone, but not him."

She hadn't either and hearing him say it made the reality of her future even more questionable. Zeb had filled the void after a lonely time of losing Caleb. She'd never really had any time in between. "He was there for me when I needed someone."

Caleb slowly turned away. "I'm sorry I left you like I did. It was the only way I could make myself leave. Even one more minute with you and I would have changed my mind."

A smoldering fire began to build in her heart. She didn't want to hear his words. They left her confused even more than she already had been. She couldn't trust herself to discern what and why Caleb was saying all this, but she wouldn't be his victim again. He'd broken her heart once. She wouldn't be stupid enough to let him do it a second time.

"Your companion is your work." She stared straight at him. "Maybe that's enough for you."

His brow furrowed, and he dropped his head and hands over his knees. When he looked up, his ruddy face was tight with either anger or sadness. She couldn't tell which. She thought of apologizing, but she didn't know what for. What she said was true.

"My bottom is wet from the snow."

A small chuckle bubbled out of him, and he held out a hand to help her up.

She reluctantly accepted and stood next to him. "Why did you come over this morning?"

He was quiet, watching the activity on the pond, and then turned to answer her. "I lost a year. For some reason I thought I could bring it back."

Her angry thoughts kept her captive as if the devil himself was willing her away from Caleb. He didn't owe her anything—nothing that could be replaced, anyway.

She physically shook and stared up at him. "I guess I'm still bitter, Caleb. I didn't realize until now."

"I shouldn't have brought it up."

She nodded. "I should go."

"Can I walk you—?"

"*Nee*. But *danke*." She found her feet moving ahead much faster than her mind, and before she knew it, she was home. In the time it took her to make it back to the farm, she'd stuffed away his tempting words. Now, she would have the noon meal to prepare. That would keep her mind off of the conversation they'd just had.

She walked into the *haus* and washed up to start making some biscuits. *Mamm* came in with bottles of milk, Maria behind her. "Where have you been?"

"Over at the pond. Did you need me?"

"*Nee*, but we did need the eggs." *Mamm* set the glass bottles on the counter and wiped her hands on her apron.

"*Ach*, I left them in the hen *haus*."

Mamm made a motion with her hand to scoot Emma along. "I hope no critters got into them."

Emma grabbed her coat and moved quickly to the chicken

coop. Caleb had put them on top of the chicken lofts when he gave her his gloves. She looked down at Hilda, who was watching her intently as Emma leaned against the doorjamb. She wondered why *Gott* had separated her from Caleb. They connected so well.

She felt comfortable going on the trip for Mark's sake and with deep hope that she might also find an opportunity to change hearts. But she was not comfortable if her desire to go was because of Caleb. How could she know? How could she be honest about her feelings? She sighed, hoping she wouldn't get into a situation that she would regret.

Something told her it might be too late.

Chapter Eleven

Caleb didn't like the way he'd left things with Emma and decided to check on her. Before he could make it to the house, he thought he heard something in the barn. Caleb moved toward the sound quickly and quietly, remaining still enough to hear the noise. A slight moan came from one of the stalls. He peered in to see Maria kneeling on the straw-covered ground. Dun, a large workhorse, stood close by. He slowly moved his huge head toward Caleb as if to protect Maria. Her eyes were closed, and her bottom lip trembled. Whatever was causing this anguish was consuming her.

"Maria?" Caleb whispered.

She sucked in air and whipped her head over toward him. "Caleb." She pushed off the ground to stand but he stopped her with an outreached hand.

"Don't get up. I'll sit with you." The stall door creaked as he let himself in and gave Dun a pat to his hide. He took her hand and waited until her chest stopped heaving. Emma had often told him how fragile she was, and he knew as much, but never like this. "Do you feel like talking?"

"I don't want Emma to leave. I don't want to go with Mark, but I don't want her to go either." She caught her breath, and a hiccup popped out as she lifted a hand to her lips.

Caleb's heart skipped when he heard those words. He'd hoped but now knew that Emma would be with him in the city. For how long and why he didn't know or care. He'd take any time she had to give.

"It would be very different without your brother and sister here. But they'll be back, sooner than you think." He believed what he said. Mark's bravado couldn't touch what was out there in the city. He would either dive in with both barrels and get himself into trouble or stick his tail between his legs and go home.

Would Emma be right behind him or would she stay and evangelize? A selfish part of him wished she was going to be with him. When they spent time together it was as if he'd never left.

"I didn't say anything about Mark. He's the reason Emma's going." She wrapped her arms around her waist. "I hate him for it."

Her pinched face and tight lips gave warning to Caleb not to correct her, tell her she might regret what she said. Maria needed to vent, so he let her, whether it was good or bad. He'd learned not to tell anyone how to feel or what to do about their situation. They knew but didn't want to say the words. *I'm sorry.* Or *I'll change.*

"Your mom and Martha are going to need you more than ever. You're a good sister, Maria. This will give you special time to bond with them." He tried to think of the positive and hoped Maria would too. But her pale skin and the dark rings under her eyes didn't give him much encouragement. She was distraught, missing her sister before she'd even left.

Maria sat back, leaning to the side and holding herself up with one hand. "You make it sound easy."

"You have to let go of this, Maria. Your sister has more of a reason to go than you know. So don't be upset with your brother." He picked up a piece of straw, wrapping it around his finger. He missed working the earth and growing crop.

There was something spiritual about the process that drew him closer to the Lord, creation, and all its bounty.

"What do you mean?" Her forehead wrinkled, her curiosity piqued.

"Has she told you she wants to go on missions?" He didn't feel it was wrong to tell Maria this. He knew if Emma had seen how upset Maria was, she would do whatever it took to make her feel right about Emma going. And he would do the same.

"She'd mentioned it, but I didn't ever expect her to." She paused and frowned. "Is that what Emma thinks she will do in the city?" She shook her head. "You can't let her, Caleb. There are bad people there. She could get hurt. You wouldn't want her to get hurt, Caleb." Her pale cheeks grew red, and she sat up, anxious.

"There are more good than bad in Philly, Maria. It's not Sodom and Gomorrah." Caleb grinned and touched her arm. "She wants to evangelize to the people there."

Maria stuck her bottom lip up, much like a child who wasn't getting her way. "I can't argue with that. I don't understand it, but it would be wrong of me to ask her not to go if that's her reason."

"So you won't go headlong after your brother over this?" Caleb chuckled, which made her grin. "Finally, a smile."

"I still blame him, Caleb." She fidgeted with discomfort. "My legs are going numb."

Caleb stood and helped her up. He hadn't seen Maria this way before. She was normally peaceful, calm, and ignorantly content. This resentment worried him, more for her sake than Mark's. Mark could care less what anyone thought—an attitude Caleb hoped would dissipate some once Mark hit the city and was humbled by the experience. "You're a sweet girl, Maria. Don't let the evil one steal your joy."

"If anything happens to Emma, I'll never forgive him." With that, she turned and walked out of the stall slowly enough for Caleb to latch the stall door and catch up with her. But the steam was rising, and he hoped it would settle before they got to the house.

"Maria." He stopped, so she did too, and stared at him with wide eyes. "You know better than to worry about that with me there with her.

She held back her emotions with her head up and stood straight. "Keep her by your side, Caleb."

The Amish seemed sure he was taking them in to purgatory rather than a city. Yes, there was more to contend with than in the country. But the country mouse came back only because he tried the city life and knew where he belonged. He was sure that would happen with Emma, and probably Mark too.

He shook his head slightly, thinking what the deacons must think of him if the Millers had issue with his ways. He hoped he didn't find out. There would be no recourse for him if they did come question him.

As they came out of the barn, Emma was approaching. "*Ach*, Caleb, I didn't know you were here." The slight chill brought out the pink in her cheeks, giving off a vigorous glow. That was one of the things he missed about the country. Clean air and wholesome food made a body feel good and healthy.

"I came to see you and ran into Maria." He glanced over at Maria, but she kept walking, her shoulders stuck straight.

Emma watched her go. "Is she all right?"

He nodded, unclear of what his role was regarding this family that he cared for so much. "Are you sure you want to do this, Emma?" It would be the last time he asked, the last time he questioned or felt the guilt for her going. What she said now was what he would go by when he was gone, when she was homesick or upset with Mark or worried about chores back at the farm.

"*Jah*, I am." She didn't waste a second with her response. He would take that response and seal it. No turning back.

"That was a firm answer." He was pleased and ready to move on, but she seemed to have something on her mind.

"I've spent time with some who are going. I see the need for me to be there. They've confessed what they want to do. Some plans are harmless, but others have ideas that concern me. I don't set out to be a chaperone, but there are some who will need one." Her smile disappeared, possibly because of what she'd learned, but she didn't shirk away from the needs she discerned from talking with them. That was a huge step in and of itself.

"So you're ready for this?" He stuck his hands in his pockets, more excited than he should be that she was going, and sure it was mostly for selfish reasons. He would need to remind himself to be prepared for when she left him in Philly and came back to the farm, but he couldn't help it.

"*Jah*, almost. I have never told anyone about my faith, Caleb. I've always had it, but I have not talked about it. How am I supposed to tell others when I don't know how?" The wind whipped the strings of her prayer *kapp* behind her as he stared into her brown eyes.

Caleb nodded and sat on an old wooden bench by the barn doors. He patted the spot next to him. "You worry too much, Emma. You live out your faith. Think about what that is and pray for guidance that you'll find the words. There is no one way. Each testimony is different. What's yours?"

She frowned and stuck out her bottom lip in thought. "I

can't ever remember not believing. I've always been a child of *Gott*."

He shrugged. "Then say that. I heard one pastor say the doctor slapped him on the bottom the day he was born and he said, 'Jesus,' and he's been saying it ever since."

She giggled. "That's the silliest thing I've ever heard."

"But it's true for those of us who were born into a Christian family."

Emma was still smiling when she nodded. "Sometimes I think it's a disadvantage that we didn't have the opportunity to think about it before we claim it."

He nodded. "I thought about that a lot when I went to the city for the first time. It all comes back around. We make it complicated, not God."

"You have the answers, Caleb. I don't." She stared deeply into his eyes.

He wished he knew what she was thinking. He hoped it was something good but couldn't tell by her expression.

"I've learned how to express what I feel and believe and why. But it didn't just happen. Only after many conversations did I feel able to tell someone my story."

They were both quiet for a moment. He was trying not to say more than he should, wanting her to come to her own conclusions. And her mind was obviously spinning with questions. "Did you ever doubt your faith?" she finally asked.

"I doubted if I was worthy. But the Word comforted me in reading some of the passages in Psalms." He paused with a new thought. "I'm sure there are many other Amish who feel the same way you do." He looked her in the eyes. "You could share your story with others. Share your love for God through words and actions here. It would be different, but there is a need here for those who want to find that personal relationship with their Savior."

"I'd never thought about that." She turned away. "I'm really scared, Caleb." She looked straight ahead at the sun rising up over the hills.

He took her hand and looked at the golden rays with her, enjoying the silence and the warmth of her hand. He'd never known of her to be scared. It wasn't in her to let fear control her. But for the first time he could see something different when he turned and looked in her eyes. What he saw troubled him enough to look away. Whatever it was that brought out those piercing eyes made him shiver. "What is it?"

She kept staring straight ahead. "You have courage to live in such a place, Caleb."

He turned his attention ahead as well.

Chapter Twelve

The next day Caleb watched the sun creep above the horizon as he strolled down the gravel road to the Millers'. As the sun rose, the snow melted, which would make for a muddy mess on the festival grounds. It was the first week of March, and the festival was being held a couple weeks earlier than usual due to the forecast of heavy rains later in the month.

When Caleb arrived at the Millers', he saw the family gathering what they were going to sell—food, quilts, and Ivan and Mark's wood working. As Caleb got closer, he watched Rebecca place two quilts in a box. She paused, and then pulled out the top one. Caleb cocked his head to see the pattern. Each square had the name of a state with the coordinating state bird and flower. The colors were vibrant, and the intricate stitching had to have taken longer than most he'd seen—and he'd seen a lot of quilts in his time.

"You shouldn't sell that one, Mrs. Miller," he said, even though he knew her well enough to guess that she would. The family surely had more quilts than they needed, until weddings and babies came. Even so, the quilts would be personalized, each one made for the special occasion.

"Caleb, I didn't know you were going to the festival with us." Rebecca smoothed out the wrinkles and laid the quilt in with the rest.

Caleb hadn't considered going, but now that she mentioned it, he decided it would be an excuse to spend more time with

Emma before he left. Despite her intentions, he still doubted she would really leave her family and the community. So he'd planned to come by and tell her good-bye, but this would work out even better. He would miss her when he left. Being outside at the festival would give him peace, plus the food couldn't be matched and the camaraderie would be comforting.

"Where is the rest of the crew?"

"Finishing up chores," Rebecca said while she resumed packing the goods. As Caleb joined in with the packing, he hoped it would be a profitable day for them. He knew this was one of the few times they would attend something this big, a once-a-year family trip that would last the entire day. A good part of their income came from selling produce and homemade items, so they needed to make the best of the opportunity.

Caleb watched Emma walk onto the porch. She had to have realized halfway down the stairs that the box she carried was too heavy, but she was too stubborn to set it down, instead wobbling forward with each step. When she set her foot down, he gently reached around and pulled the box away, peeking around it to smile at her. His heart hit hard in his chest, like it had years ago when they were together.

She stopped and stared. "Caleb?"

"You don't know your own strength. I can barely lift this thing." He shook his head as he placed it in the back of the wagon.

She stepped forward as if to see it was really him. "When are you leaving?"

"Decided to stay awhile. Can I join you? You'll need to take the buggy too, so I'd be glad to chauffeur you."

Emma scoffed. "I think my *daed* would frown on us being together unsupervised."

"He still hasn't lightened up on that? We're older than most who are married here." He knew she really meant that her *daed* didn't trust him. Before he'd left for the city, Ivan had thought highly of Caleb, but his decision to stay in Philly had soured Ivan toward him. Caleb understood to a point, but Ivan had never given him a chance to explain his true cause. Ivan had it in his head, as did many others, that he'd led the youth in the wrong direction.

If they only knew it's the exact opposite…

When he glanced at Emma, she was blushing. He wasn't sure why. Could it be she still had feelings for him? He remembered the day he left. He'd come to her to tell her good-bye, set on changing the world. His big ideals and mission to help others couldn't be denied. She reluctantly let him go with her blessing. He envisioned her stricken expression and tears trickling down her face. He'd never gotten over her. Sometimes when he was alone in the city or had a bad day, he'd wish she was there with him. But she'd made it clear she would never leave the community.

"Well, then, let's get a chaperone." He grinned, knowing who to ask. He hopped in the buggy, liking the feel of the leather reins and the sound of horseshoes clicking on the asphalt road leading into town. He watched the rest of her family in front of them in the wagon. Her *daed* didn't seem to mind that he was there to drive the buggy.

Maria happily chaperoned the two of them with the promise from Emma that she would do the same for her at Sunday singing. She sat in the back, which gave him some time with Emma, who wanted to know everything that he'd been doing, and what his plans were for the future. He humbly tried to tell her but felt like he was talking too much about himself. He had grown used to hearing the stories of the homeless, nonbelievers and downtrodden, not about him.

"You live on purpose, nothing left to chance, all for *Gott*'s glory. I don't know how you do it all in such a big and busy place." Her auburn eyes sparkled in the morning sun.

"You get used to it after a while. You learn where the safe places are and people you can trust." He turned to her. "It's really no different than anywhere else." He didn't know whether she caught his meaning. Except for the larger numbers it was not much different than living in any community—even in the Amish community he grew up in. People were people, no matter where you were.

"I still can't see you living in Philly."

"Why is that so hard to imagine?"

"I knew you growing up Amish, living on the land, not cement and skyscrapers." She looked to him for an answer, more serious this time. He wasn't sure what she expected. But whatever it was, he didn't seem to be telling her the things she wanted to hear.

They were quiet for a moment. He knew she was thinking, so he waited to hear what was on her mind.

"What keeps you there, Caleb? You would make a good minister for our community."

He scoffed. "Being a minister, deacon, or bishop are all different; so is evangelizing. The Amish live out their faith, but they don't share it with others as much as most Christian groups. I want to do both. Being in the community held me back from what I feel called to do." He gave her a quick smile, hoping she understood. This would be controversial if he were amongst the *gmayna,* the church board.

"You always did like your freedom." She turned to him,

watching as he slowly turned to look at her. "I admire that about you."

"I think you're the only one in the community who understands me."

"You might be surprised." She was silent for a moment. "But I'll always believe in you, Caleb."

The lump in his throat kept him from swallowing, much less responding. Not even his parents gave him their full support. They didn't *bann* him from their home as some did when their children decided to leave the community. But he'd decided to stay with friends until he left for the city again so as not to get the deacons involved.

He found a place to park the buggy, and they went to help with the wagon. Once they got their table set up, Caleb wanted nothing more than to walk the grounds with Emma. Maria followed a step or two behind. They watched children get their faces painted and then strolled through booths, tasting different foods. A band played, and people streamed in and out of the farm equipment tent. They laughed together as brave souls risked getting drenched at the dunking tank.

"*Ach*, look at the magician." Emma grabbed Caleb's arm and drew him to another small stage. They watched as he turned a rabbit into a bouquet of flowers and then handed them to Caleb. He, in turn, gave them to Emma. She breathed in the sweet aroma. "*Danke*."

"What a gentleman." Zeb's voice traveled far enough for the magician to hear, and they turned to see him with Maria by his side. The magician reached into his hat once more and then handed Zeb a single red rose. To Caleb's surprise, Zeb gave the flower to Maria. "You seem to already have plenty." He winked at Emma but not in a playful way.

"I have a hankering for a corndog. Anyone else want one?"

Caleb hiked a thumb over his shoulder at the food tents. For Emma's sake, he should back off. He was lucky to have gotten some time with her, even if it ended now.

"I'll go with you, Caleb," Maria offered and twirled her rose. She skipped up next to him and let him smell her flower.

He glanced around, curious to see where Emma had gone. She and Zeb were walking several steps behind them. He couldn't hear what Zeb was saying, but neither of them was smiling. He didn't want to cause problems for Emma, but she hadn't done anything wrong. He was hardly a threat to anyone; they lived in separate worlds. He hadn't seen her in over a year, and didn't know when they'd meet again.

Mark walked up with a few others and stopped in front of Caleb and Maria. Caleb had a feeling he knew what they had on their minds. "Caleb, glad we found you."

"I'm surprised you did. This place is packed." Caleb saw Emma out of the corner of his eye. She slowly went over close enough to hear them. She stood behind Mark and in front of Zeb. "Who are your friends?"

"More from the community who want to go with us when you leave." Mark introduced everyone, and Caleb asked them why they wanted to leave, whether they were planning to come home, what they would do there—anything to get them to think about their decision.

He'd seen too many who ended up turning right back around. Going to the city sounded good, especially for a teen upset with his or her parents or who was just curious, but it wasn't a good enough reason to go. It wasn't a vacation or sight-seeing trip. It was working for food and a place to sleep.

The entertainment wasn't always what they expected and got them into trouble as times. Once this was explained, a couple of them seemed leery, which is exactly what Caleb wanted. It saved him the inconvenience of hooking them up to get back home after finding out it wasn't what they'd hoped for.

"You can't run away from your problems."

Caleb turned around to see Emma talking to one of the youth who was with Mark. He stayed where he was, listening.

"But maybe you should go, so you can see that your parents aren't asking too much from you."

"Or maybe I'll find out that they are," the young teen girl spouted off. Caleb had heard the story repeatedly. They don't like the rules, so they punished their parents by leaving. In the long run they usually came back, tail between their legs. Others figured out they were wrong, but were too prideful to admit it and return home. One thing the Amish had going for them in the city was that their demeanor and hard-working upbringing got them jobs, and they kept them. But it took a lot of money to live in the city; even the dives were more than minimum wage could support.

There were so many conversations going on that Caleb took a step back, watching and listening. He'd worked with teenagers for years, but this up-and-coming group scared him. One reason he only dealt with Amish was due to their obedience, but this group seemed to have their own mind about things. They were bent on having their own way to an extent uncommon for the Amish. He prayed it would all sort out in God's favor for those who could handle what they were dishing out and for those who had no idea what they were in for.

Chapter Thirteen

"You're going to have to tell her." Caleb's direct instruction made Emma lift her eyes and stare. "If you're serious about going you need to tell your parents—and yourself."

She set the quilt that *Mamm* wanted to keep in a box, digesting what he was asking. "What do you mean, tell myself?"

"Once you commit to this, you can't go back. It's not fair to anyone when someone changes their mind."

"That sounds a bit rigid." Her feet were getting colder with every word he was saying.

Caleb took her by the arms. "I don't mean to upset you, but you have to go for more of a reason than Mark. He might disappoint you, break the rules, or get into trouble. But if you have something else taking you there, then you have a real purpose to hold on to."

She marveled at his commitment in taking this trip every year with a group of restless teenagers trying to find themselves. She felt the same concern Caleb had after what happened at the festival. It might also give her some time to think about her own future...and Zeb. But deep down, she knew what the true reason was. "My reason is the same as yours."

He smiled, melting away the serious expression he'd just held. "To spread the Word?"

She could only nod, seeing the understanding in his eyes. A rush of the Holy Spirit filled her and confirmed her purpose. Emma silently prayed thanksgiving to *Gott* for giving her the strength she needed to leave her family.

"It won't be easy for you, but I have no doubt that while you're there, you will grow in a way you never knew possible." His eyes grew soft. Then he suddenly dropped her hands and moved away.

"Am I interrupting?" Zeb's voice was flat, and he squinted as he came closer. They flickered from Caleb to Emma, and then stopped on her.

"Zeb, I didn't hear you." He must have walked on the grass to avoid the noise from the pebbles on the path. Emma felt like she was caught doing something wrong, but she also knew he purposely wanted to surprise her.

"Things are quiet down by the motel, so I thought I'd come and see if you needed help getting settled in for the night."

"I'm gonna head inside." Caleb walked up the stairs to the Klines' *haus* where they were all spending the night, giving Emma a quick look before he shut the door. He remained passive. He was by nature. But Zeb was not, so it served Caleb well to know when to leave.

Zeb watched Caleb go, and then turned to Emma. "What were you two talking about?" He stuck both thumbs under his suspenders, and she felt the full force of his attention as his eyes locked on her.

"My *mamm*. I need to spend some time with her." Emma's eyes felt heavy, and she realized how tired she was. She briefly thought of just telling Zeb right then that she was going with Mark, but she didn't have the energy to tell her *mamm*, let alone him.

"Is Rebecca feeling all right?" He rubbed her cheek with two fingers. The calluses were rough against her skin, and she drew back, thinking about what she needed to tell her *mamm* and dreading it.

She nodded.

"Emma, I'd appreciate it if Caleb didn't touch you." He kept his stare on her. She was too surprised to know what to say. Had he touched her? When she thought back, *jah*, there was holding hands, and a hug in greeting, but nothing more...at least not that she remembered.

"I didn't realize he did." But Emma did have to admit she was not uncomfortable when he held her hand or rubbed her arm, touching her skin. It didn't seem natural with Zeb, maybe because they didn't have the history together that she and Caleb did.

"I'll let you go. You seem tired." He took one step back and was about to speak, but then looked inside the *haus* full of her relatives.

"*Danke*, I am."

"Get some sleep." He took one last look at her, and then turned away, his boots grinding into the dirt road. She waited until she couldn't hear the crunching sound before going to fetch her *mamm*.

As soon as she set one foot in the door, her family was upon her. They were playing word games while the youngsters watched and the older children explored outside. Emma searched for Caleb and found him talking with one of the Kline boys. It seemed teens sought him out, no matter where he was. When she caught his eye, he came over. "Sorry to bother you. But would you mind taking *Mamm* and me on a buggy ride?"

He looked around the room. "Need some privacy?"

She nodded. "I don't have the energy for this group tonight." She started to walk away and stopped.

"Did Zeb leave?"

"*Jah*, he's gone." She could have asked Zeb, but he wasn't

supporting her on this, and Caleb was neutral. "If you're uncomfortable—"

"No, I just don't want you in an awkward situation." He grinned. "I used to be Amish."

That made Emma glad he was doing what he felt *Gott* was leading him to do, wishing she had a clearer idea of what her place was. But she selfishly wanted him back in the community.

Emma asked her *mamm* to come outside to talk. Rebecca sat down in the back of the buggy and let out a sigh. It had been a long day. "*Mamm*, I've given it a lot of thought, and I think I should go with Mark."

Rebecca's eyes widened. "You…want to go where?"

Caleb turned his head and nodded, encouraging Emma. She needed it. After the conversation at the festival, Emma knew she couldn't put off telling her family she was leaving. This was something they would take hard. They'd never expect to hear she would be going on *rumspringa*. But then, neither did she.

"To Philadelphia." Emma tried to keep her from getting too upset, but *Mamm*'s moist eyes told her she would be, no matter what she said after those two words.

"But why?" Her *mamm* laid her hands in her lap and picked at a hanky. Her graying hair and many wrinkles seemed more prominent.

Mamm's tears made Emma feel a bit sentimental…and guilty. But she knew the guilt would be worse if she stayed. "I'd like to go to the city and meet the English, just for a while." She forced a smile as if it wasn't too much to ask. Emma couldn't picture herself in such a place. She may turn a year older there, depending on how long she stayed. It would be different for everyone. She hoped Mark wouldn't want to spend a lot of time there. Her mind suddenly buzzed, thinking of all the things that could be. Where would they stay? What would she wear? She pondered whether she should have at least something that was English, even though she really didn't want to. Would that be compromising who she was?

Telling Mark earlier that day that she was going to Philadelphia had been much easier than telling *Mamm*. He fussed only a little. But she suspected he had some plans of his own once he got there. She would worry about that if it came about. She didn't think it would be all that he expected.

"I can't imagine why you would go to someplace like that. You belong here."

Emma didn't expect her *mamm* to understand. Even going for Mark wasn't enough of an explanation. Leaving brought shame upon most parents. Others in the community would wonder why the parents couldn't handle their wild children. She hated to put that burden on her *mamm* and *daed*, but she continued to remind herself this was best. She could talk herself in or out of anything. But what answer would let her sleep at night?

"How can you leave the community like that? You were going to be baptized come spring. How did it go from that to this?"

"We didn't know that things would go this way with Mark, *Mamm*. It will all work out. You'll see." Now she sounded like Zeb, giving idealistic advice, trying to smooth over the situation with idle words. She had no idea what would happen when they left. The only consolation was that Maria and Martha would be here for her *mamm* and *daed*. She dreaded telling Zeb. She'd seen him angry more than once. Crossing him wasn't worth it.

Mamm looked up. "Running around with teenagers, exploring the outside world doesn't sound like something you would want to do. You seem so content here, and you're not one to break the rules."

Emma made eye contact with *Mamm*. "I won't break them. I'll try to be an example, living as a Christian in the secular world."

Then her *mamm* wept, and Emma held her in her arms until she stopped. Caleb parked the buggy and took her *mamm*'s hand in his. "Will you walk with me?"

Emma wondered if he felt responsible for her going. Thinking back to the night at the singing, she remembered thinking that Caleb was brave to evangelize in Philly.

"Come in before you leave." Emma pointed to the *haus*.

He nodded and wrapped *Mamm*'s arm around his. Her shoulders sloped as she walked slowly next to Caleb. She didn't know how to console her *mamm*, but Caleb would.

In the morning she would have to tell her *daed*.

Chapter Fourteen

Emma walked up to their red, two-story barn, sucked in a breath, and then opened the doors. Both *Daed* and Mark were milking and stopped to look up at her. "Morning."

"Don't tell me you're going to help us do the milking," Mark teased.

She pictured *Daed* doing the milking without Mark and only Maria and little Martha to help *Mamm* around the house, and squeezed her eyes shut. She'd made her decision, and she would stick with it. "*Nee*, I'm here to talk to you, *Daed*."

He stared at her for a long moment, and then slowly walked over to her. "What is it, Emma?" He asked as though he knew. He rarely showed much expression. She was counting on that now. Mark continued to work, pulling the cups off the dairy cow's udders, but he kept an eye on them and was within earshot. She looked from him to Mark and let out a breath.

"I'm going with the others to *rumspringa*." Many words tumbled around inside her head, but nothing else mattered. There was nothing she could say to make this better. Two of his children were leaving him. There were no words strong enough to make up for the ones she'd just said.

Daed stuck his boney hands on his hips and nodded once to acknowledge what she'd said. She expected a short conversation, maybe a harsh word or two of disappointment, but he didn't say a word. That was much worse.

As *Daed* walked back over to finish the milking, Mark

turned to Emma. "You could have waited." He heaved a breath as he stormed by her.

Irritation at his comment raged within her and she had no patience left. She was counting on *rumspringa* being a huge disappointment for him. Emma prayed she was right.

Emma wanted to chase after him and give him a tongue-lashing, but instead she went over to the cows and started cleaning off their udders with some newspaper she'd brought from the *haus*. A light wind whistled through the barn and stirred up small twisters, sweeping up bits of straw and chicken feed from the wood floor.

Daed's boot slid along the floor she'd been studying, the crunching sound in her ears. Emma stood and made herself look him in the eyes.

She'd expected her *mamm* to express her disappointment with tears, and prepared herself for her *daed's* rage. But anger wasn't in his eyes.

"Why would you do this to your *mamm*, Emma?" He clenched his jaw and said something she didn't want to hear. "I expected it from your brother—always causing a ruckus—but not from you." He looked around the barn as if he didn't know where he was.

"I'm going because of Mark." She didn't have the courage to tell him about evangelizing. He believed in being a living example, not telling people about their faith with words.

Daed let out a breath and looked back down at the dusty floor. "If you can't control him here, why do you think you can out there?"

Emma hesitated, only for a moment. "Caleb."

Daed turned abruptly and stared at her, then nodded. "Never thought I'd forgive him, but I suppose I'll have to if he brings you both home in one piece."

Emma shook her head. "You might accept him if you knew him better, *Daed*."

He scoffed. "There are few men I respect more."

Emma was taken aback. "What do you mean?"

He drew his boot back and stuck his thumbs over his black pants. "When he told me what he's been doing in that godforsaken place I couldn't think anything but good thoughts about him." He wiped his nose with the back of his hand.

"I didn't know you two had talked."

"I didn't want to, but you know what a pest he can be." He grunted. "Following me around, milking, fixing the barn door."

Emma glanced at the door. It no longer dragged on the ground.

"Caught him mucking the stalls yesterday." He shook his head. "All the while telling me about the city and the people there. He's done some darn good things." *Daed* pointed to an old garden tiller. "He asked me for those sorry, used-up wheels. Said they'd come in handy for a friend of his in the city who has a wheelchair or some such thing." *Daed* cleared his throat. "I'm not going to be the one to stop him doing anything of the likes of that."

He said it like he was talking to the deacon board or the bishop, protecting his change of opinion. But he still hadn't addressed the issue at hand. She held her breath and waited.

After a time he raised his eyes to meet hers. "You go if you got to, but you come back. Ya hear?" He turned away quickly, as if guarding himself from any more conversation.

All Emma could do was try to breathe as she watched him go. She'd never in a hundred years expected her *daed* to say what he just had.

Once she told Zeb, she would be ready to go to the city.

Chapter Fifteen

Zeb paced through his barn. His boots hit the wood floor in repetition as he pivoted and then marched back to the other end. He didn't know what was going through Emma's mind, but with Caleb around some sort of problem was sure to arise. He had everything in place. Once the *haus* was built and courting started come spring, there would be nothing in his way. He was sure Emma had an idea he was making plans, but she never spoke of it. He shouldn't have to go to her *daed* concerning these matters, but Emma kept it all at bay. He didn't know whether she was just nervous or unsure he was the one for her.

He chalked it up to nerves. He would count on having her full attention once Caleb left, and Zeb wouldn't have to see the look in her eyes when she saw Caleb. He wasn't a rival, though—not with his life being in the city. Zeb wouldn't make a fool of himself by showing his jealousy. Fortunately he was a patient man.

Once the dairy cows were cleaned up and unhitched from milking, he let them out one by one. They followed each other in a long line of forty or so, blindly following the one in front. That was pretty much how he felt about *rumspringa*. He spat and put the equipment away. As he went about separating the milk, he heard the creak of the barn door opening. He stood and went over to see Emma standing in the doorway.

She smiled timidly and looked around the barn. "Do you need some help in here?"

"*Nee*, I'm almost done separating." He gestured to a milking stool. They were rarely used since the gas-run milking machines were approved by the bishop. He sat with her and waited to hear what was on her mind. Her downcast eyes were the first indication something was up. Her lack of conversation was an indicator, as well. "What is it, Emma?"

She picked up a yellow piece of hay, twirling it between two fingers. "I have something to tell you. I hope you understand and will support me in the decision I've made."

The skin on the back of his neck crawled. There were two things he thought of that would make her this uncomfortable. She didn't want to get married or she was going on *rumspringa*. He didn't know which was worse at the moment, but he started calculating a rebuttal for both as he sat and waited. This wouldn't be the first time she wanted to wait to marry. He was weary of waiting, but this time she might change her mind if a *haus* was waiting for her.

"Since Mark is going to leave, I've decided to go with him." She kept her eyes on the single piece of hay but said no more.

He sat in silence, waiting for the stream of reasons why she had to leave. The more flustered she got, the easier it would be to trip her up into what was best for their relationship. The sound of the wind outside suddenly sounded fierce, and the room seemed to grow, but she didn't speak. "Maybe you should give this more thought. I wouldn't want you to go to all of the trouble and expense and have it go badly for you."

She placed both hands in her lap. "It's not about me, it's about Mark."

He had her puzzled, which was a good start.

"Funny, how everything in your household revolves around Mark. The honoring your parents doesn't seem to apply to him." He watched her face twist. He was saying everything she was thinking but didn't dare to say. But it was working. He could see her mind churning. "He's no different than any other rebellious adolescent in the community, is he?"

Emma's mouth opened, but nothing came out. She pointed the tips of her boots together and stared down at them. "Maybe so, maybe not, but my parents are older than most."

"Another excuse." He moved in close, inches away from her. "If you want to go to *rumspringa* on your own accord, that's okay, Emma. Just be honest about it."

Emma dropped the yellow strand of hay and put both palms on her knees. "That's not fair, Zeb. You're putting words in my mouth."

He'd gone too far, panicked a little. He had to back step now. He dropped his head. "You're right. I can't stand the thought of you going to that city full of violence and debauchery." He took her by the arms. "I just don't want anything to happen to you."

He thought he had her, just for a moment. Then the strong side of her came forth. She stood and looked down at him. "That's why I can't let Mark go alone."

He kicked himself mentally and shook his head. "I can't apologize for wanting to protect you."

She let out a breath and crossed her arms over her chest. Her defenses lowered. "I know. I'm sorry. I know how hard this is for you. But I'd be worthless if I stayed."

Maybe this could still work to his advantage. Let her go and be miserable and come back. He reworked his plans and stood up to put his arms around her. "You do what you think is best. And I'll be here waiting when you return."

"*Danke*, Zeb. I didn't want us to leave one another upset."

He smiled. "That's why I gave in to your decision."

She tilted her head in thought, and he quickly changed the

subject. "Would you like me to take you to church?" He hoped she would say yes for many reasons. The most important was to keep her away from Caleb. He'd been looking forward to the day, but now he dreaded it. For the moment it appeared she'd won the battle, but he hadn't given up yet. There might be a way to change her mind.

"It depends on when we leave." Her shoulders lowered, and she looked into his eyes. "You do understand, don't you?"

He didn't but would put up with this nonsense for the moment. He'd just have to think of another way to get her to stay. "Do you want to talk about this again?"

"*Nee,* I just want to be fair to you, without being unfair to Mark."

"I think Caleb is perfectly capable of watching over Mark. I'm sure he's dealt with worse." Her forehead wrinkled, and he knew he'd gone too far again. "But it's up to you and your family to decide."

She stopped. Her cheeks turned pink with frustration. "I'm tired of everyone's opinion. I'll do what I think is best." Her head lifted and she started for the door. "I'll see you later then."

He reached out to stop her but then thought better of it. He couldn't convince her of anything right now. He'd wait until after church, when she'd calmed down. She was becoming too stubborn. That was not something he was used to. But she was so emotionally attached to this situation, it was bringing out a new side in her.

He cleaned up for church and decided to drive his own buggy, hoping she would allow him to take her home. He didn't know what to expect, so he planned to wait for her to take the first step. Deep in thought, when he turned the corner to the kitchen, he bumped into his brother, Merv.

"*Nee*, I'm sorry. I wasn't paying attention." Merv looked Zeb up and down. "You're ready for church early."

"*Jah*, well I'd like to say good-bye to those who are leaving."

"Including Emma?" He stared up at Zeb, hesitantly waiting for an answer.

Zeb pursed his lips. "At this point, she is leaning toward going. But we'll see how things end up."

"I'm sorry, brother. Maybe you can talk to her again after church, over a good meal." He scratched his tousled, brown hair.

"*Jah*, I'll see you at church." He went through the kitchen with agitation running through his veins.

He went to church alone. The men usually stood together in the back or outside to talk. The conversation went from crops and the weather to the latest activities in the community—a barn-raising or quilting bee they'd help the women organize, and the frolics teenagers took part in. Those who didn't leave on *rumspringa* hung out in groups, socialized, and the boys dared to turn the brims of their hats down. The girls would go riding with a boy in his buggy and stand next to him at a singing, showing others they were a couple.

"Spring fever." Zeb shook his head as he walked outside. He didn't miss that time of "running around," and was always glad when it was over. Emma told him she felt the same, even though he had gone through the experience years before she did. It seemed to become more of an ordeal as time went on.

"So, I hear a group is heading to the city today," one of the men informed them while hitching his horse. As he walked over, Zeb couldn't help but want to find out more information.

"You sure about that?" Zeb looked at Melvin intently. He was one of many who didn't belong with either the older men or the younger.

Melvin squinted one eye to block out the sun rising behind Zeb's back. He could feel the heat as he stood waiting for an answer. "Timothy." He called over to a wide-eyed youngster. "Those young'uns leaving for the city 'bout now?"

"*Jah*, my *bruder*'s one of them."

If Emma was going to go through with this, Zeb had to talk to her before she left, and he wouldn't see her at church. He became anxious and excused himself, not able to get to his buggy fast enough. He didn't want to stop for anything, and the horse could make double time without his buggy. So he forced himself off, unhitched his buggy, and left it in the back forty of Emma's corn field.

When he got to her *haus* he knew Caleb was there. There was no sign of him, but he just knew the intruder was nearby. Zeb jumped off his horse and tethered the makeshift reins around the nearest tree. He slowed his breathing as he neared the *haus*, not wanting to appear as frantic as he felt. This was unlike him. Nothing had happened yet. There wasn't any need to panic. No one came to the door when he knocked, so he walked in the front door. Then he heard Caleb's voice.

He stopped and listened but heard only faint murmurs. He took a deep breath and went up the stairs. When he got to the second floor, he saw Caleb standing at the landing. "Morning, Caleb." He enjoyed the look on Caleb's face. Zeb turned and took the last stair and then went into Emma's room. Her eyes were wide, and she stood frozen with clothes in her hand, ready to put in the duffel bag lying on her bed. The sun shone through her window. When he lifted a hand to block the sun rays from his eyes, she jolted.

"Emma, are you okay?" Zeb frowned, concerned at her response.

"*Jah*, I wasn't expecting you." She dropped the dress into the bag and pulled the drawstring tight.

"Were you going to say good-bye?" He wanted to hear her excuse.

Her eyes shifted her eyes downward. "I hadn't decided. You were awful upset when we talked."

He searched for a way to keep her here because he obviously wasn't enough of a reason. "Do you remember what I warned you about with your coughing spells? You wouldn't want your *mamm* and *daed* to worry."

Emma frowned in thought, as if she was taking in what he'd said. For a short second he thought he might have her attention.

Caleb stepped between them, took her bag, and went downstairs. She watched him go.

"I'll write to you," Emma said to Zeb.

He nodded and tried his best to keep the steam from rising in his head. It was bad enough she was leaving, but finding Caleb here alone with her was too much. "I was planning to take you to the bus in town. Why didn't you tell me you were leaving so soon?"

She ran a finger over the quilt covering her bed. "I didn't want to upset you."

"Well, you have." He spit out the words before he could catch himself. Her eyes widened, and she looked away. He rubbed his temples with his thumb and one finger, trying to find an ounce of patience. "How will I be able to contact you to know you're safe?"

Her eyes watered as she began to speak. "I'll find a way as soon as I get there. I promise I will." Her promise sounded unsure. He went to her and wrapped his arms around her. Her body was stiff, and he barely felt her arms around him.

"Be careful." He withdrew and walked out of the room. He needed to leave before he said something he'd regret. He didn't look at Caleb as he passed him, just simply said, "If anything happens to her—"

"Zeb." Caleb stayed put until Zeb looked over at him. "I'll die keeping her safe."

Chapter Sixteen

Maria arrived to see Emma and Mark off to the bus station, but their parents had carried on as if it were just another day and left for church with Martha. Caleb stopped by not long after they left to pick up Emma and Mark along with a few others who needed a buggy ride to town. The drive went quickly with all the chatter. There was a lot of energy in the air, everyone anticipating what the city would be like. Caleb knew to leave before weepy *mamms* and angry *daeds* would be out of church and things got out of hand with their wayward children. He stayed calm and reassured the teens that he would do everything he could for them as long as they cooperated.

"You shouldn't have expected anything else from Caleb," Maria whispered to Emma. She reached out and gave her a hug, and caught Mark's attention so she could kiss him on the cheek. A tear slipped down her face, and she walked quickly down the dusty path taking her home.

Home. I never thought I'd leave, Emma thought.

She sat quietly in one of the buggies as Caleb clipped down the road into town, and kept an eye on Mark. He seemed to think this was all fun and games. Maybe it was. Emma wasn't sure of anything, other than that she had made this decision to go, and would try to make the best of it.

Once they got to the Lititz bus station, everyone piled out of the buggies. Those who were there to drop them off said their good-byes. Not many parents came, and the few who did were there to get them to change their minds. Some of the teens were hesitating on leaving, and Caleb talked to more than a few about their decision. "If you decide to leave, you're on your own to get yourself back home." He told them only once and then went about packing up to leave.

She watched Caleb help the others store their bags under the bus and find a seat. Some knew each other and others didn't. Her community had the biggest turnout, for which the deacons would blame Caleb. The more she saw him in action, the more she understood why he felt compelled to guide these young people. But many of them just wanted to be on their own, not bothered by anyone. That was until they got into a fix they needed help getting out of.

Mark stepped up and into the bus, went straight to Emma's seat and looked down at her. "I have a ride to Philly, so I'm just gonna go with some of the guys."

Emma looked at the young man waiting impatiently behind Mark. "I don't believe that's a good idea, Mark. I think Caleb wants us all together." She should have thought of something more subtle. He looked around him at his newfound friends and grunted a laugh toward Emma.

"Don't test me by considering riding with a group that has access to a car," Emma said.

Mark turned his head to the side and glanced at the guy behind him. His hair touched his collar, and he wore jeans. He was either with a less conservative group or already taking advantage of *rumspringa*. He scoffed when she told Mark no, and Emma was regretting how she'd responded to Mark.

Mark shook his head. "You're my sister, not my *mamm*."

Before he could say more, she lifted a hand. "Can you excuse us?" she asked the young man behind him.

He shrugged and started to walk down the aisle of the bus. "Catch ya next time, Miller."

Mark's lips twisted as he watched him go. Then he bent over so only she could hear him. "You're not going to ruin this trip for me, Emma." He turned around so fast, she didn't have a chance to explain to him why she wanted him with her. She didn't know those boys, and he probably didn't either. Unless he could say differently, it made no sense for him to drive off with strangers. His harsh words embarrassed and angered her. At the moment she hated everything about her decision to leave.

Caleb finally finished getting everyone aboard and sat down next to her. "Does Mark want to sit with you?" He seemed to have a new liveliness about him. She couldn't pinpoint it, but something was different.

"*Nee*, he's not happy I'm here."

Caleb looked over to where Mark sat between two other guys. "Let it go. He'll need you sooner or later, even if it's only for a couple bucks or to take care of him."

"I don't think he wants me here, let alone to take care of him." She grunted.

"You might be surprised. Leaving everything a person's ever known changes them." He grinned, trying to lighten her up, but nothing would help right now. Not unless she could get off the bus. "Are you okay?"

"*Nee*, I don't want to leave." She kept her eyes on the driver and looked out the window as they rolled out of the station.

"Does it make you nervous to be on a bus?" Caleb put a hand on hers, and she let her head drop back onto the headrest. It was a familiar feeling for his hand to touch hers, and she needed the comfort.

"*Jah*, everything about this makes me nervous." She didn't

look at him and kept her eyes on the open spaces that were few and far between. "It's closed in, makes me feel claustrophobic."

Caleb dropped his chin so he would be eye-level with her. "You're thinking too much. Think of it as a vacation. You sit back and enjoy the ride, and before you know it, we'll be there."

She couldn't help but chuckle. "A vacation?" It was an odd way to put it to an Amish person.

"Okay, maybe not a vacation…an adventure."

"Adventures aren't always good, though."

"Well, now you're just being negative." He grinned, and she nodded.

"What will we do once we're there?" She knew Caleb ministered to the disadvantaged, but she didn't know exactly what that meant. There had to be a lot of needs in a city this big.

"Whatever needs to be done. The Stock Pot at the church always needs some helping hands, so you can pass out food." He studied her intently, waiting for her answer. His eyes flickered back and forth as if to pick up the pace in her answering.

"To the homeless?" She'd never seen a homeless person, let alone talked to one or given them a meal. She wondered how a person became homeless. That would never happen in her community.

"Some are homeless, and others just need a little help for a while. Is that something you'd feel comfortable doing?" He seemed worried about her. She knew he had better things to deal with than her insecurities, so she made an effort to think positively. When she looked over at him, a thought popped into her head. They were a lot alike—always had been. So if he enjoyed what he did in Philly, there was a chance she would too.

"As long as you're there to show me the ropes." Her request was twofold. She did want his direction, but also his protection.

As different as she was, she would be an easy target for a city person to take advantage of. As she looked around the group on the bus, there was a mix of expressions, conversations, and conduct. Some were oblivious, taking it all in as it came. Others' wide eyes and pinched faces were more like how Emma felt, and then there were those like her brother, ready for an adventure and excitement.

"I won't leave you alone. I've promised not to, and I keep my word."

"Keep your word to whom?"

He looked away and then out the window, ignoring her. "See there, milk cows. Do you feel better?" His eyes met hers, and they connected for a moment.

"Can I take them to Philly with me?" She grinned. As silly as it seemed, she did feel better seeing a farm.

With him at her side the time went quickly. Emma knew he was making an extra effort to keep her distracted, and it worked. They were close to the city in what seemed to be no time at all.

Caleb looked out the window as he spoke. "The city and country split so quickly, you could be in one and then the other simply by going through a stoplight."

Sure enough, tall buildings started popping up, and then a long bridge that took them to skyscrapers. There were all modes of transportation with the trains, waterways, mass transit, and many cars, all going exceedingly fast. Emma looked through the back window, but all she could see was concrete and steel.

"Having second thoughts?" Caleb didn't look at her when he asked, just waited for her answer even though he already knew what it would be.

Emma knew the answer too, but another thought made her

stop and discern what kept tugging at her. "*Jah*, but also *nee*. There is another reason for being here."

Caleb gazed at her. "I'm sure of that."

She opened her eyes wide. "You are?"

"There's no doubt." He said it with such confidence, Emma started believing what she was thinking.

"I can't truly believe it, but there is something nagging at me." She turned her attention to a large church with spires and golden caps. "Is that the church where we're staying?"

Caleb chuckled. "It's that one." He pointed to a much smaller building that looked nothing like a church. The dilapidated roof and tattered front door made the building look more like a homeless shelter than a church. There were a handful of people sitting or lying on the steps. Most had a bag or pillow-case that held their belongings, probably all they had.

Caleb stood to address the group. "This is where we'll be staying, at the Old Mennonite Church." The sound of seats squeaking and low murmurs were heard as they looked out the bus windows. He let them digest their new, temporary home.

For the first time Emma wished for a nicer place to stay. Her five-bedroom home on a hundred acres seemed like a palace. She hadn't thought she'd ever feel this way and felt selfish for the thoughts. Emma hoped Caleb had some better news than this, but she prepared herself for whatever came.

"For those of you who have heard this speech, plug your ears." Nervous laughter fluttered throughout the bus. "I'm not here to babysit you. But it would be to your benefit if you'd tell us where you're going and be back here by curfew, which is midnight. If you're here to do mission work, there are a lot of opportunities. If you're here to party, I can't help you. That's not what I do here. Grab your bags and get settled in." He led the way off the bus, with Emma close behind.

She blinked, digesting the set of loosely made rules and options, and then decided she liked the way he worked. Forcing them to do anything was futile. They were here to spread their wings. She just hoped they didn't fly too far.

She slowly turned around in a circle, observing the cars rushing by, pedestrians gambling to walk across busy streets, and every type of person she had ever imagined—every age, color, height, and fashion style.

Caleb came up next to her. "Amazing place, isn't it?" He shoved his hands in his pockets and watched the hustle and bustle of the city. Lights, noise, and smells lifted and were carried away, and then started again.

"*Jah*, I guess you could say that." She wasn't sure what word would describe this crazy place. It scared her, and yet electrified her at the same time. "I'm not sure what to do with this strange mixture of emotions. I'm used to everything being predictable." She blew out a breath and looked for Mark. The unpredictability he created was nothing compared to this. And she worried this would only increase his curiosity, unlike many who wouldn't feel comfortable indulging in all the city had to offer.

"You'll fit in here." Caleb looked down at her and grinned. "Let's go inside."

She doubted that was true. She'd never felt more like a fish out of water. He was just comforting her. She needed it either way, so she let him take her bag along with his and then lead her into the church.

The inside was in better shape than the outside, but it still left her wanting for home. Long cracks in the deep-yellow, stucco-covered walls made it appear as if the building might split in two. A kitchen and long tables were to her right, and a sanctuary was on the left. A stream of Amish young people walked up the stairs to find their rooms.

"Are you okay?" Caleb's voice brought her back to a place she didn't want to be—even more than before she knew about the living arrangements. She shook off the attitude, shaming herself for expecting more, and went into a bedroom with two beds. There were no sheets or blankets, only a sleeping bag, but that would have to do.

"Is this going to work for you?" Caleb gave her a sideways glance.

"This is fine, Caleb."

"Okay, there's one other thing." He almost cringed but stopped himself.

"*Ach*, what's that?"

He paused and then looked her in the eyes. "Your roommate."

Chapter Seventeen

Caleb heard the clinking of chains grow louder as Monique walked to her room. When she came in, he immediately noticed she'd added a strand of gold links to her belt, and her long, dark hair with spiked up bangs couldn't conceal her beauty. She was tall and lean, with the look of a runway model. It was both a blessing and a curse. Caleb had hoped she'd tone her look down a bit with the arrival of the Amish. But he couldn't control her.

As Monique came in, he heard Emma suck in a breath. There were tattoos on both of Monique's arms, gifts from her boyfriend. Caleb had tried to keep him away, but it was impossible.

Caleb was distracted by Emma's presence, but he'd have to snap out of it. This was going to be a bigger adjustment than many of them could fathom.

"Monique, this is Emma." He glanced at Emma long enough to make eye contact, and then turned away. "Emma, this is your roommate, Monique." He purposely kept quiet to see how they interacted. Monique hadn't bonded with anyone since coming to the Old Mennonite Church. Emma was his last shot. If she couldn't draw Monique out, no one could. Monique walked past Emma, dropped a battered backpack on the floor, and sent a fleeting glance toward Emma.

"What's wrong, haven't seen tattoos before?" She lifted her eyebrows and stuck out her chin.

"*Jah*, I have." It wasn't something Emma hadn't seen before when they went into town. Emma turned away, opened her bag, and placed some Amish clothes on one of the shelves standing at the end of her bed. Just as Caleb was about to speak, Emma spoke. "How long have you been here, Monique?"

"Not as long as some and longer than others."

Monique's quick tongue had gotten her into more scrapes than Caleb wanted to remember. As much trouble as she was, he had to believe she'd get things straightened out. She'd been around the block a couple of times, but Caleb hoped Emma could handle her. She'd dealt with Mark, which was a lower scale, but the attitude was the same.

"I'll take that as awhile then." Emma put her things away quickly, and pulled off the sleeping bag covering the bed. "Is there somewhere to wash this?"

"Down the hall. There are a couple of industrial-sized washers and a dryer."

"Do you want me to wash yours?" Emma pointed to Monique's sleeping bag, which was wadded up on the twin-size bed.

Monique stared her down. "Don't be acting like Jesus sent you here Himself." She raised a fist to her hip and stuck out one foot. "Just 'cause you wear that dress and hat don't mean you're better than me."

"*Jah*, but I know Jesus sent me to this place and you." Emma turned away and scanned the room.

Caleb kept from shaking his head. He'd likely be sending groups back home within a few days after the initial curiosity was over and they'd seen enough to appreciate home. He'd be left with the hardcore bunch who liked the excitement they found. That's when his real work would begin. He wondered if Emma would be among the first group to return home.

The entire church had the same puke color of yellow on the

walls. There was only one overhead fluorescent light. Caleb was grateful that both bulbs worked in their room.

Emma sighed and then shrugged the sleeping bag over her shoulder and looked at Caleb. "Which way?"

Monique frowned, looking confused.

The two young women stared at one another for a moment, and then Emma looked again to Caleb. "Which way?"

He pointed to the right, down the hall. He'd been so fascinated by their exchange, he hadn't said a word. It didn't seem necessary. "Do either of you need anything before I go help with the meal?"

"*Nee* I don't, *danke*, Caleb."

Monique sneered. "Don't be doing that Amish talk around me. Speak English."

Her sentences were shorter the bolder she got, to the point Caleb had to stop and figure out what she said at times.

"Monique, once you get to know Emma, you'll understand what she's saying."

Monique was one of the most untrusting people he'd met, but in knowing her history, he understood why.

"We'll see." She kicked the dark-green sleeping bag toward Emma.

Emma picked up the bag and walked out. Caleb was right behind her, grabbing Monique's sleeping bag from Emma and studying her face. "If you want a different roommate, I can figure something out."

"*Nee*, it's *gut*." Emma didn't look at him, so he couldn't tell whether she was sincere, upset, or angry.

"She can be difficult, but once she lets her guard down, she has a big heart. It's been bruised so many times, she goes on the defensive until she knows she can trust you. She'll come around." He paused, hoping she'd be as hopeful, but how could he expect that from Emma already? He wasn't being fair and knew it, but couldn't stop trying.

"I asked *Gott* to put me in the right place, with those He wanted me to be with. If this is His will, then I'll be obedient and stay with her."

Her face was expressionless, which wasn't a good sign. She was trying to take it in stride, but he knew better.

Caleb let out a long breath. "Listen, it wasn't fair of me to expect so much of you. You don't want to be here in the first place, and then I dump Monique on you. That's not right. I'm sorry. I just..." He stuck his hands in his pockets, trying to decide how much to say. He couldn't tell her how he really felt about her. That would just make things more awkward. But he knew her heart, and helping others was one of her gifts.

She placed her hand on his arm. "Caleb, I'm fine. So far, anyway." She half smiled. "Remember, I came here with no expectations."

She seemed to have her mind set, so Caleb let the guilt roll off of him. He shouldn't have assumed as much as he did, but he had a lot of faith in Emma, and he couldn't help but try and use her for the good of the people there. "I see a lot of potential in Monique. I don't want her slip through the cracks like so many have since I've been here."

"I understand." She squeezed his hand, and then gave her attention to the laundry room. He watched her scan the area as they went in. Holes were punched in the walls, with drywall falling out. The once black-and-white tile was a dingy brown, and random clothes were scattered throughout the room.

"Here, let me show you how to use this." He stuffed the sleeping bag in the washer, put in the soap, and turned the dial on. "It'll be done in thirty minutes."

"That's wonderful *gut*." She watched the bag shifting around through the circle window. "It's very large."

"Yeah, a little different than doing laundry with the hand-cranked washer back home." Caleb wondered how Emma was doing, so far. It was a lot to take in, especially for a young Amish woman who was content on a farm.

He wished Monique would give a little and let Emma rub off on her. She needed to get out of North Philly before she could get her life together, but she kept going back. He didn't understand it, but it seemed to be common amongst those in poverty. No place was home for them. "Are you hungry?"

Emma frowned. It had been several hours since they'd arrived and she'd barely noticed the time. "I haven't even thought about food. But *jah*, I am."

"They'll be serving dinner in the kitchen in a few minutes. Do you want to go downstairs and help?"

"*Jah*, should we ask Monique?" Emma kept walking to her room instead of taking the stairs to the kitchen. Caleb was tickled she'd asked. If things didn't work out between them, it wouldn't be because Emma didn't try.

"That's a great idea." He stood at the top of the stairs, not wanting to interfere, and watched Emma stop at the door and talk to Monique. He had no idea whether she'd come. The deciding factor would probably be if her belly was empty.

Emma turned away and walked back to him. "Ready?"

Caleb pushed off the dull yellow wall and started for the dingy tile stairs. "She's not coming, I take it."

"She said she'll come down when she is ready." She rubbed his arm. "You are very concerned about this girl, *Jah*?"

"I've seen her go through some tough stuff. But she's strong. She just needs to believe in herself and get away from the people she hangs out with." He shook his head. "Sorry, I get carried away. Not just with her. Any of the clients who stay long enough to get to know them and what they've been through.

"Is it her boyfriend who gives her the tattoos?"

Caleb froze at the word boyfriend. This guy didn't deserve the title. He was no more than a womanizer. "He's a former client here at the church."

"You call them clients?" She twined her fingers together behind her back, listening with interest.

"Some of them are, and the case workers like us to keep tabs on them, give information about anything new going on. Others live on the street, traveling from one city to another, and make their way back around. Some we don't ever see again. Those are the ones I hope have found their place in this world."

"You really know and care about these people, don't you?"

He nodded and watched Emma smile and then search the crowded room filled with the regulars and now with a group of Amish as well. The mix was an interesting sight to see. She was looking for Mark, so he did too. Caleb found him with a group of young men and women, laughing and picking at his food. She and Mark surely knew the food wouldn't be good here compared to what they were used to. The kitchen, which was on the far side of the room, was working like a conveyer belt, with volunteers placing food on trays and offering drinks at the end of the line. The loud buzz in the building soared to an even higher level, making it hard to hear as they got closer to the food.

"It's so noisy." Emma's voice could barely be heard with all the commotion.

"Did you notice most of the chatter is from the Amish?" He looked over at her, remembering the get-togethers they'd had when he was growing up in the community. Maybe that was one reason he liked working in a shelter like this, getting to know others, going through the good and bad of life together. He suddenly felt sentimental, wishing for those days again. He glanced at Emma, so far away from her community.

"We never seem to lack for conversation, do we?" Her eyes sparkled as she asked.

"Let's go see if they need help in the kitchen." He proudly showed her the well-oiled machine behind the scenes, cooking up a storm.

"It's about time. It's meatloaf and potatoes tonight." Alex caught Caleb's eye and started gathering the ingredients. "Alex, do you need—"

"Someone to peel these potatoes? Yeah!" He shoved a bag into Caleb's hands and took a step back when he saw Emma. "And you must be Emma."

Caleb felt the temperature on his neck warm. He'd confided in Alex about his relationship with Emma. Caleb knew Alex wouldn't say anything to her, but at the moment he felt awkward. He'd never thought she'd be here for Alex to meet. Now that he thought about it, he had told a case worker about her too. They had dated for a short time, and when he broke things off he told her why—Emma.

"Hey, over here." Alex waved to get Caleb's attention. The beads at the tip of his dreadlocks clicked together as he slapped the bag to get Caleb's attention, and it did. Alex's strong hand about knocked the potatoes out of Caleb's hands. Alex's tall and sturdy frame kept away the stragglers who came around to pick a fight, but he had a temper. It didn't take much for him to blow if injustice was taking place.

"Are you with us?" Alex teased, but Caleb was getting

uncomfortable. Alex handed Emma a vegetable peeler and a knife. "I'll put you in charge until Caleb gets himself together."

"Sorry, got preoccupied for a minute." Caleb pulled out a cutting board and took the knife. The emotions whirling inside him slowed as he got into the rhythm, cutting potatoes to mash after Emma skinned them. Alex looked over at him and chuckled. He had some explaining to do, but he'd ignore it as much as possible. He didn't want Emma to know he still had feelings for her, at least not yet. She was here to watch over her brother and spread the Word. Time spent with him was secondary.

Chapter Eighteen

What am I doing here?

Emma didn't know if she could last at this place. She'd hidden her emotions well, not wanting to disappoint Caleb, but she couldn't stand how the people lived here. *Gott* help her, but she didn't see the hope that Caleb had for this Monique person. She was so hardened, Emma couldn't imagine her ever coming around. Worst of all, she reminded Emma of Mark in many ways. She shamed herself for the thought, but it was true.

She'd hardly slept the night before. The sounds of cars, people yelling, and others walking up and down the stairs all night had kept her under her covers with a pillow over her head. A group of Amish wanted to go exploring around town, but by the time they all got together, it was late, and so Caleb suggested they stay in the building or out front until daylight. Mark went out with a few others, and Caleb told her not to smother him. She agreed, and went to her room to get ready for bed. Monique didn't show up until the morning and went straight to bed.

Emma put both hands on the dryer, closed her eyes, and let out a long breath. She had come up to the laundry room to put Mark's sleeping bag in the dryer but had forgotten how. She was reading the directions and punching the dials when Caleb walked in.

"You got it figured out?" Caleb bent over to see whether she'd pushed the right buttons and nodded. "Bet you wish you had one of these back home." He grinned. He must have been waiting for her to get up. He'd walked in right behind her to the laundry room.

Emma thought about life at home when she had to bundle up in her warmest coat to go out to the clothesline and gather the laundry on the cold days. The summer heat wasn't much better, with the sun scorching her as she plucked the clothespins off the line as fast as she could to get out of the heat. "Some days, it would be nice," she finally agreed, but she didn't like the tempting talk about English machines, especially coming from Caleb.

"Did you get enough to eat last night? You hardly touched your food. It's not Amish-made, but it's all we got around here." He grinned.

"I didn't expect it to be the same. Nothing will be, I suppose." She tried to lighten her responses. She didn't want Caleb to suspect anything was wrong. "Do we need to help with breakfast?" She liked keeping busy. It was what she was used to, and there was an even bigger need here than at home due to the number of people who came for meals.

"Yeah, they've already started, but I wanted to make sure you got this figured out." He tapped on the dryer and leaned back against it. "Are you sure you're okay?"

"I'm *gut*, why?" She shouldn't have asked a question. But it was too late now.

"Nothing. I worry too much about you. And I'm sure you're tired because you probably didn't sleep well."

"*Nee*, I didn't." She'd meant to ask about that. She was used to an early-to-bed-early-to-rise routine. The late nights would wear her out. "Does everyone always stay up late?"

He crossed his arms over his chest. "I'm afraid so. You'll get used to it. I did." He pushed off the dryer and led her out of the room and down the grungy stairway. Emma had an impulse to grab a rag and cleaner so she could scrub the place from top to bottom.

The cafeteria was almost empty. Only a few people were there talking, and the staff gathered to discuss what they would need for dinner. Only breakfast and evening meals were served. Emma could see why. There were a lot of people who came for a meal, and with the Amish it had grown almost twice in size. She was grateful for the two meals, but she and Mark had a limited amount of money. She hoped he used it wisely.

They made their way through the room and were almost in the kitchen when Emma heard a booming voice thunder through the air.

Caleb stopped in his tracks. He waited until the voice trailed off, but he didn't say a word about it.

Strange things happened here. She was more certain of that every minute.

"Who was that?" Emma asked Caleb, but he'd disappeared. She looked around the kitchen, but he was nowhere in sight. She saw only two women stocking food in a pantry. One woman told her to get some breakfast, so she grabbed a plate and sat down to eat.

Caleb still hadn't returned when she'd finished her breakfast. Wanting to make herself useful, she went over to the sink and let the hot water pour from the tap, so she could wash the dishes that were already beginning to pile in the sink.

Alex entered the room with a slight swagger. He seemed tough, like he knew the streets.

"That's quite a pile of dishes to wash." He went over and rolled up his sleeves. "Where's Caleb."

"He left after he heard someone yelling outside. Do you know who that was?"

"Caleb didn't tell you?" He scoured the plates as if he was trying to scrub off the blue color.

She shook her head and reached for a towel.

"Well, if he didn't tell you, I shouldn't either. Just watch your back when you hear that voice." He lifted his eyebrows with a seriousness that she hadn't seen from him.

"Do you live here, Alex?" She washed the big pots and pans while he filled the large dishwasher with utensils and serving dishes.

"Just moved in recently. Lost my job, so Caleb put me on the team here. I came around enough that it wasn't any big change 'cause I was a client here, but I sure appreciate it all the same." He didn't look up from his work. He did a fine job, and worked quickly. "What about you? Why are you here?"

She wasn't hiding anything, but now that she was telling someone who lived in the city and was making his own way, she felt silly for coming to watch over her brother, and she wasn't ready to tell anyone about evangelizing.

"It about broke my parents' hearts that my brother was leaving. And he can be a handful, so I thought I'd tag along."

There—she'd said it. He could think her a caring sister, which was who she was trying to be, or he could think she was being overprotective like Zeb did.

Now that she'd thought of Zeb, she questioned whether she should try to contact him or her parents to tell them they'd arrived safely. Then again, maybe it would just make things worse to hear them encourage her to bring her brother home.

She looked at the Amish sitting around talking and eating, going in and out of the church, and scouting out the area. She hoped this wouldn't be as bad as she thought it would be.

"I haven't had time to get to know any of this crew. I usually wait until it narrows down to the hardcore group before I bother with names and faces." His dreadlocks fell forward around his face as he leaned over and dried off a large metal pot.

She was too polite to ask but was very curious as to how and why he wore his hair that way. But he could be thinking the same about her *kapp*. She'd gotten plenty of stares but was prepared. She'd decided not to wear city clothes unless Caleb thought it was necessary because she wanted to feel comfortable in her own skin. That could only happen if she wore Amish clothes and shoes.

"I have a feeling you'll get to know my brother then." They worked in silence. She wanted to ask him questions but didn't feel she knew him well enough yet, so she decided to ask just one. "Do you think it will make a difference for Mark that I'm here?"

"Heck, no! These kids do some crazy things while they're here. You gotta be ready for that. Drugs, girls, vandalizing—"

Emma put her hand up. "No more, please."

"I'd say I'm sorry, but I'm not. You have to be aware of all he might do."

"*Nee*, he knows I'll stop him if he falls into temptation." She felt her cheeks flush. She was talking big. Emma had no idea what she would do if Mark did any of those things. She couldn't stop him. She could only pray and be there if he fell.

"Good luck with that." He shook his head, making the beads dance around his head.

Caleb came in, which made her pause.

He knew why she was there.

Would he tell me if it was pointless?

He was a kind and gentle man, but she'd also seen him stand up against others when he needed to. She understood why he'd come to this place and why he stayed. His fair-yet-direct approach created trust between him and the restless adolescents who came here. "You seem to be everywhere all of the time," Emma said.

"Making the rounds," Caleb answered.

"For what, or whom, I should say?" she asked.

"Checking to see if everyone is staying out of trouble, at least when they're in the building. And making sure no one is here who shouldn't be." He glanced over to Alex, who was looking right back at him. There was something between them—that was obvious—but she didn't want to know what it was. If there was danger, Caleb would tell her. Otherwise she would continue to turn a blind eye to their silent communication.

Mark's laugh caught her attention. He glanced at her as he walked by but didn't stop or say hello. She didn't want to deal with him at this point, anyway, but at least she'd seen him.

"Mark!" Caleb's voice was so loud she put a hand to one ear. "Sorry." He rubbed her arms, adding comfort to the apology.

She tried to ignore the tingling sensation of his hands, but she couldn't deny the spark she felt.

Caleb went over to Mark. He said only a few words, and Mark was on his way. "He's going sightseeing with the gang."

Emma nodded. "Thank you for letting me know. Since he doesn't tell me much of anything." She set the last pot on the counter and wiped her hands on an apron. "I don't know what I'm supposed to do."

"You're doing it. The kitchen staff loves it when someone like you comes along who can do anything that needs to be done."

She knew what he said was probably true, but she was restless to do more. "I do this at home. And Mark is obviously going to go his own way, at least for a while. How do you reach people?"

He leaned against the steel countertop and cocked his head to one side. "That comes with time. You'll know when you see an opportunity." A slow grin was fair warning he had an idea. "How about I show you around the area."

"Yeah, show the lady the sights. I'll hold things down here," Alex piped in.

"Are you eavesdropping?" Caleb grinned at him, and then pushed off the counter and took Emma's hand. "You ready for this?"

She felt self-conscious only for a moment, but then let herself enjoy the gesture. She felt safer too when she looked at the open front door "*Jah*, as much as I'll ever be." She took in a breath and went out onto the sidewalk.

Cars sped around by the dozens, going every which way. Lights blinked red, yellow, and green. People walked quickly or ran, not noticing each other as they passed. One slammed his hand down on the front of a car as he tried to cross the street.

"Emma."

Caleb was saying her name, but she hadn't heard. There was too much to watch to take her eyes away from so much action, so many diverse people.

"Are you ready to see more?

She nodded.

How can there possibly be more?

Chapter Nineteen

Zeb woke up early again. He rolled out of bed, thinking about what Emma was doing, wondering if she was safe. He didn't even care that she was with Caleb. He would actually be glad to hear it. At least he'd know someone was looking after her.

Communication with the outside world was difficult, he understood, but any word would be appreciated. The thought of her in a place with so many strange people, crime, and unsafe environments zipped through his mind.

He dressed quickly and scrubbed his face and teeth, ready to start his day. He'd heard bits and pieces of information from parents whose children had gone on the trip but nothing of any significance—just that they'd arrived safely.

When he opened the door, he smelled bacon, and as he made his way down the stairs, he heard it sizzling on the stove.

The *haus* had a masculine feel considering there were three men and his *mamm*. They took precedence. Their hunting gear was supposed to be locked in the mudroom, but was frequently left out for cleaning. A calendar and a welcome sign in German hung on the walls. A table for four was all they needed, as they infrequently had guests. *Mamm* enjoyed her kerosene glass lanterns and used one in most every room.

Mamm didn't look up from the skillet. "You're up early." Her tall yet sturdy frame was much like Zeb's, as was his father's, but Merv was stouter. She turned quickly to glance at him. "You have bags under your eyes."

"Nothing a little nap under the maple tree won't cure." He ignored her studying eyes. It was obvious he wasn't sleeping and why. He didn't need to be told.

"Except that there's snow on the ground." She grinned at him, but it didn't cheer him up.

"*Daed* still asleep?"

"*Jah*, he's an old man. I say let him sleep." She cracked a couple of eggs, turned the gas down, and poured him some coffee. "You're going to be before your time if you don't get things in order with Emma." Her tone was matter of fact.

"She's doing what she feels is right. She'll be back soon." He hoped. The time spent away seemed to vary when the youth went on that trip. He never could understand why the deacons didn't keep it more restricted. The youth could just as easily do their adjusting close to home. Sometimes Zeb felt their community was giving up too many of the old ways.

Soon there will be phones and big, blue buggies approved.

He finished his breakfast and made his way to the barn. With so many cows, milking was a major production. They had a system that worked well. It was just time-consuming, even with the gas-powered machines doing some of the work. As soon as one group of cows was done, they were sent out to pasture and another set were hooked up. Zeb had finished one group and was just ready to hook up the next round.

"You're making me feel lazy." Merv's voice was welcome. "Can't sleep?"

Zeb frowned. His *mamm* must have said something, the way mothers do. "Did she tell you to check on me?"

"*Jah*, of course. You know I don't care one iota." Merv grinned. "But you might give me a bit to go on so I have something to tell her."

"Tell her everything's fine. She's just itching to get me

married off." Which was true in a way, but Emma's resistance to spend time at his farm had his *mamm* worried. There was no way to explain it to her or to himself, as far as that went. And now he was more concerned than ever. He didn't need anyone else worrying with him. "You gonna pull that wagon over from the Zimmermans'?"

"*Jah*, sure. If you got this handled." Merv seemed happy to do something other than milk cows. He was half Zeb's age, and Zeb tried to remember that when there were chores to be done. Zeb had talked his *daed* into purchasing a wagon due to the number of Holstein they had. It made good sense, and took half the time to make hauls. What they'd failed to do was make sure the wagon purchase was approved by the deacons.

When Deacon Reuben had found out, he'd threatened to tell the bishop. Now Zeb's hands were tied. Did he go to the bishop, confess that he hadn't disclosed the information, or wait until it was found out and deal with it if and when that happened? He didn't know whether it was against the Ordnung, but not knowing would be his fault, as well.

"Zeb." Merv's voice rang in his ears. "Where have you been? Thinking of Emma?" He grinned.

"*Nee.* Actually I have a lot on my mind. Only some of it is about her." Which was the truth. He thought about telling Merv, but then he might be held responsible, as well.

"I'm gonna go." He pointed toward the barn doors with both thumbs over his shoulder. "See you at the noon meal."

"*Danke*, Merv." That was one thing off his mind, but without Merv's company, he'd sit and brood over things he didn't want to think about, and the milking would take longer.

But soon enough it was time to eat, and Zeb was ready for a break. He'd finish with the last of them after the noon meal.

As he walked to the *haus,* he heard loud voices—Merv's and his father's. He jogged to the back door, kicked off his boots in the mudroom, and entered the kitchen.

His father and brother scowled as they turned his way.

"What is it?"

"Ask your brother." *Daed* came over to the dark wood table and sat down.

Merv's pink face and pinched forehead spoke without words. "I got pulled over."

The words weren't familiar and muddled in Zeb's mind. "You mean the police?"

That irritated Merv even more. "Yeah, the officer said I couldn't haul the wagon or be on the road with either vehicle that has steel wheels."

"I told you to watch your back." Zeb shook his head. "They gave the Beliers a hard time of it down south."

Merv's cheeks reddened. "He would have said the same thing to you."

"*Nee,* Merv, I would have found another way to move the wagon."

"What were you hauling it for in the first place?" *Daed*'s face was almost as red as Merv's. He lifted his elbows and placed them on the table, waiting for an answer.

"I needed to haul off some of the cow dung. With so many cows, we have too much to spread come planting."

"Well, it needs to be done then, and we'll explain things to the police department. I remember something about this down in Kentucky with an Amish farmer, something about the steel wheels tearing up the roads. We'll have to make a visit to the church board before we go."

Zeb tensed, wondering how much would come out of this meeting. If Reuben was there, a lot more could be divulged.

He felt he was already in the hot seat. "Let's not waste any time. The rumors will start flying as soon as word gets out."

Mamm, who had been quiet through the conversation, jerked back. "I don't know that to be true. Who would know, and why would they bother?"

Zeb was spinning a web that could get him snagged if he wasn't careful. The possibility of gossip wasn't likely but would be a way to lessen some of the blame on him. "We don't all need to go."

His *daed,* who was halfway out of his chair, sat back down. "The more of us, the better to explain."

His *daed*'s confused expression filled Zeb with more guilt. "Merv will go with me. There are a few cows that need milking, anyway, *Daed*. If you can manage."

With that he turned and walked out, not leaving room for any objections. His hazy mind, full of deceit, held answers to questions that he might be asked. He wanted to go alone, but they would need Merv's account of what happened. He kicked at the dirt clods beneath his boots and stuck his hands on his hips to keep from hitting something.

Merv hitched up the buggy as he came around the barn, and Zeb helped him along. He took the driver's seat, pushing Merv to the passenger's side. It irritated Merv, but Zeb didn't care at the moment. When they got on the main road that led to the bishop's farm, Zeb took a right to the highway instead.

"Where are you going?" Merv frowned.

"Show me where you went down the highway." Zeb tensed, but try as he might, he couldn't get his heart to stop thumping in his chest. The only other time he'd felt this way was when he was with Emma, when he could get her alone. But that wasn't worrisome like now.

After a couple of miles Merv pointed. There's the spot, right over there, before those oak trees."

"Stay here." Zeb jumped out of the buggy and examined the roads, walking a good way down and back. "I don't see any damage, so that much is good. Hopefully, there won't be a big fuss." Merv's eyebrows pinched together, making his baby face appear chubbier than usual. "I thought we were going to the deacons."

"They don't need to be bothered. We can take care of this."

They weren't more than a few miles from Lititz, but it would take over an hour to get there. That was a whole lot of time to think.

They didn't talk much, but when they got to the courthouse, Merv started in. "Can we just walk in and do this?"

"You got the warning he gave you?"

"*Jah*." Merv tapped the straw hat that had seen better days. But Merv wasn't prepared for this today, and neither was Zeb. Nevertheless, he felt responsible, and couldn't rest until he'd had a chance to plead his case.

Merv tried to keep up with Zeb's long strides, tagging along behind. The tall building with a sharp, red roof stood boldly in the center of the town square. Statues of politicians or other noteworthy individuals who'd led the city stood on either side of the sidewalk leading to the front doors. When they got there, Merv pulled on the handle. It didn't budge. Zeb gave it a yank and scowled, and then looked at a sign on the door. "They're locked."

"Why's it locked? It's early enough."

Zeb shook his head and leaned over, placing his hands on his knees. Church was every other Sunday for Amish, but every Sunday for the folks in town. "It's Sunday."

Merv groaned, and Zeb shamed himself for being so rash,

driving them all the way to town before stopping and thinking about it. If he'd been a cursing man, that's what he'd be doing about now.

Chapter Twenty

Walking around the city with Caleb turned out to be much better than Emma had expected, but only because she was alone with him. They went through Fairmount Park, sat by a fountain watching people walk by, and enjoyed gazing at the huge museum of art with its pillars and many steps.

One place had blocks of boathouses, behind which was a river where people rowed their narrow little boats down the winding waterway. She and Caleb sat on a park bench and watched as the boats paddled out of sight one after another.

It was a peaceful place, considering they were in the midst of a metropolitan area. Tall trees lined the streets, and patches of grass popped up between the cement sidewalks.

"You see, it's not so bad." Caleb grinned and took her hand to walk across the six-street intersection. The red and green lights were confusing as to which of the six lanes could go and which ones had to wait.

"*Jah*, but I could never get used to this."

Even if I could, I don't want to.

There was nothing here that Emma desired, and she already regretted coming. She was curious, and still hoped to share her faith, but keeping an eye on Mark wasn't going to happen as far as she could see. It was a learning experience, and she would leave it at that.

Deep down Emma knew she had come partly for Caleb, as well. She had feelings for him that would probably never dissipate, and this was the only way she could be with him. She had to confess that she'd had a crazy notion that they could work together at the church or that he would someday come back to the community. But she could see now that wasn't going to happen.

Then she thought of Zeb and guilt flowed through her. He had no way to receive any communication from her, even if she did find a phone, so she decided to write him a letter. Caleb would know how to send it to him. It was the least she could do after she'd left him the way she had.

"You look tired. I'll walk you up." He let go of her hand when they got to the church and opened the door for her.

The late nights had taken a toll on her in the short time she'd been there. Maybe she would get used to it like Caleb said, but she didn't want to. There was nothing here she wished to conform to.

"Caleb, who was that person you went to see this morning? Alex wouldn't tell me."

Caleb stopped and stood on the stairway, eyes downcast, and then slowly looked up at her. "I'm not sure I want to tell you, and I doubt you want to know."

Emma perked up with an anxious feeling in her stomach. "What is it, Caleb?"

He looked back at the large room they'd just went through and held out his hand to her. Quietly he led her to a table in a corner dark enough they wouldn't be noticed easily. "I haven't told anyone in the Amish community about this. I trust you will keep this confidential."

"Of course." She leaned in, ready to listen to what was so heavy on his mind.

The doors flew open. Loud voices engulfed the room. A

group of street kids walked in, knocking over chairs and overturning tables.

Emma put her hands over her ears. Her heart raced and her chest heaved. She turned to Caleb, who was closing the door to keep any more from coming in. He grabbed a nearby broom and slipped it through the handles. His face contorted when he looked at her sucking in air.

Another crash sent him flying over to a young man in a leather jacket and shaved head who seemed to be the leader of the group. He barked orders, and then watched as the gang carried them out. "Guys on one side, Gals on the other. She's gotta be here somewhere."

Caleb grabbed his shoulder to get his attention.

The leader held up his hand. The others stopped and waited while he gave Caleb a slimy grin. "Look who's here. You came back from Amish land. I thought you might stay, go back to the Amish ways. You always were more them than us."

"You've had your fun, now go." Although Caleb's tone was even, controlled, Emma saw his hands tremble, and he stood ramrod-straight.

The leader's eyes scanned the room and froze on Emma. "And who is this?" He looked closer, but Caleb stopped him.

"Keep your distance." Caleb's voice was louder, more urgent. That made the leader smile a crooked sneer.

The leader stared at her until Emma looked away. His strikingly handsome face burned into her mind, and his crystal-blue eyes seared into hers. The vision was familiar, like someone similar who she knew but couldn't place. Emma wanted to look up, to study the face again, but then shuddered, thinking about the image she'd just seen, and kept her eyes shut.

"Why so protective, brother?" The gravelly voice seemed closer or was she just so scared it seemed that way?

"Take what you will and go." Caleb's voice didn't sound like him.

She lifted her head and watched as the two stared at each other.

"Give me Monique, and I'll be on my way." He bit hard onto the toothpick in his mouth.

Caleb crossed his arms. "I don't know where she is and wouldn't tell you if I did."

The leader's upper lip lifted, and he let out a long breath. Emma felt her own breath leave her lungs as she watched the two square off. Neither one was ready to back down as what seemed to be hours passed by.

Emma gathered her nerve and stood.

Like a dangerous animal waiting on its prey, the leader's head snapped over to her. His clear, blue eyes made her shiver and knees wobble.

"Why, it's little Emma." He looked her up and down. "But not so little anymore." He chuckled, like the sound of crackling kindling in a fire. He motioned with two fingers for her to come over.

"Go upstairs, Emma, and finish the laundry." Caleb didn't look at her, keeping his eyes on the leader.

All four of the young men stared at her as she took slow steps to the stairs. She felt the nagging cough begin to burn her airway. Caleb followed her with his eyes as she passed by him. Emma could feel their stares as she took each step, not turning to look back. She went right, instead of left to her room, remembering seeing a lock on the door to the laundry room. When she went inside, she quickly shut the door and pushed the metal button in the doorknob to lock it.

She stood against the door to catch her breath. Finally, the coughing began to subside. She could hear metal chairs being knocked about, followed by a low rumble that faded into the distance. Fear and disgust rose in her chest, the raw emotions threatening to drown her. The fright writhed and morphed until she was left with a longing for something familiar. Home. It was one thing to work hard and help others on this trip, but to put herself in danger was another.

After resolving to pack and walk to the bus station, Emma noticed the new sounds, or rather the absence of noise. She strained to hear through the door, but only silence reached her.

Has something happened to Caleb?

She wanted to open the door and see if she could find him, but was too scared, and she shamed herself for it. Just as she was about to open the door, she heard a light tapping.

"Caleb?"

"It's me."

His voice was like a sweet hymn. She took a deep breath, ready to open up the door and let it swing open.

"Are you all right?" Caleb walked over and embraced her, holding her so close she could barely breathe.

"*Jah*, I'm fine. Are you?" She pulled back and studied his face. She hadn't seen him so worried. This was too much for him.

"I'm sorry. That must have really upset you. It isn't usually that bad." He pushed away the hair that had fallen out of her *kapp* and held her face with both hands.

"What was that about?" Her voice cracked and was soft as a feather.

"He and Monique get into a fight, she leaves, and he comes to find her. It's a pattern. It's gotten out of hand. I'm sorry you had to see that."

"That man is with Monique?" Hearing that made her wish she had known so she could have a good look at the despicable man who treated her roommate poorly. No wonder Monique was so angry and on guard.

"Unfortunately, yes."

"Can't you make him stop?"

"No. He's been arrested a few times for other incidents, but he never stays in long. He's smart enough to know how far to push things before getting in real trouble."

"Why doesn't Monique stay away?"

"She's tried, but he finds her. He's got a lot of cronies who do his bidding."

It confused and scared her that someone as horrible as him could have that much power over others. And that Monique was trapped in his web. "Why do people listen to him?"

He shrugged. "People get brainwashed. Others have no family or home and get caught up in it. Some have his same mentality and like to control people."

What a horrible feeling to be running away from someone all of the time and never able to get away, to be trapped.

"I wonder where Monique is. We have to find her."

Caleb shook his head. "It's not that easy here, Emma. It's not like the community, where the word gets passed along and eventually all know what the problem is and they work together to remedy it. Here everyone is pretty much on their own."

That made her homesick all over again. She thought about the leader and the others who were with him.

Why would someone want to do what they do? Were they trapped too?

"Was he who you talked to this morning?"

"Yeah, he was looking for Monique, threatening me if I was harboring her."

"Were you?"

He nodded. "I've set her up with every women's shelter in the area. He finds her."

They were both quiet for a long while until he broke the silence. "I shouldn't have put you together as roommates. Monique doesn't usually stay here. She has to stay with Abe most of the time. But it still wasn't a good idea." He leaned forward. "I was hoping I could get you to talk her into leaving. But I put you in danger. I'm sorry."

She thought about what he said. "If I had known what was going on, I would have agreed to have her as my roommate. I wish you'd have told me. I would have tried harder to connect with her."

"I knew you'd feel that way about it. But I shouldn't have assumed." His gaze dropped as if he felt ashamed, but she took it as a compliment. He knew her well enough to know she'd help someone in need. Emma had to admit, though, she didn't think she had the courage to help someone in the city. Evangelizing was one thing, but physically hiding someone from a man like this was totally different.

"Emma, what's causing you to cough?" He held up a hand. "Be honest, and don't hide anything." He tapped her nose. "I know you too well."

Emma closed her eyes, realizing she was relieved to not try to keep her secret from him. "I don't know for sure. My throat closes."

There she'd said it. The secret she'd held to have the freedom to come on this trip and not worry her *mamm* and *daed*. Most of all she wouldn't be beholding to Zeb.

"That's asthma, not difficult to manage if you treat it right. I can help you with it."

"That would be wonderful-*gut*." He was so tired and

burdened with so much she decided to agree with whatever he said. At least for now. Her nod was all she gave him but it was enough.

He took her hand and went to her room. "I'll be right outside your door. Try to get some sleep." He squeezed her hand and walked out the door.

She heard the chair knock against the door and his shoe tapping on the ground. He wasn't an anxious person, but tonight's fiasco must have brought him to a level he couldn't suppress.

Emma heard voices as she got ready for bed—others, who must have been nearby, asking what happened, but not one came out from hiding. She couldn't blame them. This leader person obviously had a reputation.

She peeked her head outside the door and looked to see whether anyone was nearby. When she found the hallway empty, she stood next to Caleb. "*Danke* for keeping me safe." She paused, looking at the brown fold-up chair she'd seen up against the wall. "You were here last night too weren't you?"

He nodded.

"*Danke*, that makes me feel better."

"You're welcome."

She turned to go back into her room, but stopped. "I heard you call that man by name. What was it?"

Caleb looked away and then stared at her for a moment. "His name is Abe. You might remember him better as Absalom, my brother."

Chapter Twenty-One

Emma was exhausted when she went to bed but was awakened by movement in the room. She lay stock-still, barely breathing. The smell of tobacco wafted through the room, and a tall figure fell into the bed next to her. She knew Caleb wouldn't let in anyone but Monique, so she sat up and tried to see with the dull light that shone through the dingy window pane.

"Monique?" Emma's voice was just above a whisper.

The dark silhouette didn't move. "What?"

Emma jerked, surprised at the sound of Monique's voice, rough and gravelly. "How are you?"

"Humph." She grunted.

Emma sat up. "I'm worried about you." She slid off the bed and moved toward her. Understanding the truth of what Monique had been through gave Emma newfound empathy for her.

"Don't be." She rolled over and lay on her back.

"Can I turn on a light?" Emma didn't want to pry but couldn't stand by and pretend nothing was wrong, either. After seeing Abe in action, she wouldn't put anything past him. She never would have realized who he was if Caleb hadn't told her. It wasn't just his appearance. His eyes were cold and unfeeling, unlike Caleb's, which showed every feeling in his heart. The shock of Abe being the man who stalked Monique was stuck in her mind. She couldn't get her head around the change in him. He'd always been a troublemaker, but this was so far over that line, she couldn't see the end of it.

"I don't care," Monique mumbled.

Emma was about to flip on the light when Monique sat up. "Don't. I like the dark."

"Are you okay?" Emma could hear in Monique's voice that she wasn't, so she flipped the switch, only long enough to see for herself that she was okay. The one lightbulb shone against the darkness. Emma squinted just long enough to see a bruise. The dark color of her skin made it hard to see.

"I told you not to." Monique squealed at Emma and covered her eyes with her hands.

Emma turned off the light. "I'm sorry, I just knew something was wrong and I want to help."

After a long pause, she heard Monique sigh. "Did your boyfriend tell you about me?"

"Caleb is a friend."

"Whatever you say." She lay back down with a groan.

Doubt raced through Emma. Monique was obviously in pain, but she didn't know how to help her. Even if she did, Monique probably wouldn't cooperate. No matter how many times this happened to a person, it had to be embarrassing or maybe it was more frustration. She could only imagine how Monique was feeling. "Can I do anything for you?"

"I just need some sleep." She took in a sharp breath.

Emma went to the door and slowly opened it. "Caleb."

He stood. Dark bags under his eyes showed his fatigue. "How's it going in there?"

"I need some bread, hot milk, pepper, and a bowl."

"Go back in and lock the door. I'll be right back." Caleb hurried to the stairs as she closed the door behind her. When he knocked a few minutes later, sh the items he brought.

He lingered in the doorwa on the light."

There were so many street and car total shock when Caleb flipped the switc plained again all the same.

Emma ignored Monique's mumbled cursing making a poultice with the milk, pepper, and b kneaded the ingredients together, adding bits of milk bread until she had a pasty substance. Monique, with no id what Emma was doing, made repulsing noises when she saw what Emma was making.

"That's disgusting. I'm not eating that." She wrinkled her nose and turned away.

"It's not for eating."

Caleb grinned. "This is a poultice."

"Your *mamm* made it too, *jah*?" Emma smiled, enjoying a memory of something at home.

Caleb smiled as he watched her, and she thought he may have suppressed an emotional response. His lips tightened, and his head was down as if to hide his face. "It doesn't taste good, but it sure does the trick on wounds."

"Let's see how it works for you, Monique." Emma offered a small amount to Monique. She slowly reached forward toward a bluish mark on Monique's arm.

Monique frowned and pulled away. "What is this, voodoo?"

"*Nee*. It's a home remedy. I've used it many times. It usually helps." Emma looked into her eyes, and Monique stared back. A few seconds ticked by before she finally nodded.

"It smells funny," she said as Emma applied the gummy

to her bruise and a small open wound. "What does

ws out the pain in those scratches, keeps it from getting ted. It's harder to move a bruise along. It heals in its own e, but this will help a little." Emma examined her work d glanced at Monique. "The cuts are small, so they should eal quickly." She paused and looked away. Monique seemed to do better when she didn't look her in the eyes when she asked her questions. "What are they from?"

"A scratch."

"From Abe?"

Monique sat up straight. "No, from my pet cat." Her voice rose with annoyance. She tried to cross her arms over her chest—a gesture Emma had seen her do before when she got angry—but winced when she touched a sore spot. "You say his name like you know him."

"I do." Emma began to clean up, avoiding eye contact.

Monique's eyes squinted. "'Course you did. You're from the same farm?"

"The same community, *jah*."

"He ever your boy?" Monique grinned a little, but not in a kind way, and looked at Caleb, as if she wanted to make trouble.

"*Nee*."

Monique looked at Caleb and then back to Emma. "Caleb was."

Emma's cheeks warmed as she finished cleaning up. "Leave it on as long as you can stand it. It tightens as it dries." She didn't look at Caleb when she handed him the bowl. "*Danke*, Caleb."

"Thank you for helping Monique."

She felt his eyes on her but didn't look up until he turned away.

When she glanced at Monique, she was smiling. "He's a good guy—puts up with me and every other messed-up person around here."

"You're not messed up, Monique."

She grunted. "Then what am I?"

"Alone." Emma didn't know where the word came from but thought it was all that was needed at the moment.

"I ain't alone. You're standing right here." She scowled.

"People aren't enough."

"You got that right," Monique scoffed.

"Even good people."

Monique's eyebrows drew together. "What's left?"

"Christ." Emma had so many verses memorized and speeches to say, but all that was coming out were one or two words. When she started to panic, a cool calm surrounded her. She waited.

"Don't know Him. Don't want to, neither."

"Why?"

"I'm what people call a lost soul. Not all good and righteous like you Amish folk who are on the *right* side of God."

There it was—what she'd worried about. How could she explain herself to someone who saw her in that light? Her life was so different than Monique's, and her faith had been grounded at a young age. *Gott* was surprising her with this conversation, so she took in a breath and let Him work through her. "Being born into it has made me question it."

Monique blinked. "What do you mean?"

"If you don't make it your own, it's not for *Gott*. It's for others."

"I see that every time these Amish kids come around every spring. Ones like you don't usually talk this way though."

"Ones like me." Emma thought about the words. She'd always been considered a strong Christian in her community. Being here made it easy to think that was true. But *Gott* was pushing her to live it and show it to others. For the first time in her life she had to explain who she was in her faith, not just say she had one.

"There's ones like you all over here every year. They try to help the wild Amish. They're the ones who usually go home crying." Monique lifted her brows in confirmation, and Emma believed it. She was exactly what Monique was talking about. No wonder Mark resented her, being the "good" older sister, there to keep him from sinning.

Caleb walked in. "Everyone all right in here?" When he saw Emma's face, he stared.

"I open my mouth too much," Monique confessed.

"It's okay. I was talking to Caleb about it the other day." She could see that *Gott* was preparing her back then and probably long before that. Emma had to do it His way, not her own. She heard the lines in her head that she'd prepared to say, and shook her head. "Thank you, Monique."

Monique frowned, always suspicious. "For what?"

"Helping me see myself from the outside in."

Monique turned her head to the side, absorbing what Emma said. "I don't know what I did. You're kinda freaking me out."

Emma shook her head, unfamiliar with her words, but figured out enough to know it was a joke. "I have a lot to learn."

She meant that in many ways. The people, the culture, the purpose, but most of all, what *Gott* wanted her to do here. It was obviously much different than what she had planned. It scared her and excited her at the same time.

This trip has been a journey into the unknown from the beginning. Why would that change now?

Chapter Twenty-Two

Zeb stopped at the post office for the second time that week. He'd never spent so much time in town. The small city of Lititz had become somewhat of a tourist attraction, not like it had been when he was a kid. The population was twice the size, and everyday stores had become novelty shops that had everything from tacky Amish postcards to chocolate figures depicting an Amish person. The store owners defended selling them by saying there were no faces on anything they sold, so it was all fair game.

He made a point to put his head down and keep going when tourists were around. Most respected his privacy, but others were incredibly rude.

A woman discreetly took a picture, and then stopped in front of him. When he tried to ignore her, she fell into step with him. "Can I have a picture taken with you?"

He didn't say a word, just kept walking. She eventually drifted off. With the mood he was in today, he hoped for their sake no one bothered him. He'd heard through the grapevine that Emma made it to the city, but he hadn't received anything from her.

"Zeb."

His head snapped up at a loud voice. "Merv, I didn't see you."

"Or hear me. I called your name a couple of times." He shook his head with frustration plastered all over his face. "You were fretting over Emma again, weren't ya?"

"*Jah*, as a matter of fact I was." Zeb stood tall, bowing up a little to remind his kid brother he was the elder of the two. "If I didn't know better, I'd think you were scolding me."

Merv shrugged. "I guess I was." He looked at him sideways. "But don't you think you deserve it? You said once she left, you'd let it go."

Zeb started walking, done talking about it, and Merv followed like a pup after its mother. Zeb didn't want to be reminded of what he said he'd do. That was before she left, when he'd thought he could follow through with supporting her decision to leave. But Merv was right—he couldn't stop pining over her. There was too much of the unknown, and for a young Amish woman to be in such a place was ridiculous. The worst part of it was that she hadn't really wanted to go. This could have been avoided, except for Mark. And in Zeb's eyes, Mark wasn't enough of a reason for her to go. She either had another reason he didn't know about or it was his worst nightmare—Caleb. If there was a connection between them, it could ruin everything he'd planned.

"Someday, when you can find a girl, you'll understand," he said.

Merv stopped for a second and stared at him. "What do ya mean, *can*? I could get any old girl any old day." He frowned.

Zeb could see he'd struck a chord and was enjoying the response. "I'll believe it when I see it, or *her*, I should say." Zeb waited for the retaliation, and sure enough it came.

"I courted David Barkman's daughter all last spring. Your memory's going." Merv huffed out a breath.

Now he'd struck a chord with Zeb, although Merv wasn't aware of it. Zeb worried about the age difference between him and Emma. Although he didn't look it, he was ten years her senior. She was soon to turn a year older, but so was he. He'd always be a decade older than his wife. That didn't resonate well with him.

Merv hurried, trying to keep up with Zeb. "Where are you headed?"

"Post office." He knew Merv would figure out what he was doing, again. But he didn't care. Emma had promised she'd write, and he believed she would. He'd waited three days, which was maybe too soon, but by the end of the week he'd expected some sort of response.

"So that's what it is. You haven't heard from her." He slapped Zeb in the back. "Don't worry, big brother, she'll be back soon. Emma's not one for the city."

He hoped Merv was right but didn't want to seem too eager. "*Nee*, she's not. I'm interested in contact information."

Merv followed at his heels as Zeb went to his mailbox and slipped in the key. He didn't get enough mail to bother with a box at his farm, so he just came into town now and then. He could see a white envelope through the small glass area above the key.

"Well, is it from her?" Merv was breathing down his neck, literally.

Zeb shrugged him off and pulled out the mail. He then looked at the handwriting. "*Jah*." Zeb wished he were alone so he could read it privately, but he didn't want to wait. He ripped it open as calmly as he could and read the two paragraphs she penned.

Zeb,

I'm sorry I didn't send this to you earlier. It's been quite an adjustment, one I'll never fully make but am trying my best. At first, I was ready to leave at a moment's notice, but as long as Mark is here, I have a reason to stay.

I suppose you are all getting ready to seed the fields. I enjoy planting even more than fall harvest and am disappointed I'll miss it. I miss the food even more. I'm hoping to help improve the meals here. If I leave this place accomplishing only that, it will be a great feat. But I'm hoping for much more to happen before I come home. Pray for me.

Yours,

Emma

At the bottom, she'd made a sketch of what looked like a rundown building. Then he noticed a cross on top of the roof on the second floor. If that was where she was living, he'd go and pull her out right that minute. He hoped it was only a hostel where they were housing the less fortunate, or a soup kitchen where she volunteered.

"Is that a church?" Merv was so close, Zeb felt his breath again.

"Did you read this whole letter?" Zeb was irritated enough that others in the post office stared at him.

"Just parts." Merv backed away.

Zeb took in a deep breath. "Gotta run a couple errands. You coming?"

Merv nodded and went ahead of Zeb. "*Jah, Daed* needs some feed."

Zeb hated his temper flying off that way. Sometimes he thought he'd be better living on his own with only a wife to tend to. Maybe that was why *Gott* had never given him any children. He'd never known whether it was him or his wife that kept them from conceiving but decided he didn't want to know.

The fact that Emma had written only a few words bothered him. What was she doing that she couldn't take a little time to write in more detail about what was happening? Her message was confusing, one minute saying she wanted to leave, and the next saying she had something to do there. The unknown filled his mind with negative thoughts. Worst of all, Caleb was there with her. Memories still went through his head when Emma and Caleb were young, hiding behind the haystacks and fishing together down at the creek. Now they were together again. How could he not wonder and worry?

They stopped at the seed and farm supply store to place their orders. They'd planned to buy feed for the livestock, as well, but the prices were too high. Zeb decided to shop around before making the purchase.

As they were leaving, Merv pulled out an envelope from Zeb's pocket. "What's this?"

Zeb squinted to read the return address.

The City Ordinances Municipal Offices, Lititz Pennsylvania.

"What's that about?" Merv looked over Zeb's shoulder.

"I have no idea." He ripped it open and read silently, knowing Merv was too. "Steel wheels banned, Ordinance No. 41, on hard surface highways?" Merv said it loud enough to make some heads turn as they walked out of the building. "Why did we get a letter? It was a warning, right? And I thought Reuben said we had to have steel wheels."

Zeb's blood pulsed with every step as he remembered his conversation with Reuben, who'd promised he'd let the bishop know about the situation because it affected everyone in the community. It was a cheap way out of dealing with it himself, but if Reuben could take care of it, the burden would be lifted from Zeb.

"I thought it was taken care of, but apparently not." Zeb turned on his heel and headed the other direction.

"Where are you going now?" Merv tried to keep up, but Zeb didn't slow his pace.

"To the courthouse." He turned at the corner and crossed the street. Zeb opened the double doors and went up to the security desk. A tall, unsmiling officer stood and waited to hear his question.

"Where do I go to take care of this citation?" Zeb stood almost eye to eye with him, unable to hide his irritation, which put the guard on the defensive.

"Through the foyer and to the right. You can make an appointment there." He crossed his arms over his chest, waiting for Zeb to leave.

Zeb shook his head. "I want to talk with someone about it now, today."

"You'll have to ask the court secretary." The guard eyed Zeb, obviously done trying to reason with him.

Zeb let out a breath, containing his temper, and headed for the hallway where the guard had told him to go. He'd lost Merv somewhere along the way. He'd catch up with him later. The woman who sat at the secretary's office was an attractive blonde with long nails. He couldn't help but stop and study her, so different from the Amish women in his community in their dress and plain faces.

"What can I help you with?" Her blue eyes flashed at him, taking him off guard momentarily.

"Who do I need to talk to about this?" He handed her the citation and watched as she read.

"You'll need to make a court date so you can meet with the

members of the County Board of Supervisors, or you can pay the fine and show proof you have done everything required." She slowly handed it back to him. He begrudgingly accepted it.

"Is this a common problem?"

"I can't comment on that, Mr. Bowman."

He frowned. "That's confidential information?"

"I'm not allowed to talk about any of the situations that come up. I'm just the secretary. Would you like to make an appointment, Mr. Bowman?"

She seemed to be suggesting it without telling him to, so he decided to accept. He didn't care to spend more time in town, but maybe another diversion would help get Emma off his mind.

Chapter Twenty-Three

A group of the Amish finished breakfast and walked toward the front door. Mark was one of them, and Caleb knew Emma would want to know what they were up to. She had done well to give Mark his space. More so than he thought was possible for her, but she seemed to have her own agenda now that she had seen Abe and was caring for Monique. He couldn't have been more proud of the way she treated Monique with dignity and respect, both of which Monique hadn't had for a very long time. He didn't know much about her past, and she didn't share any information, so Caleb had stopped trying.

"Mark." Caleb came around from the kitchen as Mark waited. "What's going on today?"

Mark didn't respond well to Emma, but he did with Caleb. It was all for the better. Emma could get the information she needed without the attitude from Mark, and Caleb kept a finger on him so they knew where he was and what he was up to without Emma's involvement. It seemed to be working well, as far as they knew.

Mark looked back at the other five or six teens about his age waiting for him. "The museum of art is close, so we thought we'd go over that way and look around."

"Really? The museum?"

Caleb didn't mean to act smug, but he rarely heard of groups going to the museums.

"*Jah*, maybe." He grinned. "It's kind of a cool place to hang out around the park in front of it."

"All right. Take care."

Caleb had learned to use the right words when talking to them. If you sounded like a parent, they thought you were being too paternal. With those who were homesick, he had to be the opposite, so he treated them like their parents would. The more he thought about it, the more he knew how complicated it all was.

Mark was learning the local lingo, as well, which didn't surprise Caleb. Some would try to fit in any way they could. Others were repulsed by it, like the group of girls sitting together at a nearby table with forlorn expressions on their faces. They had already asked him how it worked if they wanted to go home.

"What are you going to do with them?" Emma's voice was like sweet music to his ears. He'd never get tired of hearing her laugh, either.

He looked over at the miserable young ladies and decided it was time to do a group project. The independent ones might not be interested, but for these girls it was just the ticket. "If you could pick something to do today, what would it be?"

They all looked at one another, waiting for someone to speak up. Caleb wanted to smile at their *kapps*, blue dresses, and white aprons, which were all the same. Yet he'd never laugh because he knew each of these girls by name, and who their parents were. "What about gardening?"

That created a few smiles and raised brows. "But where?" one of the girls asked with a serious tone.

"There are flower beds on either side of the stairs as you walk up to the church. You probably didn't notice them because the beds haven't had anything in them for a while." He looked at each one of them. "Are you interested?"

Half a dozen *jah*s went up at the same time. The girls were up and ready before Caleb had a chance to give any instructions. Other than telling them where the tools were, this group didn't need much guidance for planting anything. Then came the questions.

"Do you have soil?"

"Where do you get flowers from around here?"

He held up his hands to make the chatty girls stop so he could answer. "There's a shed out back with some tools. Alex will pick up some flowers and seed down the street." He turned to leave, but Emma was standing in front of Caleb.

"Are you coming?"

"This may be the best part of the trip for me." She smiled, but Caleb felt there was some sorrow mixed with the excitement. "I asked Monique to come down if she felt comfortable."

He was grateful that Emma had asked her but cautious as well. "That's probably a good idea. We just need to stay close to her."

"Of course. But she can't stay up in her room all day and night." Her tone lifted.

"Is something else on your mind?"

Of course there was. It had been from the moment she'd gotten here. It was a silly question. He knew she would enjoy gardening, but this wasn't the typical planting like they did back home. She knew that, he was sure, but he would be curious to see how they improvised with what little they had to make this work.

"I'm torn. I thought my place here was something different than it started out to be. But now I feel it's about Monique." She stopped and looked straight at him. "But am I fooling myself to think I can really do anything for her?"

"Of course you can, and you will. I knew you would from

the moment you talked about coming. I selfishly had you two together from the time you said yes." He paused. "I've never seen her let anyone get near her, physically or emotionally, until the other night with you."

Emma smiled. "*Jah*, and her wounds are healing, just like she is, if Abe would stay away. Do you think he will?"

He hadn't been around the last couple of days, but Caleb had no doubt that he would be coming for her. It was some sort of power thing he had with Monique. There were other women out there he could go after, but there was something about Monique that kept him coming back.

"No, one of them will end up in the hospital or, dare I say it, killed before they stop."

Emma startled when he said the word, but if she was going to get involved, she needed to know what she was up against. But something unexpected shone in her eyes, and she boldly answered him.

"That can't happen." The wheezing in her chest started up again. If she wasn't mistaken she was sure stress made it worse.

Caleb blinked a couple times. "I'd like to think it wouldn't, but I've seen it for too long to think it will end any other way." He took her hand, understanding that Emma was beginning to bond with Monique. The protective side of her was starting to bloom. When he thought about blooming, he decided the garden was in good order for her too. "Shall we go out with the girls?"

Emma bent her head. "What happened to Abe?"

Caleb rubbed his face as if to brush away memories of his brother. "We came down here for *rumspringa* a while ago."

"I remember. You didn't want to go, and I was surprised that you went." She looked away for a second. "I'd hoped you'd stay with me on the farm."

He grunted. "Believe me, that's what I wanted too. But my folks asked me to go. They knew Abe would go and that I'd watch over him." Caleb took in a breath and let it out slowly. He didn't like to go through this again but needed to for Emma's sake. She needed to know.

"He went crazy here, causing all kinds of trouble. Even to North Philly, the roughest part of Philadelphia." Caleb shook his head, trying for the umpteenth time to figure out why Abe had that streak in him and why he couldn't get it out of his system. "When I saw what he was capable of, I felt too responsible to leave, and even more so when I learned what he was fighting against."

Emma took his hand in hers, a familiar gesture he remembered from when she was consoling others. "You don't have to tell me any more, Caleb."

"He's destructive, Emma, to himself and everyone around him. Just know that. Maybe that's enough." He didn't want to scare her, but at the same time, he wanted her to be wary. Abe was after Monique, not Emma, so if she stood clear, he would leave her alone. Caleb started walking again, and she followed.

They strolled silently to the front doors, and as soon as they went outside, Emma turned to Caleb and stopped. "He was so handsome, and had that head of thick blond hair. What's made him so angry?"

"He cut it all to show his disobedience to God. He blames everything on God."

Emma frowned and moved back. "Why would he turn against *Gott*?"

"He's sick, Emma. The cancer is as deadly as he is."

He could see the shock as her eyes opened wide and her mouth fell open. "*Ach*, Caleb. I'm so sorry."

"They say it was the pesticides from working the farm."

Caleb shrugged. "But who really knows? What I do know is that it made Abe bitter against his people and his faith when they told him. It was one more reason to disown everything Amish."

"Can he get treatments?"

Caleb shook his head. "They say it's not curable. He couldn't if he wanted to, which he doesn't. No insurance or money. Doesn't even have a job. He takes what he wants."

She was quiet for too long, and Caleb was worried he'd said too much. It was a lot for a young Amish person to swallow. He had become accustomed to the harder side of life since coming here, but he'd also seen a lot of lives changed. He had many reasons to praise God each day. "I'm sorry to have to tell you all of this."

"I asked you to, Caleb. I wish the community could know. They would help him."

Caleb scoffed but didn't comment. He knew Abe would never accept help from his community like most Amish did.

"He may still come around, when it gets bad enough." Her bright, brown eyes poured into his, hopeful and naive. He discerned the cynical thoughts and pushed them away. Emma had always been good in that way, thinking the best of people. He needed to be around that attitude and her.

He conceded with a nod. "You never know. He's still able to function really well right now, but eventually he'll get weaker." He took her hand and led them outside, needing to get outdoors. When the blasting horns and hordes of people surrounded him, he wished for the quiet solitude of the farm. It was difficult to clear his head with all the commotion.

He dragged out the dirt that was desperately needed in the old, empty flower beds that lined the stairs of the church. When he came back, the girls had cleaned out the cement boxes and were ready to pour the dirt into them. Then they planted a variety of flowers of red, yellow, orange, and purple. Some of them had a sweet scent to them that Caleb could smell as he went up the stairs. This would give him something to look forward to each day, as well as being a visual welcome for the homeless and residents there.

"You've all done good work here today." He stood, hands on hips, and encouraged them on a job well done.

Emma had been quietly working, talking with the girls, but not with her usual friendly enthusiasm. He had put a heavy load on her, maybe too much, but he was glad to have her to confide in. What brought her to a smile was when Monique joined them.

"I got something for you." Monique handed her a small white bottle with a hole at the bottom.

"What is this?

"It's an inhaler. Caleb told me you needed one." Monique looked from Caleb to Emma and frowned at Caleb. "It's from the clinic, over the counter. We got the same thing going on." Monique grinned. Caleb nodded, wanting the answer but not sure how to ask if it was from the street.

"*Danke*. Here, Monique. I have a few left for you to plant." Emma took out one of the black plastic trays with the flowers that she'd saved for her.

Monique scanned the area and then looked down at Emma, who was sitting on a cement step, holding the spade up to her. "I don't know how to do any of that." Her almond-shaped eyes peered down at the bag of dirt at Emma's feet.

"There's not a lot to it. Here." Emma patted the spot beside her.

Monique hesitated, but then sat down next to Emma. Reluctantly taking the spade, she dug around in the dark soil.

The two of them talked and planted the rest of the flowers, taking their time to enjoy the process.

Caleb felt like an intruder, not taking his eyes off the scene. Never in a million years had he thought he'd ever see this sight. He leaned against the red brick wall that led up to the church and enjoyed watching the Holy Spirit move and grow such an unlikely friendship.

Chapter Twenty-Four

It was a sunny, blissful morning with just enough breeze to keep the temperature mild. A visiting choir was coming to the church to spend the day with them. Emma looked forward to hearing them sing, although she was unsure of the accompanying instruments they used. But this entire trip was about new things, so she learned to be open to whatever came her way.

Emma placed the inhaler in her dress pocket. She'd tried it once and it worked well, but she wasn't comfortable using it. Just having it at hand made her feel better.

When the group arrived, the Amish came down to greet them. The African American men and women ranged from teenagers to young adults, much like the ages of the Amish.

They awkwardly introduced themselves to one another, the Amish offering their one hand pump and the English accepting with a grin. Once they sat down to share lunch, things seemed to lighten up a bit. One young man made an extra effort to meet as many of the Amish as he could.

"I'm Adrian." He shook Emma's hand and then Mark's.

"This is the way you do it where I come from." Mark offered his hand to Adrian and pumped his hand once. "That's it. None of this sliding palms or bumping fists." Mark grinned, egging him along.

"This one is even better." Adrian put his fist up, and Mark mimicked him.

"Peace." He hit the top of Mark's fist.

"Love." He hit the bottom of Mark's fist.

"Unity." They bumped fists.

"Respect." They touched thumbs. "That's what they do in Jamaica."

Emma watched Mark's face glow as he learned a new custom and made a friend in the process.

They ate together, laughing and sharing stories. It was as if they'd known one another for a long while, rather than the single hour that they'd just spent together.

The group put on shiny blue robes and gathered together on the church stage. Being used to good craftsmanship, Emma worried the old stage might fall into pieces with the large number of them, but no one else seemed concerned. The choir participants moved around, clapped their hands and lifted them as high as they sang.

"They sing *gut* for English," Mark commented with a grin.

Emma absorbed the music when they sang "What a Friend I Have in Jesus" and "Amazing Grace." "I really like that one. I wish they'd sing it again." They also sang some songs that reflected their culture, which were interesting, but not what she preferred. Dancing and shaking their bodies while clapping were a bit much. Mark, on the other hand, seemed to love each and every song as he clapped along with a smile plastered across his face.

Caleb came over and sat with her. "I thought we'd take them to the park."

Emma brightened at the idea. She had noticed how well they were doing together and hated for them to leave. She could see how well Caleb dealt with these groups. Being flexible and spontaneous was a must, and she was learning how to respond as he did when surprises or changes rearranged the order of things. "That's a wonderful *gut* idea."

"What's a good idea?" Monique sat next to Emma. She didn't look as tired as usual, but she didn't smile. Not that she ever did, but her features were grim. Emma remembered back to the first day they met, when Emma had been sure they'd never come to a good place. Yet after much prayer and the opportunity to help heal her, here they were, sitting side by side. Emma hoped nothing would happen to reverse things back to the way they were.

"Let's go to the park and fly a kite." Caleb said it so enthusiastically, Monique rolled her eyes and shook her head. She seemed to be in no mood for playfulness.

Emma hoped she hadn't had contact with Abe. He had control over her in a way that couldn't be undone—at least, not yet. Emma would do whatever she could to help the vicious cycle end, but it all depended on Monique. She would rise above it or get swallowed up again.

Emma had grinned when Caleb suggested flying a kite. She'd never flown one but had always wanted to. Of all the things she was curious about, this was one she was truly interested in. It was silly, she knew, to want this experience more than others, but it freed her to think of maneuvering something up so high in the air.

Caleb moved closer and squinted his eyes. "You really want to do this, don't you?" He seemed amused, yet serious about it at the same time.

Am I being obvious?

Monique rested her chin in her palm. Only her eyes moved as she scanned the room, always leery of her surroundings. She was completely uninterested in their conversation, bored with it, even. The young woman didn't hold back her feelings and could be outright rude, but Emma understood, as Caleb did, that she'd been through a lot.

"Do you really have a kite?" Emma asked.

"Yes, I do. Also a volleyball net, Frisbees, and a soccer ball." He lifted his brows. "Watch this." He jogged up to the stage and waved his hands, a gesture to which the teens seemed to respond.

"Listen up. We're going across the street to the park. Anyone who wants to join us is welcome." He directed his attention to the visiting group and jogged back to Emma.

She couldn't help but smile as he ran to her taking her to a large closet down the hall, where he dug around until he found the equipment he needed.

"We'll grab this, just in case." He pulled out the air pump and held a Frisbee in the other hand.

Some of the young men grabbed the rest and headed for the park.

She watched them cross the busy street and then scatter around the park. Some sat and talked by the tall fountain with statues of famous historical figures surrounding it. Others set up the volleyball net or played a game they called Frisbee golf. The weather couldn't be more perfect, with a slight breeze and white, fluffy clouds overhead.

An alarm went off in Emma's head when she didn't see Monique. She turned around and went back into the church. When she passed through the lobby and to the eating area, she went to find Alex.

"Haven't seen her since you left." He stopped cleaning and looked around the room and back to Emma. "That's not a good sign."

"What do you mean?" Emma's stomach began to roll, feeling something was off.

"She always goes back, Emma. It's just a matter of when." He handled a towel nervously and shook his head.

She took in a breath, frustrated with him for giving up so quickly. She didn't care what the history was. "Maybe this time it will be different."

"I used to pray for that, Emma. Now I pray for safety."

"So you give up, just like that? You don't try to keep her away?" Her face twitched with frustration, partly at Alex but more with Monique. She'd heard of women in her own community who were abused, but the bishop didn't let it continue. They tried to work through the church to remedy the problem, not look the other way.

She turned and walked away before he could respond. Emma glanced back as she climbed the stairs. He was still watching her as he continued to wipe down the bench seats. He was obviously concerned, which fed Emma's concern.

When she made her way up to the room, Emma was relieved to see Monique on the bed. One foot on the floor, tapping the wood beneath her high-top tennis shoes. She didn't acknowledge Emma and kept her eyes fixed on the dingy, popcorn-textured ceiling.

"Are you going to the park?"

Monique scoffed. "No, I don't play Frisbee. You Amish are so easy." Her moods were as unpredictable as Mark's, but at least it was something Emma was used to and had learned to live around.

"*Jah*, I suppose we are…but it might be good to get out for a while." Monique was probably right, but Emma took no personal offense to it. She would rather be easily entertained than in the fast pace Monique was in. Deep down she wondered whether Monique felt the same but was so caught up in the only life she'd ever known that she defended it.

Monique sat up abruptly, her eyes narrowed. "Go play with your new friends." With that she stood and left the room.

Where the sudden bitterness came from, Emma didn't know. Maybe something was said that triggered negative feelings, or maybe she just didn't feel like socializing.

Now that Mark was being somewhat reasonable, Emma was put in a familiar position with Monique. At least it wasn't both of them at once. Emma mustered up some strength and went to find Caleb.

When she got to the top of the stairs, she noticed the place was almost empty. All that remained was the staff and a few lingering teens and the group who wanted to go home that Caleb would be taking to the bus station soon. She found Caleb sitting in an old, tattered beanbag chair, and plopped down in an avocado-green one.

"Comfortable?" He grinned as he watched her squirm around, trying to adjust to the strange chair.

"*Nee*, not really." She let out a sigh and looked upstairs for any sign of Monique. "She's not going to the park."

"So you're not, either." He said instead of asked.

"*Nee*, I would worry."

"You're not her mother, Emma. It's good of you to care for her and be there for her, but you have to let it go. She's going to do whatever it is she's going to do. And all you can do is be there for her again when she falls."

"That's negative—for you to be so sure that she'll fail."

"I hope I'm wrong. But I doubt it. This is all she knows. The only way to change that would be to modify her environment and keep her away from the bad things she's been involved in."

"I can't think about it that way. I have to have hope she'll change her ways."

"I hope so too. But she has to want to change." He reached for her hand, and she responded without hesitation, almost expecting the common gesture. She had grown accustomed to him clutching her since she'd come here. He'd done it since they were children—instinct, she supposed.

"Everything is so much better with you here, Emma." He looked up as if to see in her eyes whether she was comfortable with his words.

She slowly turned her head, trying to think of the right response. The one that immediately came to mind was how she felt when he was at the farm with her.

"I feel the same when you're home." They seemed to both want to be together, but in their own worlds. Being with him now was good only because she was with him, but if she wanted him in her life, she would have to compromise, and living in the city wasn't something she could do.

His bright eyes dimmed at the words. His struggle was the same as hers, and neither could give up where they felt they belonged. She closed her eyes in silent prayer, asking for strength and wisdom. *Gott* had brought her there for a reason, but now so many reasons competed that she wasn't sure which was the most significant.

"I get confused as to what I'm supposed to do since I've come here."

Caleb looked to the floor. Disappointment or just plain sadness seemed to penetrate him.

"Maybe you're trying too hard. Maybe you just need to *be* and not worry about the rest."

She didn't totally understand what he was saying, but it was enough to let her know she should slow down and take it as it came. At a place like this, that was about all you could do.

She noticed his eyes shift and look behind her. Monique swung a bag over her shoulder and moved quickly down the stairs. As she got closer, Emma waited for her to stop, but she didn't. Emma saw her eyes, heavy and bloodshot, and knew something was on her mind.

The front door opened, causing Emma and Caleb to look that way, away from Monique. Wherever Abe was, his followers were too, harassing anyone who was vulnerable.

Abe stood with his back against the glass door watching Emma's reaction as Monique went past him and down the stairs. A toothpick stuck to his lip as he smiled. He shoved his hands in his jeans pockets and leaned back to hold the door open. His eyes followed Monique until she was out of sight, and then looked at Emma.

"You're done babysitting. She's mine now."

At that moment, some in the group came back from the park, talking about Abe as they went up the stairs to the church. As they passed Abe, he grinned and watched each of them stroll by.

The Amish frowned and tried their best to ignore him. The city kids showed more anger toward him, but neither had an impact. Abe had apparently accomplished what he'd set out to do—discourage the Amish, anger the group of city kids, but most of all, to capture the pawn. In either place she went, Monique was a hostage.

Chapter Twenty-Five

Caleb gave the Mennonite driver some cash to pay for taking a group of Amish girls to the bus station. As he walked up to the church, he knew there would have been another load of guys, as well, but they were too prideful to admit they wanted to go home. He could see it in their eyes and lack of enthusiasm that a few weeks in the city were more than enough. He listened in on a conversation as he took a seat in the kitchen, waiting for Emma.

"It's boring in the city. There's not enough to do." A blond-haired kid who still wore a bowl haircut looked unhappy.

An older girl tucked her palm under her chin, not used to idle hands. "*Jah*, and they live in small areas, right next to each other, but are isolated from one another."

A tall lanky Amish boy nodded. "It's strange, the men and women work together, doing the same things. And when they go on that subway, they all run together, but no one leads.

"They stare straight ahead and don't talk." Another young man paused. "I feel sorry for them."

Caleb felt sorry for *them* sitting around and complaining instead of practicing what they were preaching. But after the situation with Abe, some of them had been scared straight. Although Abe was forbidden to come back to the church, it didn't stop him.

Caleb opened the paper like he did every morning to read the obituaries. Occasionally there was a name he recognized or a call from the morgue when one of the homeless had passed away. He would notify any friends or families if he knew of them, and offer the church if a family member didn't have a place to hold the funeral. It was just part of what he did. He couldn't get to know these people without feeling responsible for them.

"Our group is dwindling." Emma scanned the room as she sat next to him. The smell of her hair, the way she talked, and her presence alone stirred something inside of him that no other person could. He made a point not to stare, sniff, or hang on her every word, but at times it was impossible.

"Most of the girls are gone. There's still a dozen or so boys. They're the ones who will usually stick it out." He folded the paper and poured more coffee into her mug.

"Unless Abe keeps coming around." Emma looked down at her cup and then took a sip. "Some of the Amish didn't know who he was or the others he was with. They tried to evangelize to them."

Caleb's brows furrowed, and he gave her his full attention. "Do you know what came of it?"

"*Nee*—nothing good, anyway. Those young men scared them, taunting them, flirting with the girls, and picking fights with the boys." Emma shook her head. "What's the point of all this? It only makes the Amish look weak and stupid when all they're trying to do is talk to people about their faith."

"They're not as well-equipped to evangelize as they should be with a crowd like there is here. But then we talked about that, remember?" Caleb searched her face, knowing she was discouraged. "It's going to come naturally or not at all. People here are skeptical, so don't expect it to be easy."

"Everything is so negative. Why do we just give up when we have *Gott*'s work to do?" Tears built up, but she blinked them away.

He reached for her, but she pulled back, angry. He knew it wasn't directed at him. It had been a long few weeks, unexpected for her once she'd gotten involved with Monique. Mark seemed to be doing better, so that was one positive. He and Adrian spent time together when they could. For the most part, though, she was right—a lot had happened that was difficult, if not impossible, to solve without the help of community.

"I'm sorry, Caleb. If it wasn't for you, I wouldn't have come here at all and met Monique."

"Sometimes I regret getting you two together. It's been harder than ever since you got involved. It's almost like Abe's competing with you for her."

Emma took her time to respond. "He knows we've become friends. He's threatened by it."

He was surprised at her confident reply, and he could see how it could be true. Abe had let up on Monique until Emma started a relationship with her. How would Emma take that information? He didn't want to make her feel responsible for Abe coming in strong again once she got here. "He's a possessive man. Maybe if we let go a little, he'd lose interest."

"And let Monique fend for herself?" Emma shook her head.

He'd figured she would balk at the suggestion but wanted to throw it out there. He just didn't see how they could do anything to help Monique at this point.

Mark distracted them from their conversation. He was dressed more like Adrian than Amish, in jeans and a T-shirt, but his work boots gave him away.

"New clothes?

"Adrian let me borrow some while I'm here." Mark looked over at Emma. "I knew you wouldn't like it."

"I like the boots." She smiled. "Are you going somewhere?"

Mark remained unsmiling. "I'm meeting up with him." He

held up a hand when Emma sucked in air. "I'll be back before dinner. Can he eat with us?" Mark turned his eyes on Caleb.

"Sure, it would be nice to see him again. Be here by six to help set up?" Caleb gave him a chore so he'd be back well before dark and Emma wouldn't worry so much.

"Sure. Later." He turned and walked away with a bit of swagger.

"What kind of word is that?"

Caleb grinned. "It's just a condensed way of saying, 'see you later.'"

"There's nothing funny about any of this." Emma stood and rushed after Mark. Caleb was caught off guard and decided to stay put. Emma was too emotional to reason with. She'd probably had her fill of Philly, something he was avoiding dealing with. This wasn't the place for her. She would need to go home soon, and he would be here without her. Nothing would be the same once she left.

He decided to find her and tell her she should go whether Mark left or not, because he didn't want to see her miserable. But when he went through the front doors there was no sign of her or Mark. He knew she wouldn't have gone with him, but he scanned the area and neither of them were anywhere in sight.

Caleb took the steps two at a time and went from one end of the block to the other and then made his way to the park. He'd barely hit the grass when he ran across a group of Amish guys walking over to him. They were unusually quiet, and not one cracked a smile as they approached.

"What's going on?" He waited for an answer, but they all looked at each other, not wanting to be the one to tell.

"We're in a bad spot." One blue-eyed young man spoke up,

but he glanced at his friends as he said it, not at Caleb. Their approval obviously took priority over his.

"Spill it, guys. Whatever it is isn't important, so don't waste time."

A few seconds went by, and finally one of them spoke up. "Adrian's gonna show Mark where Monique is."

He couldn't meet Caleb's eyes, but that didn't matter to him. He was just glad they told him. He was also scared. Anywhere Monique was, Abe would be, and that meant danger.

He clasped the boy on the shoulder. "*Danke.*" Speaking in the boy's own tongue made him smile, and Caleb had to admit it felt good for him too.

"Can we help?"

"Tell Alex and Emma I've gone to find them." He didn't know the street, but he knew the area, and everybody knew everyone else's business in those neighborhoods where people lived in small row houses.

But he wasn't thrilled going alone. He wasn't too proud to admit it, either. It wasn't a good part of town.

"Emma went with Mark."

Caleb's chest contracted. The air in his lungs stuck. Nothing moved for a long, drawn-out minute.

"You!" He pointed to the dark-haired kid who'd said the horrifying words. "Which way did they go?"

He pointed in the direction Caleb had planned to go but was the last place he'd want to be. There would be no mercy once they set foot in the area he figured them to be in. A hand slapped his back, and he turned to see Alex. He didn't dare be so bold as to ask him to go with him but having a black man with him would help. And it was Alex's old stomping ground.

"Let me take you home." Alex's voice was strong, not intimidated.

"No, I'm doing this."

"I mean my crib, where I come from."

Caleb nodded sheepishly. Although he knew Alex's history, he knew him in a very different way.

"You do what I do, how I do it," Alex ordered in all seriousness. His concern made Caleb worry more. "You boys go to the church and stay there."

None of them balked at his directions.

"Let's do this." Alex made his way through speeding cars, angry taxi drivers, and crowds of grumpy people getting off work.

Caleb panicked a little, realizing the early shift was over and after the next group was off work, it would start to get dark.

"Keep up." Alex was as serious as Caleb had ever seen him, and his pace was faster than Caleb could keep up with.

The subway stifled Caleb, who wanted to move his own two feet. The train stopped twice before they finally got off.

When they got to the top of the stairs, Caleb felt the oppression immediately. He sensed a heavy weight was pushing on his chest. Negative thoughts circled around in his mind.

Why did you let Emma come here? You can't help Monique, stop trying. Just try *to find her here.*

"Which one?" he said to himself.

"What are you mumbling about?" Alex stared at him, trying to tell him something. "Move your feet, man."

He went halfway down the block and stopped at one of the skinny, rundown homes, and knocked on the door.

Their words blurred in his mind. He couldn't stand there and do nothing, so he started down the narrow road that divided the two sides of row houses.

"Abe!" He kept his eyes peeled and continued to yell his

name. Alex frowned at him, but then continued his conversation with someone at the door.

Out of the corner of his eye, Caleb saw movement. A door opened and Mark came out, waved Caleb over, and waited. Caleb's legs felt like putty as he made his way a few houses down.

"Where is she?" Caleb asked.

Mark shut the door behind them. "Which one?"

The small two-story home was filthy, with sparse furniture and a rank smell. Sleeping bags, food packages, and bottles were spread out throughout the living room and kitchen.

Caleb hadn't thought about the possibility that although he'd meant Emma, Monique was there too. He couldn't help but think of Emma. Not only was he responsible for her, he also knew he was in love with her.

"Are they both here?"

His eyes wandered up and down as he saw Monique. Most of her hair had fallen out of the clip that lilted to the side, and it hadn't been washed in days. She'd stopped trying to keep her clothes clean. There was no way to do that without shelter. The dark bags under her eyes made her look even worse.

"Monique." Caleb went to her. Her usual resistance was gone, defeated like the rest of her.

"What happened?" Alex went over and stared at her sorry state. He balled his fists. "Where is he?"

"Abe? We don't know." Emma's voice was calm in the midst of the chaos. "We should go before he comes back."

Caleb and Alex each put an arm around Monique, helping her walk, and took her out of the place of rubble she was living in.

When they got outside, Adrian followed and handed them a jug of water. "I can't be seen with you."

"Get outta here. Go!" Alex shooed him away with a protective gesture. They knew the rules of the street that Caleb and Emma couldn't fathom.

Adrian lifted his fist. Mark smiled slowly and raised his hand. They did a Jamaican handshake, then Alex nodded as Adrian walked away.

Chapter Twenty-Six

"*Danke* for breakfast, *Mamm*." Zeb placed the handmade napkin on his empty plate and walked to the door.

His *daed* turned around to see Zeb. "What time is the meeting?"

"Not until later, but I'm going into town early. Gotta take care of some business." He still hoped he could take care of this without a long procession of Amish getting involved. Zeb had a knack for talking himself in and out of tight spots. The only part that bothered him was that Merv was involved. He could make things worse with his ignorance alone.

"Sure you don't want me to go?" His *daed*'s gray hair and peaked complexion was an answer in itself. *Daed* didn't have the energy or stamina to spend the day riding in the buggy and sitting in a courthouse all day, but he would be glad to get it behind him.

"*Nee, Daed*. Merv and I can handle it. We'll need a hand with the milking, though." They honestly did need assistance because they would need to start early to get to town in plenty of time. And it would give *Daed* something to do to feel helpful.

"You ready?" Merv ate the egg sandwich *Mamm* had made him and washed it down with a glass of milk.

"Here are a couple more for the road." She handed each of them a jug of water and sandwich wrapped in a towel.

Zeb and Merv were silent during the drive to town as green

fields turned to cottages that turned to business offices until they were in the heart of town.

They looked for a place to park that wouldn't bother other drivers if the horse made a mess, and then found their way to the courthouse, waiting for Merv's name to be called.

They sat on wood benches that were placed against three of the walls in the room with a long table of men facing them. As the time came to start the proceedings, more people started coming in, both Englishers and Amish. Zeb had expected some to show up, but not this many. But then the meeting he'd had with the deacons may have piqued more interest.

Reuben hadn't been at the previous meeting, and that was no accident. Knowing he was away visiting family in Ohio, Zeb had taken advantage of the opportunity and called for a meeting with the deacons during that specific time. *Gott* help him for being so manipulative. At times he felt if Emma were there his conscience would take second place to hers. She had a rock-solid honesty about her.

He scanned the room, but didn't see Reuben there today either. It seemed too much of a coincidence, but it was still early, and he could show up. Zeb sank down in his seat.

I'm being paranoid. If Reuben had a problem with our milk farm, it would have been brought up by now.

"Mervin Bowman." An older gray-haired man looked through his bifocals at a paper as Merv moved forward.

"A police officer pulled you over for failure to use required towing equipment, failure to display a reflective device on a slow-moving vehicle, and having steel wheels." He looked down over his glasses at Merv.

"*Jah*, sir." Merv stood and twisted the brim of his hat, nervous as all get-out. Zeb had put him in this spot and wished he was the one standing there, not Merv.

"Permission to speak." Zeb stood, not able to sit by and watch his brother go through this alone. He was representing the entire community, after all. "I'm Merv's brother."

"Yes, Mr. Bowman."

"I came into town when we got the notice and explained to the officer that the wheels are a part of our religious beliefs, as is not using a slow-moving vehicle sign. We don't have the privilege to change two of the three, but we will use a different towing device."

The man took off his glasses. "And why do you feel the need to speak for your brother?"

"I should have been driving that day. I asked Merv to do a chore I should have done." If that sounded genuine enough, Zeb may have swayed the group of decision makers enough to consider a lesser punishment.

"Would the outcome be any different?" The older man's fuzzy brow furrowed with question.

"For the most part, no. But I have been attending the meeting over this matter and want to know what's been decided. I'd like to help with anything to remedy the situation." Zeb wouldn't have used the towing device Merv used, but that didn't need to be brought up unless necessary.

"It has been decided that steel wheels are not allowed due to the damage they cause. We spend millions every year on resurfacing highways in this area. The only option we can offer is rubber tires over the steel wheels. The other recourse is for you to challenge this in court due to your religious beliefs, according to the freedom of religion act." The mediator grinned. "I hear you have a history of that."

"May I add something here?" The bishop stood to face the group of men who oversaw the conversation. Zeb let out the air in his lungs, glad he was present to help move this in the direction necessary.

The gray-haired mediator grinned. "Ahh, yes, Bishop. Why is it that you have to use those blasted steel wheels?" They seemed to know one another. Zeb hoped it was in a good way, and not some other tussle the Amish had for the old ways.

"We're not meaning to be above the law. It's a sign of humility. Any advancement in our community can cause *schism* in the church. We can't make changes without going against the mother church." The bishop's reddish beard and hair shone under the fluorescent lights as he waited for a response.

"The members of the Lancaster County Board of Supervisors want to take care of the roads. It's our responsibility. If there are any damages from this incident or in the future, you will be responsible."

"I will personally pay for any damages." Zeb may have spoken too quickly and out of turn, but he wanted this off his back and everyone else's. It would go against their principles to change anything they were doing, and if money could appease them, so be it.

The older man nodded. "Yes, Mr. Bowman, you will pay, or whoever is responsible." He looked over at Merv.

Zeb treated him like a coddled child, but better that than Merv saying something that would get them in any trouble.

The group of Amish men gathered once outside the room, discussing the issue. Hearing their remarks made Zeb realize they'd opened a can of worms. The problem had only started to bubble up to the surface and would surely affect them all until things could be ironed out with the city and the *gmayna* board. Then the Amish pulled together.

The bishop walked over to Zeb before he left, pulling him to the side. "Take care of this, Zeb. We don't want it turning into more problems. We'll pay whatever fines come up as a community. You're not alone. It could have been any one of us. But until we can work this out with the mother church, our hands are tied."

"*Nee*, Bishop Bender. We have the money to pay what is owed." Zeb wasn't that out of the way. The dairy farm was doing well enough, it wouldn't gouge their income.

The bishop leaned in closer. "I hear you're doing well with your dairy farm."

Zeb's mind tingled, a warning that this might be a new set of problems. "*Jah*, it's a change from growing crop, but it's worked out for us."

"*Gut*. It's a good thing to have a dairy farm that's done so well in our community. Doing well enough to give up growing crop, even?"

A flag went up. Knowing he'd been the topic of conversation in the presence of the bishop was not a good sign. Zeb's throat went dry.

He waited long enough to reply that the bishop spoke up again. "Or are you still deciding?"

Reuben walked through the doors, scanned the room, and made eye contact with Zeb. As he began to make his way over to them, Zeb felt trapped by either side. There was no way out of this conversation. He had to tell the truth within the few seconds before Reuben told the bishop.

"That will only happen if I'm able to use gas pumps to speed up the process. We have too many cows to do it any other way."

There it was, out in the open. He'd have the bishop's blessing or be denied. But even if he was given permission, he'd have some explaining to do as to why he already had the equipment.

Ivan stopped Reuben, said a few words, and Reuben

continued over to them. The bishop's answer couldn't come quickly enough.

"Hmm, sounds like we have another meeting to tend to." He twirled his beard, a sign he was thinking, sizing up the circumstances and probably working out an answer as they spoke. "We'll talk later."

"*Jah.* The sooner, the better." That wasn't the closure he'd hoped for, but at least it was out there, and Reuben was no longer a threat. He wanted this over. It had been hanging over his head for too long. Between that and Emma's distance, he was about at his wits' end.

"How's Emma doing? Have you heard?" Bishop placed his black felt hat on his head and tapped the top once.

"Not recently. Just one letter. I'm heading over to the post office, so hopefully there will be some good news." Any news would be just fine about now. He'd been patient long enough.

Bishop made the soft humming sound again and then shook his head. "They always come home again. And I wouldn't be worried about Emma. I'm glad she's there. She'll bring those young'uns back where they belong."

"If anyone can, it would be her. I just hope it's soon." Zeb was antsy, now that the post office was open and the meeting was over. He tipped his hat to the bishop and told Merv to meet him at the buggy. He wanted to be alone this time if there was a letter, and for some reason, he felt sure there would be.

When he got to the mailbox, he looked through the glass window to see two letters. He pulled them out and noticed they were both from the same address—the Mennonite church address Emma had used. He ripped open her letter, hoping he was reading them in the correct order.

Dear Zeb,

I hope this letter finds you well. I've adjusted to the church where we're staying. Everyone is friendly and helpful. I especially like a man named Alex. He has helped me learn how the Stock Pot runs and how to help. Mark seems to be enjoying his time here, which is good for him but hard for me because he's difficult to keep track of and is fearless in this big city. He has made a friend here, a nice young man, but I worry Mark may stay because of this friendship. Regardless, I hope to be home soon.

Tell my family Mark and I are well and hope to see you all very soon.

Yours,
Emma

Zeb stuck out his lower lip in thought. This letter was more insightful than the last, but still not what he'd hoped for. There was another, though, so he couldn't complain. He thought about whether she'd received the letter he'd sent to her. Maybe that explained her short message. He would send another one as soon as he got back to the farm.

He opened the second letter, but it was written in Caleb's penmanship. His head snapped back in surprise. He read quickly and faster, completely still as he kept reading. His pulse pounded. Worry and fear engulfed him.

He walked quickly to the door, and when his boots hit the concrete he took off to the buggy.

Merv was in the buggy waiting. "What's wrong?"

"I'm going to the bus station. Give me any money you have

on you." Zeb cut off drivers and urged the horse into a fast trot when he had the space.

"What's going on?" Merv stuck a wad of bills in Zeb's coat.

Zeb handed him the second letter, trying not to panic. "Emma is in trouble."

"How do you know?"

"That letter is from Caleb."

"What's it say?"

Zeb swerved through the traffic as horns honked. "He wants me to bring Emma home."

Chapter Twenty-Seven

Emma's hands shook, shaking the coffee she held in her hands. She looked up at the stairs in the church for the tenth time, hoping Monique would come down so they could talk. Emma wanted to find out what happened, but then she didn't. None of it would be positive, and she didn't want Monique to relive it all again. Maybe it wasn't as bad for her, having lived in that neighborhood all of her life.

Emma had never been so scared or been in a place that was so rundown and broken. To think that people actually lived there was difficult to comprehend. She wasn't completely naive to such a life but had never experienced it firsthand. It gave her a new perspective and way of thinking about the downtrodden. The situations in her community couldn't compare to what went on in the city.

"I can't wait any longer." Emma set her coffee on the table and stood. "I'm going up to see her."

Caleb looked at her with bloodshot eyes. Neither of them had gotten much sleep. The coffee wasn't keeping them alert enough to do much else than wait for Monique and guard the doors. Emma wouldn't put it past Abe to boldly walk through those doors and steal Monique back again.

It didn't make sense to Emma. If he wanted her, why did he treat her so badly?

"I'll stay here and keep an eye on things." Caleb grabbed her hand. "Don't be disappointed if you don't get much out of her. It's difficult." His smile didn't reach his heavy eyes.

She pulled away and took her time climbing the many stairs up to her room.

When she opened the door, she saw Monique gazing out the hazy window. She appeared to be somewhat better after taking a shower and getting some fluid down her, but she refused to eat. Emma hoped she would, once her nerves settled.

"You're looking better." Emma glanced over at the empty glass of juice she'd brought her earlier. "Would you like more—"

"Stop babying me. I'm not dying." Monique put a hand over her eyes as if wishing Emma wasn't there. Even her dark skin took on a lighter shade. Her gaunt figure was alarming. Within just a short time with Abe, she'd become withered and hardened. Emma understood to a point but was tired of her rude behavior.

"I'm only trying to help." Emma meant for her tone to be direct, but Monique's reaction took her off guard—she had started to cry softly but didn't seem to have the energy. Her chest moved with effort, and Emma could barely hear the sobbing sounds. She went over and sat at the end of the disheveled bed. The sleeping bag still held an unpleasant odor despite a washing. "I'm sorry."

Monique sat up. "Don't apologize! Gosh dang, you freaking Amish people. Don't you ever fight back?" Her knitted brows and rigid face gave her a ghostly appearance.

"*Nee*, we don't." Emma didn't hesitate to answer, proud to be part of a group of people who didn't settle things with violence.

Monique balked. "Where has that gotten you?"

"Peace," Emma answered without thought. It was plain and simple to her, and she was glad that it was. Being here and seeing this made her more homesick than ever, but Monique needed her now. No matter how obstinate she got, Emma wouldn't leave until she knew Monique was safe. "Why are you angry at me? All I want is to help you."

Monique had been quiet, digesting what Emma said. "I don't want your charity."

Emma frowned. "It's not charity. You're my friend. And friends take care of each other."

Monique turned away. "I haven't exactly done my part."

"There will be a time."

Monique's expression was like none Emma had seen before. She wasn't sure what it meant or what she was thinking, but she thought it was something good. She stood and pulled the sleeping bag off her bed and went to the door. "It's a beautiful day outside. I'm going to make a picnic. Are you coming?" It was throwing caution to the wind but staying in day and night wasn't healthy, either. A few minutes outside would do them all some good.

Monique tilted her head. "Okay." She slid off the bed and pulled her hair into a ponytail.

"I'll take those." Emma grabbed her roommate's sleeping bag and turned to go to the laundry room. Maybe things Emma felt were harsh but that seemed to be exactly what Monique responded to.

When Emma came downstairs, she found Caleb with his eyes closed, holding up his chin with his hand. "Ready for a picnic?"

He jumped, with a glazed-over stare. "Do you think that's a good idea?" He rubbed his face to wake up, and then stood next to her.

"I think it's a great idea." She spun on her heel and made her way to the kitchen. No one was going to change her mind. She was tired of hiding like a mouse and fretting over Abe. If it was time for David to fight Goliath, she needed to be prepared—in a nonresistance sort of way.

Caleb went in and leaned on the doorjamb. "You're determined." He grinned. "Can I help?" He was already opening a cabinet, pulling out a large basket.

They both made sandwiches, and Caleb filled a chest with drinks. As Monique came down the stairs, Caleb looked at Emma. "Remember, this was your idea."

"But you're coming along on your own accord." She corralled a few of the Amish who were bored to tears, ready to go and do anything but stay inside any longer. "Fetch those throwing discs."

"You mean a Frisbee?" Caleb chuckled and sent a couple of the young men to grab some.

Monique followed right behind Emma as they went to the park. Emma could feel her nervous vibes, but Emma was determined not to let Abe or anyone else intimidate them. He preyed on people's fear, but she would not be one of his victims. If she could be that example for Monique, maybe, just maybe, he would finally leave her be.

Emma laid a blanket on the grass and took out the food and drinks. Monique helped but kept an eye out. Emma couldn't imagine living that way and questioned whether there was any hope of Monique's life changing. Emma's thoughts came to a halt.

Of course it can. That's what having a Savior is all about.

Her role wasn't just to be Monique's friend or protector. It was to bring her to the Lord.

"Emma!" Monique's voice penetrated her ears.

"Sorry, what did you say?" Emma looked around the park, watching their small group play a different version of Frisbee golf.

Monique pointed to a woman close by who'd set up a canvas and was painting with chopsticks. "I'd love to do that."

"Paint with chopsticks?"

Monique actually grinned. "With anything. I've always loved to draw and paint."

"Why don't you pursue it?" Emma thought about how much she loved to sing, but it was forbidden except when praising *Gott.*

"With what? How?" She lifted her palms up, frowning.

Emma looked back over at the chopstick lady. Her long, salt-and-pepper hair was braided, and hung down to the middle of her back. She looked to be about her *mamm*'s age, only skinnier. "Ask her."

Monique shook her head as a couple of girls came over and sat with them. They were the only girls who hadn't left and seemed to be holding on pretty well. They enjoyed volunteering, and now that the other girls were gone, they kept busy, unlike the boys, who seemed to want to be entertained. Caleb didn't partake in that, only providing good, hard work helping the community.

When Emma looked at the girls closely, she noticed their lack of conversation and appetite. "Do you girls want something to eat?"

They shook their heads. "*Nee, danke.*"

"What's wrong with you?" Monique asked in her forward way.

"We were talking to some boys about our faith, and they shared theirs. I'd never heard such things." The blonde girl was clearly upset. Her eyes brimmed with unshed tears.

"Why did it bother you?" Emma felt a pang of guilt. Sharing her faith was what *she* had come here to do.

"They have a different religion. I asked them what happens

when you die. They said nothing." The blue-eyed girl's sadness made Emma feel for her. Caleb was right—it was hard for them to talk to others when they only know about their own religion.

The handful of young men came over to eat, catching the end of the conversation. All admitted they were a little homesick.

Caleb sat down, having listened to them talk. "What would you be doing back home?"

"Singing." One of the boys took out his harmonica and began to play. It wasn't like being at a service back home, but it was the next best thing. *Gott* was being lifted up, and that was what was important.

Emma gazed over the park. People were moving their bodies with the beat of the rapping songs that she'd come to know, street dancing, open sin that made her feel dirty inside. They showed no shame in flaunting themselves.

She closed her eyes, feeling her parents close to her, praying for her as they bowed their heads before each meal. Emma missed them. She missed the farm, her sisters, and even Hilda, the ornery chicken.

Emma started cleaning up, speaking Pennsylvania Dutch. The others looked at her with wide eyes. They'd been speaking English for weeks, very little Pennsylvania Dutch. The look on their faces as they rattled off the words was revitalizing.

Maybe that will be enough to keep them steady until they go home again.

Chapter Twenty-Eight

Caleb wanted Emma out of harm's way, and he didn't know whether he could keep her safe anymore. She was stubbornly attached to Monique, and that friendship had become dangerous for her. He would never forgive himself if anything happened to her, and neither would Zeb. He turned his attention to Mark, who had been quietly waiting for Caleb.

Mark's tight lips made Caleb suck in air. "Be strong for Adrian, Mark. Pray through this so you have the courage you need to get him through this." The news of a fire in Adrian's neighborhood had hit them hard. Not so much for Caleb—unfortunately it wasn't uncommon for him—but that Adrian was taken to the hospital was heart-wrenching for Mark.

"Is he hurt bad?" Mark used as few words as possible, keeping himself intact. Caleb had never seen him this vulnerable, which made it even harder to talk to him about it.

"I don't know, Mark. I only found out about him through the grapevine—people know who I know and tell me when something's up. I'm hoping it's not as bad as it sounds." Caleb hesitated about Mark going to the hospital with him. He needed to make a couple phone calls first, anyway, so he had time to figure out what was best.

"I want to see him." Mark lifted his head, keeping himself together as determination began to take over. Caleb didn't know how Emma would feel about Mark going, but could see in his eyes that Mark wouldn't take no for an answer.

"Let me do some networking first." Caleb was rather short

with him, but he had to be. A lot more things could be involved that Mark couldn't even imagine with gangs and vendettas, not to mention there was the possibility of Abe being involved.

Mark stood. "I'm going to see him whether you're with me or not."

"Don't think for a minute that I don't want you to be at the hospital at Adrian's side. But it's different here than the community where you can trust everyone." When Mark rolled his eyes, Caleb stood, facing him, standing within inches of each other. "Mark, don't test me on this."

Mark took a step back and huffed out a breath. "Then I'll go myself," he mumbled.

"No, you won't." Caleb stood his ground verbally and physically. He wasn't much taller than Mark, but he used every advantage he had to let Mark know that this time, he wouldn't get his way.

Mark balled his fists, turned, and walked away.

"What happened?" Emma stood staring at Caleb in disbelief.

"He wanted to take himself to the hospital."

Caleb wasn't in the mood to explain more. There were times when he got tired of naive Amish kids who had to learn everything the hard way. Sometimes he didn't know why he even bothered with the annual ritual of *rumspringa*, but they were his people. Even though the community didn't consider him part of their fold, he treated their sons and daughters as his while they were with him.

"That was wonderful *gut*." Emma still had a shocked look on her face. "I wish it was that easy for me to deal with him."

Caleb shook his head, switching gears to locate the hospital Adrian was at. It was privileged information, and there were over three hundred hospitals in the Philadelphia area, which could be narrowed down easily due to Adrian's indigent status.

Once Caleb found the right one, he asked Emma to find Mark, though Caleb wouldn't be surprised if he'd left, which would be futile—Mark would never find Adrian's hospital.

Caleb got ready to walk out the front door when he saw Mark coming up the steps. "They won't let him see visitors, only immediate family. There's an investigation involving the fire. They think it may be arson," Caleb explained.

Mark shook his head. "Where is he?"

"Philadelphia General Hospital in West Philly. But there is something we can do in the meantime."

"What?" Emma walked up behind Caleb.

"His place is beyond repair, and we can't get on the property due to the investigation. But we can help rebuild a place for Adrian's family to live, one down the street from his that's been abandoned. I'm waiting to hear back from the city to see what they say."

Emma looked at him like he was crazy, and Mark grinned from ear to ear. "There's nothing we Amish do better than build things."

Caleb smiled. "Think of it as a barn-raising."

"Where would we get the material?" Emma seemed to come around. She had a gleam in her eyes that surprised Caleb. It was a bold move, but there was something about the Amish way of helping those in need and building, just about anything, that made Caleb think it might not be so far-fetched after all. He thought sure Emma would worry about the area close to where Monique was, close to where they would be working. Maybe she was getting past that.

Caleb lifted his hand up toward the broken down old church that had become his home. "This place runs on donations. I'll just be asking for a different kind."

She smiled at Caleb. "This would be an incredible gesture to Adrian and the community where he lives."

Caleb nodded. "This is a good project. It will keep the guys busy."

Emma's eyes widened. "And for the girls."

Caleb cocked his head to the side. "Emma, I don't think it's a good idea for you to go. "You'll be safe at the church and needed—"

"I'm not going to live in fear." Emma placed her hands on her hips and raised her brows. "Caleb Lapp, I will be going to this *haus* raising."

And with the look in her eyes, Caleb knew it was futile to try and convince her otherwise.

Emma shut out the noise as they went down the busy street. No one said a word. What had started as a chance meeting with the church group had turned into friendship, Christian fellowship, and that had led Mark to have a strong relationship with Adrian. Once they got the permit, they wasted no time gathering together to help build Adrian's home. She reminded herself of that as they started their way back to that godforsaken neighborhood. Fear rose in her remembering the horrible incident when they found Monique. She'd hoped never to be here again. But with Caleb by her side, she felt safe.

Emma stepped into the subway train and held tight to a steel post. The seats were all taken. Even an older lady clung to one of the poles to keep from falling. Flashes of words were painted on the cement walls that surrounded them. She didn't know some of the words, and others, she chose not to see.

How do people come down in these tunnels and paint walls

with the large, noisy trains going by? And why do they write on walls at all? If they have something to say, they should speak it.

"Hang on, there's a corner up here." Caleb clasped his hand over hers to keep her steady. Emma swayed and grabbed Caleb's arm with her other hand. The sensation of his strong arm made her heart skip. As much as she tried to avoid it, her feelings for him were as much there as they ever were. She'd done well to push the thoughts away, but after being with him during this long period of time, her resistance was beginning to wane.

Emma looked out the window as the train flew through the tunnel. There was so much to see, and different people to observe, although she'd noticed people here didn't like you to look at them. They would frown and look away, giving no opportunity to converse. Most didn't talk, avoiding others as much as possible. There was very little laughter. She felt sad for them.

If they were happy, she sure couldn't tell. Emma expected the different clothing but not to the extent she'd seen here. Skin was exposed to an embarrassing level. There were low-cut necklines and pants that hung down as if they would fall off. She wondered what the women's faces really looked like beneath the color and marks around their eyes and lips.

"South Ninth Street," a monotone voice announced over the intercom. When the doors opened, everyone rushed out to be first, instead of letting others go before them. Caleb lifted a hand so the others who were with them could see that they weren't moving. Once everyone got off the train who were going to, the Amish walked onto the platform. Emma missed the dirt beneath her feet that gave with her steps, unlike the hard concrete here. "How much farther?"

"A couple of blocks. Not far."

Caleb grabbed Emma's hand and held tightly. He looked back frequently to see the group of a dozen Amish who were trailing behind them. They were getting as many looks as they were looking, a mutual curiosity between them and the natives.

Caleb thought it best Monique stay at the church with Alex and the other staff of volunteers who were there. Monique had told Emma she wasn't ready to go anywhere even close to Abe's home, and Adrian's neighborhood was far too close.

Caleb led them to Adrian's burned-out house farther down from the residential area. Black scorch marks randomly covered large areas around the windows and doors. The houses beside his were brick and also had dark marks. There were areas where the fire had taken down walls and floors. Most of the place was covered with black soot.

Rows of houses lined both sides of the streets. Most were in need of repair, others were more cared for. The closeness made it hard for Emma to breathe. There was only cement in front and a small yard in the back with a chain link fence a few feet away from the house. Neighbors were inches away, with no privacy once you set your foot out the door. Steel bars covered the lower windows that looked out at sidewalk level. It was so similar to Abe's place, she felt the same fear climb up her spine.

They approached a beat-up wooden home. "This is it." Caleb looked down at her. "Adrian's family will live here."

She heard him, but she was too busy trying to inhale to respond. The asthma was kicking in again. But why? Without any reason.

Caleb watched with concern until she seemed to catch her breath, then turned to the group and motioned to them by clapping his hands. "All of the materials are in the back yard.

Your job here is to rebuild the shell of this house. It's a good thing you're doing here today."

Caleb stopped and scratched his head. "Adrian's family couldn't afford to have their home repaired. Without your help, they would have few options of where to live while they waited for the outcome of the investigation."

"Who builds the rest of the *haus*?" Mark asked at the same time Emma thought of the question.

"An organization called Habitat for Humanity will help with the rest. So let's get to work and make it the best it can be, for Adrian."

The looks on their faces showed determination mixed with sorrow. Each of the Amish young men collected his tool belt, hammer, or saw, depending on his assignment. The young women set up the sawhorses and kept the men supplied with whatever they needed—more nails, boards moved, or a cold drink when needed.

The weather was a little warm, but not so much that it was uncomfortable. Neighbors came by and watched as they worked. Caleb greeted the passersby to explain what they were doing. Most were interested, and many were surprised. Emma could hear one very loud man as he talked with Caleb.

"You all don't even know how much Adrian's folks will appreciate you fixin' this place for 'em." He shook his head. "That don't happen 'round here. When your house gets vandalized, burned, or just plain falls apart nobody gonna help. You on the street or in a shelter."

"We're glad to help. Adrian is a friend of ours." Emma looked at the man's shocked face and wished it wasn't such an unusual thing to help when people needed it. But a group of Amish doing it would be unusual for sure. Then she thought of Caleb. He used what he'd learned growing up Amish.

Maybe that was why God had put him here—to spread the idea around in a place completely different than what he grew up with.

They worked into the evening, until it started to get dark, without taking more than a few minutes' break. By the time the sun went down, they had the wood-frame walls in place, and once the cleanup was complete, they'd finished what they set out to do. The interior was left up to the next crew.

As they packed up, Caleb heard grumbles of empty stomachs. They'd taken a short break for lunch, but they'd earned a good meal. Emma wasted no time getting out of the area before dark. She'd looked over her shoulder too many times today and was ready to leave.

Emma noticed Caleb lead them down a different street on their way to the subway and stopped at a restaurant that made her stomach growl. Caleb told them he wanted to have a special dinner so they could bond after doing a good deed. They all pitched in, and Caleb made up the rest with the slush fund.

He stopped at an area that was only mildly better than where they were and opened the door of a crowded restaurant.

"Here it is. Geno's! They have the best cheesesteaks in town. My mouth is watering already." Caleb waved the group in and explained to them how to order as they passed him. The men of every color and size who worked there stared at the group, and the Amish returned the stares. Most of them had traded in their Amish clothes, but they still stood out with their hair and the way they talked, and even more so, their manners.

"You ever had a cheesesteak at Geno's?" one of the men asked in all seriousness, as he flipped strips of meat on a large, hot griddle with a spatula. He pointed to Emma, who was standing in front of the group with Caleb at her side.

"*Nee*, I haven't, but we make something similar—a

hamburger sub that looks similar to yours." She liked this man and was enjoying the banter. He and the other cooks around him chuckled but continued their work. More people came in, and they all got down to business. Some were brave and got the works, and it looked good enough for Emma to delve in, as well.

Emma noticed Mark quietly sitting among the other Amish teens. It wasn't like him not to talk or join in the fun. He looked up and met her eyes, and for the first time since they'd been in Philly, she knew he missed being home.

Chapter Twenty-Nine

The bus turned off the highway, and Zeb paid his share of the toll. He was low on money, unprepared for the trip, but nothing could have kept him home even one more minute.

I knew something like this would happen. This is Caleb's fault. I should have never let Emma go, and neither should Caleb.

All he had to say was no, but Caleb's intentions weren't pure. His feelings for her were beyond good reasoning, and now she was in some sort of trouble.

Zeb snapped out of it and tried to pay attention to the surroundings. He didn't have much interest in the city life, but as they started over the Benjamin Franklin Bridge, he had to admit that he was impressed.

He'd never seen so many vehicles. He looked out the window at the Delaware River that was almost as wide as the nine-thousand-foot bridge. He'd picked up a couple brochures and a map at the bus station so he would know how to get to the church where Emma had sent him letters. Having nothing better to do, he read them on the drive.

Once off the bus he found a taxi. He had no bag, no change of clothes, and hadn't eaten since breakfast. All of that just added to his frustration. As soon as he got a hold of Emma, he was turning right back around and going home. He watched people rush down the streets and cars speed past them, everyone in a hurry. He'd expected as much after hearing from others what it was like here.

When they got close to the church, Zeb recognized the building by Emma's drawing she sent in her letter. Actually, the picture looked better. Zeb winced as he glanced over the rundown building. Cracks showed foundation issues, and age had worn down the wide steps. The bushes and flowers around the front helped redirect a person's attention, and he was sure Emma had a hand in planting them.

Zeb paid the driver and took a deep breath then prayed for a peaceful departure from this place. He didn't feel anything was safe here, even the church he was about to enter. He walked in and held up a hand to his brow, adjusting to the low lighting.

The sun shone outside, but it felt like sunset in the building. He should call it a church, he supposed, but it didn't look or feel like one. But then he'd only visited a couple because Amish services were held in people's homes. He understood it was a nonprofit, struggling to make ends meet, but it didn't seem safe or clean, even for the downtrodden who lived on the streets. He knew his feelings all came from wanting Emma to be back home with him and tried to stop himself.

"You here to see Caleb?" A tall, mulatto-skinned man came up beside Zeb. He seemed confident, with his hands on his hips and staring him in the eyes.

"Actually, I'm looking for Emma." He'd deal with Caleb later. Right now he needed to see Emma's face, to touch her, hold her, and make sure she was safe. "I'm Zeb, and you are?" Zeb offered his hand.

"Alex. Caleb told me about you."

Zeb frowned. "*Ach*, what did he say?" He wasn't certain if he really wanted to know, but he wanted all of this behind him.

"He said to come get him as soon as you got here. He's been waiting. Take you awhile to get here?" He widened his stance, relaxing a little, but Zeb couldn't—not until he had Emma by his side.

"*Jah*, by bus. I left as soon as I got Caleb's letter."

"Yeah, there's been a lot happening." Alex tilted his head as if thinking. "But there's been a lot of good things too. It's not all bad here like you Amish think." He grinned pleasantly.

"We just do better in a different lifestyle. I don't mean to be rude, but I am anxious to see Emma."

"Oh yeah, sure." He snapped to it and took long strides like Zeb did. They stayed in sync until they got to the top of the stairs. "You can keep up." His smile relaxed Zeb a little. He seemed to be the man in charge, and Zeb could appreciate that, being in somewhat the same role.

A door opened, and Emma walked toward him. Her eyes widened, and a small sound came from her throat. She wrapped her arms around him and wouldn't let go. When her soft cries began, Alex slapped his shoulder and went back downstairs. Emma didn't move or stop the tears until Zeb tried to pull her away, but she held on ever tighter. She'd never shown this kind of affection toward anyone. Not that he could remember. He hoped it wasn't this one time, when she was desperate, needing someone stable, but for the moment, he'd take what he could and hold on tight.

"I guess you didn't know I was coming," he whispered in her ear.

She slowly pulled away, wiping her nose. He handed her his handkerchief and waited patiently until her shoulders stopped shaking and her hiccups ceased. It was probably a long while, but he didn't notice. It gave him time to look at her without her seeing him staring. Her cheeks were sallow; the color of her skin wasn't sun-touched as it usually was. The more he looked at her, the more he noticed nothing seemed usual. She was wearing English clothes, and her hair was in a strange twist under her *kapp*.

"I'm sorry." She let out a long, harsh breath.

"Don't be. You're upset about something, and I'd like to help any way I can."

"*Nee*, I'm sorry for leaving, for thinking I could take care of everyone. Being gone so long, not telling you more—"

He held up a hand. "That's not why I came."

She looked up at him with bloodshot eyes underscored by dark bags. "Then why did you?"

"Caleb sent for me." He waited to see her response. He didn't know whether Caleb had told her, but this would show Zeb how she felt about him...about both of them. He couldn't compete in this contest over Emma. That was why he let her leave. He wanted her, but if she didn't feel the same, he would be done.

"I'm glad." Her sad smile gave him permission to take care of her, in his mind, anyway. She didn't always accept help, but this time there was no doubt. Whatever had happened here had left her distraught.

Going on *rumspringa* was one thing, but going into a city like Philadelphia was asking for trouble for a group of Amish. He was sure she was feeling that way right now, frustrated and regretful she'd come. But now choices would have to be made. He felt more confident than he ever had about their relationship.

Caleb stopped cold. Seeing Zeb holding Emma burned a fire in his gut. He turned away, dragging his hand over his face. When he turned and looked up to see Emma go limp against Zeb's chest, it was all Caleb could take. He walked away, but the image was ingrained in his mind. She'd never touched him or looked at him the way she just had with Zeb. Had the relationship they had all been in his mind? He felt like a failure. But not just with Emma, it was Adrian too, and Mark, for that matter. There had been too many close calls, unlike any *rumspringa* trips before. He had to take responsibility for it. He wished he had insisted that Emma not come. He'd known there would be more danger if she was here, but he let her come anyway, putting others at risk.

How could I be so selfish?

"Stop it." Alex's voice was right behind him. Caleb went to the kitchen in a daze.

He didn't even try to pretend nothing was wrong, but he didn't want to talk about it, either. He just shook his head and started checking inventory.

"Don't you want a pencil and paper?" Alex handed both to him and crossed his arms over his chest. "You did the right thing, ya know."

"Hope so." Caleb stopped to write down the needed items, hoping it was accurate.

"It's gotten out of hand, never been like this before." Alex didn't move, or stop talking, which is what Caleb wanted, to shut this all out so he could think.

"Yeah, I know. I take full responsibility." Caleb felt sick to his stomach. Seeing Zeb had awakened something down inside—denial that was sitting in the bottom of his belly beginning to churn.

"That's not enough. This thing with Abe ain't going away."

Caleb rubbed the stubble on his chin, ready to explode. "I'm aware of that. She's going home with Zeb."

Alex whistled. "She know that?"

"No, she doesn't." He took three long steps and stood nose

to nose with Alex, fuming that everything Alex was saying was another example of what he'd done wrong. "Any more questions?"

Alex looked down at Caleb, who had been standing on his tiptoes. "Don't ya think you should tell her?"

Caleb threw the pencil and paper onto the counter. "I'm going for a walk." He stormed past Alex and headed for the door.

The picture in his mind of Emma's face when Zeb had held her flashed through his mind. Emma looked like she did when she was on the farm and there was no threat to worry her night and day, no friend at risk of a stalker.

She's at peace in his arms.

Caleb went past the park and the river where they'd watched the boats when she first came. It seemed like such a long time ago. Maybe it was. He was so enamored with her, he couldn't think straight. She had fit into his life too easily. He'd lost sight of the fact that this life didn't fit her at all. She'd made an effort to stay and do what was needed, but she'd done more than she should, and if he had been in the right frame of mind, he would have taken action earlier.

He'd gotten on the subway, and listening to the whir of the train, drained his mind of thoughts. Now aware of his surroundings, he watched an elderly gray-haired lady bounce with the motion of the train, her eyes shut, oblivious of a hungry-looking young man watching her. Caleb wasn't sure why. One thing he did know: you had to watch your back or you come up short of your wallet, purse, or the purchase in your hand. He questioned more than ever why he was there. He'd had doubts from time to time, but they'd quickly passed. Having Emma here and seeing the city through her eyes made him think long and hard about his purpose.

As the train stopped, he glanced at the street sign. He was almost there. It was no coincidence. He was being tested by God or the devil. He'd find out which soon enough. He lived amongst the worst of it, but his faith held strong. He honestly felt that the more evil crossed his path, the firmer he became in the Lord. It was as Emma had said—it's more difficult to share your belief and grow a personal faith when the obstacles are few and far between and when the Bible is studied by the bishop and shared with others, instead of the people studying it themselves.

Caleb got off at the next stop. The unsettling neighborhood shot adrenaline into his veins. This was part of him, to go to these places, talk to these people, and try to make sense of their world. It was hard—more so than he'd ever anticipated. But helping the downtrodden was coursing through Caleb, as much as the blood that pumped through his body.

The clink of an empty can startled him. He looked down at the end of the street. A bonfire glowed as the last specks of the sun hid behind the housing projects.

He wasn't ready for this. It wasn't planned, yet here he was, alone in the slum.

As if he was thinking aloud, the appearance of three dark, alkaline souls slunk in front of him. He couldn't make out their clothes or faces, and they all seemed similar in height and build, as if the three were all the same person.

"You're either brave or stupid to come here." Abe's gravelly voice sounded deeper, slower, and more powerful.

"Probably both." Caleb didn't know for sure why he'd come. There were too many reasons to pick from. Maybe it was to finally take a stand or to do what he should have done a long time ago—have the guts to keep Abe away from Monique. The cruelty she'd suffered plagued Caleb, and Abe terrorizing the streets had to stop as well.

And then there was Adrian. Caleb wanted vengeance in a bad way, but if he was going to be honest, he was there to cleanse himself from guilt.

The men's shadows didn't become any clearer, as if there was a sheer separating them from him, but Abe's voice was distinguishable. The sound of Abe's tone had kept Caleb up at night when Monique was with him, helpless until they'd found her. "Stop hurting my people, Abe."

Abe chuckled, a crackly, dry laugh that made Caleb's skin crawl. "You sound like Moses. Trying and failing."

Caleb could feel Abe smirk. "Ahh, you do remember your Bible. Moses succeeded in the end."

Another rumbling noise made its way up Abe's throat. "But not you—not tonight."

Caleb's heartbeat pounded double-time as they moved toward him. As they did, courage born of peace came over him, and he bowed his head to pray.

Chapter Thirty

The room was spinning. The emotions seeing Zeb brought out in her had caused a reaction Emma didn't expect. All of her grief, fear, and energy were on overload. The minute she'd seen him, all of those pent-up emotions grew stronger, tensing every muscle in her body. She went limp in his arms, defenseless against him touching her.

"Emma, come sit down." Zeb practically carried her to the bed. He scanned the bed and the room, and then pursed his lips. Emma knew that to be a sign of concern. She felt sure he was disgusted with where she'd been living. He didn't know about the good things that had happened. At the moment she couldn't appreciate them, either, but knew in her heart she had changed lives even during the short time she'd been there.

"Are you ill?" He lightly brushed his fingers across her cheek.

As she looked into his blue eyes, she found him studying every inch of her face. Not like her *daed*, *mamm,* or even Caleb. Zeb's controlling and judgmental ways stressed her, and at that moment, it was the last thing she needed.

"Can't believe you're here." Her words came out as a slight whisper, her energy spent.

His eyes sparked with frustration or maybe anger. "I should have come sooner." He stared down at her. "You're so pale."

This time of year with all the planting, she was usually in the sun, helping and preparing the picnic at whosever *haus* they were at that day. "Did my *daed* get his planting done yet?"

He lifted one side of his cheek, not enough to be a smile.

"*Nee*, the heavy rain held us up a bit."

"You'll wish for it once you're finished." She liked the talk of crop and the farm, her *daed* and *mamm*. "How are the girls?"

He sighed. "They're as busy as ever. I think Martha is becoming a tomboy."

She frowned. "*Nee*, why do you say that?"

"She follows Maria around now that she does Mark's work. They work in the field, the barn, and the outbuildings. She even wanted to help with the silo."

She tilted her head to the side and thought about it. "She actually put the corn on the conveyer belt?"

"That's not the point. She's doing Mark's chores so that he can be here wasting time away." A line grew deeper in his forehead as he spoke.

Emma grunted. "I miss them."

"And they miss you. We all do. You should be home, not here in this..." He scanned the room and then looked back at her "...place."

She put her arm over her face, holding back the tears. She didn't know how homesick she was until this moment. It was best that way or she never would have stayed. But Zeb only made her feel guilt-ridden.

Alex knocked on the open door. "Can't find Caleb. Have you seen him?"

Emma sat up straight.

I hope he didn't do something rash. It had to be difficult for him to send that letter to Zeb. He might want me gone for another reason.

"He surely wouldn't go far in this area?" Zeb stared at Emma, but Alex answered.

"Actually, he does, but he left in a hurry." He glanced at his watch. "It is kinda late too."

"If you want to go, we'll hold things down here." Emma honestly didn't know whether she had the strength, but she worried about Caleb. He wasn't usually out this time of night. Emma stood to show Alex she meant it.

"All right." He lifted a hand, making motions for her to move slowly. "As long as Zeb is with you, I'll go take a look around."

"I'd like to help you, Alex, but I think you're right. Emma needs someone with her," Zeb responded before Emma had a chance to speak.

Alex took a long moment to hold his gaze, their unspoken communication stronger than words. The trust wasn't there. Neither of them was comfortable with the other. Emma wished Caleb was there.

She heard people talking in the hall, and soon Mark appeared. "Hey, Zeb."

He pumped his hand but gave him a questioning glance. "Hey?"

"*Hallo.* Is that better?" Mark responded after a slow stare. She knew he was bothered. Something had changed, and they both seemed to notice it right away. The experience here had forced Mark to grow up, and that came forth even more at that moment. He expected respect from others—demanded it—but it wasn't earned, it was forced. It wouldn't matter to him whether they were on *rumspringa* or not.

"Much better. How is it here?" Zeb gestured out with his hands and winced, as if the place hurt him.

"It was good for a while. Then things got tough." He looked away. Emma listened as he spoke of his experiences, hoping he would be ready to leave when she did.

Zeb looked back at Emma. "It seems it's been that way all around."

Mark plopped onto the bed. "It's weird to see you here, Zeb."

"We'd all be much better off if we were home again, on the farm. The ground is ready to plant. Your *daed* needs your help about now." Zeb kept a steady eye on him, challenging him to offer an excuse.

Mark looked down at his able hands, which had been idle too long. When he lifted his head, he stared at Emma. "I'm not ready yet."

Emma's heart sank. He left her no choice but to go and leave him here. Her time was up, and so was his.

"I have one more thing I have to do."

"*Ach*, what might that be?" Zeb seemed curious, and impatiently waited for Mark's reply.

"A friend of mine is in the hospital. I'd like to see him one last time before I go." Mark's facial expression resembled one Emma hadn't seen for a long while, so she paused long enough to see the boy in him again. She missed how he'd been when he was younger, before adolescence had taken over and he decided to grow up right that minute. She would imprint that image in her mind, as a reminder to a better time between them.

"Is this person Amish?" Zeb glanced at Emma.

She shook her head.

He slowly turned to Mark with the authoritative stance she knew well. "Well, then, it's not your responsibility, Mark."

Mark stood, frowning. His eyes shifted to Emma. "I'll be ready before sunup. And when I get back, I'll go home with you." He turned away.

"Spoken like a true Englisher." Zeb shook his head as he watched Mark walk out. "I'm sorry to see that he is still causing you trouble."

Being away from Zeb made her think about what it would be like to be married to him. Before she'd found comfort that he was older than she was, but after being away Emma found him to be rigid and judgmental. After what she'd been through, that was exactly what she *didn't* want.

He stuck his hands on his hips. "So who runs this place if Alex and Caleb aren't here?"

The door creaked open, and Monique came in, but then stopped short when she saw Zeb. "I heard you were here."

"Zeb, this is my roommate, Monique." Her skin looked healthier and her hair well-kept, braided down her back.

"Monique, I didn't know Emma had a roommate." He glanced at Emma. "I'm finding out all sorts of things." He forced a smile, but she didn't.

"Emma didn't tell you about me, huh?" A tinge of bitterness seeped into her words.

"I haven't told him a lot of things." Emma didn't want to get into it at that time. She would need to prepare Zeb before telling him everything that went on here. Some of it bad, most good, but for an Amish man with his life experience she felt sure he'd be upset. When she let herself think about it, she would be too.

Zeb turned to her, all facial expression gone. "What happened here?"

This wasn't how she wanted to tell him. Emma wanted to be far away from here when she told him, back at the farm, sitting on the porch swing creaking, drinking lemonade, knowing it was all over and she was safely back home.

"A lot, Zeb. More than you want to know." Emma looked down at the floor, knowing how she would feel if the tables were turned. She'd have wanted to know, to help, to be there to support him. She hadn't let him do any of that. He had every reason to be upset with her.

Why didn't I ask him for help? Why did it come down to Caleb asking?

She let out a long breath, tired, but knew it was only right to tell him. "Monique, can you get us some coffee?"

Zeb held up a hand. "Get some sleep. You're exhausted. We'll talk about it in the morning on our way home."

She didn't miss the last words, but decided she would deal with that later. "It's time you heard the truth of what the last few weeks have been like." She paused, unsure of how he would respond to her next comment. "I won't be able to sleep until Caleb is back, anyway."

She waited to see if he was offended or jealous, and received confirmation in the way his eyes widened and his nose twitched.

"You haven't been here that long, Emma. Six weeks and five days, but that's longer than you should have."

Had it only been that long? She didn't know. It had all become a blur. "Seems longer."

She led them downstairs and grabbed two mugs full of hot coffee. Her body surged with a reserve of energy. She'd pushed herself to a place where her body floated through the exhaustion—a strange feeling that she couldn't compare to anything other than manual labor on the farm, but this wasn't the same. "Please don't blame anyone for what's happened here. It's no one's fault. If it wasn't for one person, everything would have been manageable."

"But still not good?" he said as a question but meant as an answer.

She nodded and continued. "Monique is in a rough relationship." She waited to see how that bit of information affected him. He sat quietly. "We've all done what we can to help her, but he won't leave her alone." It was so unlike him not to share his opinion or ask a question. He either didn't care or was trying to be polite.

"Can't the police deal with this?"

"They have, but he knows the system and has connections. Besides, the police don't bother with this type of situation here." She stopped and watched his brows pull together. "What is it?"

"You sound like an Englisher in the way you talk about these things."

They were speaking Pennsylvania Dutch without her even thinking about it. It was so natural, she hadn't noticed when the English stopped and Pennsylvania Dutch began.

"I've asked all of the same questions you probably have. What it comes down to is, the English don't take care of their people the way we do."

"*Jah*, I believe that to be true. But we slip up at times too."

She wondered what he meant by that, but he didn't continue, so she did. "It's been a tug of war since I got here, and I don't see an end to it." She wanted a magic answer to appear. She'd thought maybe it would be Zeb, but all the things that had concerned her about him before she left were now twofold.

What would it be like to leave this place?

Leaving Monique would be hard. Emma would have to know she was in good hands. But that was just one of many different things and people she thought about here.

"Who is this man who has you all under his thumb?" Zeb leaned forward, not knowing what he was asking. She hated his name rolling off her tongue, and she wondered whether Zeb would have the same reaction once he heard it.

"Caleb's brother, Absalom." His expression changed from a curious frown to angry red. Everyone in the community knew of Absalom but didn't speak of him. His *mamm* and *daed* considered him dead to them.

"This is no place for any of us." He pursed his lips. "We leave at daylight."

Chapter Thirty-One

Abe took one shot to Caleb's gut.

Caleb bent over, gasping for air.

One of Abe's goons stepped forward, but Abe put out a hand. "He's mine."

Caleb tried to stand upright, but the ache stopped him. He took a couple deep breaths and stood against the pain. He met Abe's eyes, standing firm.

Abe's irritation grew when Caleb didn't respond. "Don't just stand there, make a move!" He punched him in the jaw. Caleb's head snapped to the side. His eyes watered, but he stood his ground.

Abe chuckled with a bitter tone. "What is this? Your vow of no resistance? You're not Amish anymore. You don't have to follow their rules." His ghostly pale-blue eyes pierced Caleb's.

The comment stung as badly as the hit Caleb had just taken. He may not be considered Amish by the bishop's terms or Abe's, but Caleb would always consider himself so.

What Abe didn't understand was it wasn't just the Amish vow he held strong to that kept him from fighting back; it was also Emma. With no hope of being with her, he had no hope at all. The minute Zeb had shown up, it had all come to a head. She would be gone come daylight, and he wouldn't see her again. He couldn't; seeing a home that he didn't build, seeing children that weren't his. Zeb's, of all people.

A sting brought him back to the moment. Abe's blow to his cheek brought out such anger he raised his fist. Abe grinned and stood there waiting. But Caleb would never be like him, no matter what he had to lose.

He dropped his fist and took a step back. Abe reached for him, but Caleb yanked away so hard Abe's smug expression morphed into shock. That was a vision Caleb would keep tucked away in his mind. He heard Abe cussing and hitting one of his thugs.

"This is over, *bruder*." Caleb turned away from Abe's foul response and continued walking until he got to the subway. The whizzing sound and motion of the train made him tired. His body was spent, and his mind was a blur.

How could I have lived such different lives, growing up Amish and then as an adult living in a metropolitan city?

He made the decision to come. Thought he could be his brother's keeper. But it seemed nothing could make him change.

The train came to a halt. The doors opened, and Caleb climbed out. The air was warm—too warm for his liking. The adrenaline still pumped through him. He wiped the sweat off his brow.

He went into the building and took the elevator to the fourth floor and was glad he had something to smile about when he went into the room. Mark's head drooped to the side as he sat in an avocado-colored hospital chair, snoring.

"Hey, Caleb." Adrian held up his fist to do the Jamaican handshake.

"You feeling better?" Caleb knew he shouldn't sit. He'd never get up again, so he fought through the exhaustion.

"A lot better. Going home tomorrow."

The word *home* sang in Caleb's ears. Thanks to his crew at the Stock Pot, Adrian had a place to live with his three siblings and parents, and Caleb would go back to the church.

The room spun a little.

"You don't look so good." Adrian frowned and stared. "What happened to your face?"

"Ran into a door." Caleb grinned. It hurt, and he winced.

"You better sit down." Adrian pointed to another chair beside him.

"I think I will. *Danke*." Caleb didn't know where the Amish word came from, but Adrian got a chuckle out of it.

Caleb's cheek throbbed, and his stomach was empty. Emma was with Zeb, and Abe would be after him sooner or later. For the first time in a long while Caleb felt distant from God, at a time he was in need, when everything was going wrong. He shut his eyes.

If you're pulling away from me, Gott, at least tell me what You want me to do.

Caleb heard a voice in his head. *Sometimes I calm the storm. Sometimes I let the storm rage, and I calm My child.*

That was the last thing he remembered.

Caleb woke to a slap.

"Wake up!" Mark tapped him again as if he were putting on cologne.

Caleb's eyelids stuck together, and his mouth was dry. He rubbed his face with both hands. "What time is it?"

"It's morning. What are you doing here?"

Caleb sat up and leaned over, staring at the grimy, white linoleum floor. "I could ask you the same thing. You're supposed to be leaving this morning."

"And what happened to your face?" His eyebrows furrowed as he inspected Caleb.

Caleb lifted his head. "Your sister know you're here?"

"*Jah*, I do now." Emma walked to Caleb, put both hands on either side of his head, and stared at the shiner on the right side of his face. "Abe?"

Caleb nodded, increasing the headache that already pounded in his head. When he looked up to see Zeb leaning against the doorjamb, the throbbing increased. Caleb wished he could curse at Zeb, tell him to leave, and make Emma stay. None of that was going to happen, but it made him feel a little better to think about it.

Emma came back with a cloth, bent over, and pressed it on his cheek. His eyes bulged when he felt the chill and the pain. When he looked into her eyes, she was staring back at him. He'd gotten used to seeing those big, brown eyes.

"How could you be so careless?" She held the cloth with one hand and covered her face with the other, holding back tears. "I was up all night worried about you." Her whisper rose to a low growl. "I'm sorry. I had a lot of thinking to do, and—"

"*Jah*, well, so do I, but I didn't leave and worry everyone to death." She closed her eyes and took in a breath. "Oh, Caleb." She stood and rushed out of the room, leaving him with only the sound of her shoes clacking behind.

Zeb watched her go, and then stared at Caleb. "What did you say to her?"

Caleb ignored him and stood to find her. When he got to the door, Zeb put out a hand. "I'll go fetch her. You've obviously done enough."

Caleb slapped his hand away and mustered up the energy to catch up to her. "Emma, stop this." When he got close enough, he took her by the hand, led her outside the hospital and to a bench. "Come sit down."

"*Nee*, Caleb, there's nothing to say." Her eyes filled, and she wiped her nose with his handkerchief.

"Yes, there is. I did a lot of thinking after I sent that letter. I know you're set on going back to the farm. I told myself I wouldn't try to change your mind. But are you sure?" He waited to be chastised for asking, but instead her tears fell.

"Being here has been hard. I know it's not always this way. Abe makes it harder than it needs to be." She looked down at her hands, folded in her lap. "You serve a purpose here, Caleb, but if your brother wasn't involved would you still stay?" Caleb started to speak, and she stopped him. "What I'm asking, Caleb, is would you ever come home?"

Just hearing the word almost brought tears to his eyes. She had no idea how much he'd love to grow a family on a farm. No one had the faintest inkling of what he really wanted. He didn't believe it himself, at times. He was so sure this was his calling. If it wasn't for Emma, he might still feel that way, but after the damage that had been done, it was more than he could handle.

"If things were different," Caleb said as Zeb's face flashed in his head, telling him to tread lightly. "But they're not."

She wiped away tears before he saw them fall and nodded. "Then I should go."

"How is your asthma?"

She furrowed her brow. "It's better. You know that."

"Does Zeb? Did he even ask?" Caleb moved his hand forward. She was so close, reachable to touch and hold. But did he have that right? "Was there any other choice for you to marry?"

She held up a hand to stop his words. "I don't know, Caleb. Was there?"

His mind tinged, going back and forth with mixed emotions. "I don't know if you want what I do."

Emma took a second to look him in the eyes, as if she could

see the regret he held. "Why did you send Zeb that letter?" She stood and ran quickly to the door where Zeb was waiting and never looked back.

Chapter Thirty-Two

Honk! A taxi flew by bringing Emma back for a moment, as she waited for Zeb to take them back to the church.

Her heart broke a second time. The first was when Caleb left. Now, feeling she had no choice but to leave him, it shattered again.

You knew better than to come here in the first place. It wasn't about Mark so much as it was about Caleb.

She had lied to herself about her motivations for coming to the city and look what it had done to her. Their time together at the farm before they both left had given her hope about what it would be like, but being in his world did not sit well with her. She understood that it wasn't always this intense, but she couldn't reconcile living this way when she had a peaceful farm to live on. It would just be with Zeb, not Caleb.

That thought made her cry again, which would make Zeb even madder at Caleb.

Zeb walked with her to the subway, which he had made known he detested.

"What did he say to get you so upset?" Mark grudgingly followed behind them and found a seat.

"It doesn't matter," she said firmly, not wanting to talk about it with him.

"I don't know what's going on here, but I'll be glad to get you and Mark safely home." Zeb kept a protective gaze on her until they got to the church. He wasn't street savvy but at least he was trying.

"There's one more thing that I need to talk to you about." She sighed.

"*Ach*, what's that?"

Mark stared out the window, having left his friend who he would probably never see again.

"We are ready to leave," Emma said. As a matter of fact, she was looking forward to it. Or was that just the disappointment of Caleb's answer?

"*Gut*, because I'd be bringing you both home even if you weren't."

"Zeb." She squeezed her eyes shut and said what she needed to. "I want to bring Monique with us."

There it was, out of her mouth and flying into Zeb's mind. She waited, praying for the best.

The train turned, and Zeb lost his balance. He grabbed one of the steel poles to hang on. "You mean that girl who caused all these problems?"

"*Jah*, Monique." She didn't try to explain where the blame truly went. Emma just wanted to make sure Monique went with her.

He was either shaking his head or it was bouncing along with the movement of the train. "I don't know—"

"Zeb, it's the only thing I ask of you. Please, I can't leave without her." She was begging and shouldn't have to, but right now what mattered was that all four of them went home.

"*Ach*, Emma." His face tightened and his mouth opened and shut quickly.

He had to know her conviction to making sure everyone was safely home with her. "All I care about right now is getting you and Mark back to the farm." He paused. "Soon enough, we will have our own *haus*."

She didn't know whether he meant the situation wasn't

permanent or his words were just a reminder of their commitment to each other. Emma had questioned her life with Zeb, but there was not another option anymore.

When they got to the church, Alex motioned for Emma to come to him. He went around the kitchen door to meet her. "Abe is on the prowl."

Biting fear pumped through her arms, and they started to tingle. "Where's Monique?"

"In your room, scared as a mouse." He looked over to Mark.

"She needs to be someplace safe," Emma thought out loud. It was ironic that Monique couldn't stay protected in a church, but then for some, like Abe, it was a perfect way for them to show their disdain of their former religion. Violence and fear were the complete opposite of what this building represented. It was at that moment she found the solution. "Mark, get your things."

Mark frowned and stuck his hands in his pockets, something he'd grown to like while he was there. "Right now?"

"I gather we're ready to leave?" Zeb seemed more than happy to go. It wasn't that easy for Emma. As much as things here rubbed her the wrong way, she'd learned a lot and made some life decisions along the way.

"*Jah*, all of us." She looked at him long enough for him to understand her meaning. Now it was a matter of convincing Monique. With Abe on the hunt, she just might agree.

"So when Abe's name is mentioned, everyone runs and hides?" Zeb shook his head.

Alex squinted and answered with a warning tone. "We look after our own here, Zeb. That's what we do."

"I wish I had that kind of power," Zeb scoffed.

Emma didn't have time for this conversation, but she wished she did. Zeb's arrogant ways left her angry and frustrated. He was talking about things he didn't understand, and she wondered if he ever would. It took a certain kind of heart to bleed for the less fortunate.

Emma went to her room to talk to Monique, hoping she wasn't in a stubborn frame of mind. She seemed to get mad rather than sad when danger came her way—defenses up, ready to fight back.

She caught Monique at the door.

Monique pushed up her lip and let out a breath. "Is he here?"

"Not yet. It's only a matter of time when you stay here." Maybe this time Monique would finally make a change, leave this place, and start over. "Mark and I are leaving with Zeb."

Monique wrapped her arms around her stomach. "When?"

"As soon as you're ready."

"What?" Monique moved back. "For what?"

"To come with us."

Instead of seeing her defenses go up, Monique seemed curious. Her eyes widened, and she turned her head to the side, thinking. "I can't leave here."

"What do you have to stay for?"

She shrugged. "What would I do on a farm?"

"What we all do. Live as a community together. It's quiet and safe." She paused, waiting. "Just for a while."

"I don't know..." Monique frowned, and Emma thought she might be losing her, so she backed off a little.

"Stay the night or two, and if you don't feel comfortable, we'll bring you back. You couldn't be anyplace safer. Abe would never come back home." Emma prayed for discernment, made herself be patient, and waited.

"Isn't that what the prodigal son said?" Monique said in all seriousness.

Emma was caught off guard just long enough to stop rushing and think on Monique's words. "*Jah*, I suppose he did."

Monique looked at Emma and then up to the dirty window to see the bustle of the city, and then turned back to Emma. "Only if I can come back. I'm not gonna convert, just so you know that right now."

Emma pushed up onto her tiptoes and hugged her. "*Danke*, Monique. I feel better already."

Monique shied away, and her eyebrows lifted. "Are you doing this for you or me?"

"Me," Emma said, half-seriously.

Monique's smile was an unexpected ray of sunshine in this dreary place. Talk was sparse as they gathered their belongings and then went downstairs.

"I'm gonna miss you around here." Alex engulfed Emma into a hug, dwarfing her with his height. "Take care of Monique."

"You know we will," reminding him that it takes a village where she comes from.

He grinned and pursed his lips. "Are you sure you want to go?"

"It's time. Thank you for having us, Alex." She couldn't say more without emotions bursting forth, so she left Mark to say his good-byes.

Emma sat on her bag, looking at faces while she waited. The footsteps and voices slowly stopped as most everyone left the building. She didn't expect to see Caleb, which was good, because he never came.

Chapter Thirty-Three

Caleb moved toward the window but remained hidden. Outside Emma, Mark, and Zeb loaded a car that belonged to a local Mennonite. Their conversation was subdued, and Emma's expression was somber. His heart beat faster when she turned toward the window. He didn't know if she could see him, but he quickly moved away.

What a coward.

He bent over and stared at the worn linoleum. It was tattered and used up, just like he felt.

Alex walked in and leaned against the counter. Caleb kept his head down, looking at Alex's sneakers, but then stood and stared at his friend. He was as much of the Stock Pot as Caleb, maybe more so. He'd been there before Caleb, as a resident, but had shone through and ended up being one who helped instead of needing help. Caleb admired his friend, enough to see him standing in Caleb's place.

Alex frowned when Caleb turned his head. "You get in a brawl?" His forehead creased. "With Abe?"

Caleb nodded but didn't want to talk about it, again.

"Why didn't you come and give Emma her good-byes?" Alex's wrinkled brow and stern air let Caleb know he was irritated.

"You had it handled. Thanks, Alex." He pushed off the counter, done with the conversation and hoping Alex was too. "I'll get the soup pot out and start cutting the potatoes."

The large, beat-up, steel pot had seen better days, but they would use it until it fell apart. The last time he'd had anything different than soup was when they went to Geno's for a Philly cheesesteak sandwich. Then he started thinking of the food his *mamm* made, and Caleb's mouth watered. He poured in the chicken broth and some noodles, stirring methodically.

"Hey!" Alex's voice brought him back. "I handled it because you didn't. They're your people, Caleb." He took a step closer. "And Emma deserved better."

"She's with Zeb. She's fine," he said with uncalled-for and uncharacteristic sarcasm. "Sorry, Alex. You're right. I should have seen her off, but I couldn't, not with him standing there."

"That's another thing. Why is he in this at all?"

"What do you mean? They're in a relationship, probably to get married come harvest." Caleb almost choked on the words. He could think them, but hearing them made him sick.

"You two are the ones in a relationship." Alex leaned back and half-smiled.

Caleb scoffed. "I doubt that."

"The way she looks at you. Your long conversations. Sinking into the Word like it's your own private Bible study. Sitting around with a cup of coffee, cup after cup, until you were both too exhausted to talk anymore?" He shook his head. "No, my friend. It's you and Emma who are the ones. Not Zeb."

Caleb looked at the ceiling and remembered each of those moments with her. He fought to keep his emotions intact, but it was harder now, knowing she was gone. "I didn't think you'd noticed." He grinned to make light of his struggling composure.

"To tell you the truth, I was jealous."

Caleb drew his brows together. "Why?"

"You don't see that every day, Caleb. I've never experienced that kind of a connection. I didn't even know it existed until

I watched you two." He glanced over at him. "I wasn't eavesdropping. Couldn't help but notice, though."

"Well, since you seem to know more about Emma and me than I do, why don't you tell me how I move on."

"You don't. You get what's yours before it's too late." Alex was so matter of fact that Caleb started to believe what he said.

"She's made her choice, Alex. And I have a responsibility here."

Alex leaned back and stuck out his jaw. "You took your hits from Abe, which I don't agree with—you following the street rules. But at least now you're no longer his keeper. You're free from him."

Caleb shook his head. "I did that for Monique."

"That was secondary." He slapped Caleb on the shoulder. "It's time for you to find your place."

Caleb's resolve waned. This place was all he'd known for years, with his mission to bring his brother back, away from this sin he lived in. But maybe Alex was right. "And that would mean to be with Emma."

"Right." He stretched out the word.

"On the farm, with the Amish, which would be awkward, especially with Deacon Reuben on my tail." Caleb compared Abe with Reuben and decided he had nothing to worry about.

"So you're thinking about it—going home?"

Alex wasn't going to quit, and for once, Caleb was glad. He hadn't ever thought the Stock Pot would be the place he would stay forever, but now, really considering it made him a little sentimental.

"Yeah. I'll start making some plans."

Caleb took the soup out to serve the guests. One of the homeless guys Caleb knew well came over for a helping. "How ya doing, Albert?" Caleb sank the ladle into the pot of steaming soup. The older man nodded his thanks. He hadn't talked since he witnessed a violent crime against his daughter. When Caleb looked around the room, he realized he knew most everyone's names.

"Don't start…make 'em." Alex pulled him back to the conversation.

Caleb thought of the perfect answer. "That goes for you, too." A slow smile stretched his face.

"What do you mean?" Alex opened a bag of corn bread muffins and poured them in a basket. Then he froze. "What goes for me?"

"If I leave, someone has to take my place." To his surprise, Alex didn't respond the way he expected.

He lifted his chin slightly and met Caleb's eyes. "I can't do what you do." He glanced around as if to measure the responsibilities involved. "I wouldn't know where to begin."

"You do what I do every day. I just wouldn't be here to tell you." Caleb understood Alex's hesitation, but what he'd said was true. Alex knew what to do, he just didn't believe it. "Name one thing I do that you don't know how to."

Alex took a long while before he answered. "I don't know the lock to the safe."

Caleb frowned. "You got me on that one, but that's only because you don't trust yourself." When Alex was a minor, he had been caught stealing from a corner grocery store where he worked after school. The stealing had continued into adulthood and hadn't stopped until he spent some time in jail. But that was what Caleb loved about this place—second chances.

"This time, you can't say no when I try to give you the combination." Caleb was seeing God in these decisions they were making, and he felt good about what was happening. But he wouldn't be honest if he didn't admit a part of him didn't want to let go.

Emma will make it easier, right?

He sure hoped so. He could be wrong.

And then what?

"So is this the changing of the guards?" Caleb asked.

"You were saying no fifteen minutes ago. Now you're ready to saddle me up while you're running out the door?" Alex responded.

"No, I'm just not sure I'll follow through if I don't do it soon." Caleb wagged his head. "It's too easy to stay and hard to say yes to go back."

"You doing it all for Emma?" Alex lifted one brow. "Is that enough? What if it doesn't work out with her? Will you stay?"

"That I don't know. Without her in the picture I would find it hard to deal with a few of the rules they have. I always had a problem with some of them—still do." He didn't want to think about it. He'd deal with it, come what may.

"Can't say it's all good and rational here, either."

Alex's words made him think. It was what you made it to be. He hadn't been baptized, so there shouldn't be a problem, but then you throw in someone like Reuben, and things start tumbling down. It would be difficult enough to show up and just start living the life. He had a lot or thinking and praying to do. The Stock Pot was just the beginning of changes he was ready to make in his life, whether it was here in the city or there in the country.

Chapter Thirty-Four

"We're out in the middle of nowhere." Monique adjusted herself in the backseat of the buggy in between Emma and Mark. "Is this as fast as this thing goes?" She looked up at Merv and Zeb, who didn't appreciate her comments.

Merv was at the bus station to pick them up. He was the first of many who would stare, ask questions, and whisper when they saw Monique. Emma decided to ignore most and tell only a select few her story. The deacons would also want to know, but she would share Monique's story only with one she trusted most.

"I'll have you know this horse could beat most any in our community," Merv said with pride, but Monique just rolled her eyes.

At one time that would have bothered Emma, but she'd learned some things just won't change, especially with Monique. This was going to be quite an adventure with Monique around. That made Emma smile.

"There's nothing to look at." Monique searched the pastures, planted for the fall crop.

"That's the beauty of it." Emma smiled and breathed in the fresh air. "No concrete, cars, or polluted air. It's wonderful-*gut*."

"Ahh, and that crazy way you all talk." Monique's voice carried, even when she had a normal conversation. This level was more than Merv could take. Emma had known it was just a matter of time.

Merv pulled back on the reins and brought the horse to a

stop. Then he turned around to face Monique. "Are you about done complaining?"

Monique's brows went up, a sign Emma had learned meant she was ready to have a war with words. "And what if I'm not?"

"You can get out and walk—that's what." Merv's eyes squinted as if studying her, and then he turned to get the horse moving. Emma wasn't exactly certain what the encounter was about, but she would be sure to keep an eye on the two of them.

"I'd like to see you make me," Monique said under her breath.

Emma chuckled to herself that Monique had been so quiet about her remark. She had been praying this place would make her a gentler person.

They drove through the serene countryside and then a pleasant stroll along streets to downtown Lititz. Before she knew it, they were passing through town. She appreciated the shops, restaurants, and museums that complemented the old heritage and architecture. The small town was a breath of fresh air. Home. It would be even better when they rode out of town and the sprawling farms started popping up. She began to relax and unwind like never before. No filthy bed, bad food, noise...and most of all, they were safe. That had become an important word to her.

When they got to Emma's farm, Mark got out first and ran up to the *haus*. *Mamm* and Martha came out with Maria behind them. "Come on, I'll introduce you." Emma encouraged Monique. She knew it would be awkward. They were already staring.

"*Mamm*, girls, this is Monique."

The girls didn't stare for long, as they'd been told that it's rude. But this time it was a bit harder for them. Emma squeezed Maria in her arms and reveled in her laughter.

"She's pretty," Martha whispered in Emma's ear.

Monique stood upright, showing her height, and there was no hiding her attractive face. Her mocha-colored skin stood out, so beautiful, along with her almond-shaped eyes. One couldn't help but admire her. Before anyone even said it, Emma decided she would try her best to make Monique plain, though it wouldn't be easy.

She looked at her *mamm*. "*Hallo*."

Mamm looked up at Monique from her five foot height. "Well, aren't you a sight to see."

Emma cringed and mouthed *sorry* to Monique, but she didn't seem to mind. Her *mamm* meant it in a positive way, and Monique seemed to understand that. The real test would be her *daed*.

"Monique and I shared a room together."

Her *mamm* nodded once as if to say she approved and then started wringing her hands. That meant she wasn't feeling busy enough. "Well, you must be hungry."

"We can make something, *Mamm*," Maria, who had been unusually quiet, offered.

"Are Merv and Zeb going to eat with us?" Monique's interest made Emma wonder. If she didn't know better, Emma thought she did want them to, or should she say, she wanted Merv to.

"*Ach*, no. They have all those milk cows to tend to." Emma was actually glad they were leaving. Her family needed time to adjust to Monique. So did she, for that matter.

"We can all chip in. Idle hands are the devil's playground, and all." *Mamm* marched to the *haus* as she spoke.

Zeb went toward the barn to greet *Daed*, and Merv took their bags up to the *haus*. *Daed* stopped when he saw Monique, but then picked up his feet again and started over to meet her. "And who might you be?"

"Monique. I stayed with Emma while she was in Philly." Monique didn't have the same relaxed demeanor around *Daed*, and Emma thought she understood why. Her relationships with men seemed to be negative. Even the stories she'd told about her own family were heartbreaking.

"Philly?" *Mamm* questioned but no one answered, she'd be used to the term soon enough. They were more interested in what *Daed*'s response would be. He slowly walked over and gave Emma a hug, which was rare for him.

"Glad you're back in your own *haus*." Then he turned to Monique. No one moved or spoke. They waited and watched as *Daed* took her in. "You Emma's friend?"

Monique shrugged at Emma and then nodded but didn't talk.

"You in some sort of trouble?" He hadn't taken his eyes off her. Monique looked down, which cut the tension. Emma wished he'd leave her be, but she knew better than to ask.

"Run into some hard times." Monique glanced at Emma.

He grumbled something under his breath. "Hungry?" He closed one eye to block the sun.

Monique didn't respond right away, probably unsure of *Daed*'s curt conversation. She would have to get used to that. "Yeah, I guess."

He dropped his arm down to his side. "Well, are ya or aren't ya?"

His rough tone didn't reflect his genuine hospitality, and Emma marveled at it. She took Martha's hand and started to walk to the *haus*. When they reached the porch, Emma turned back to see Monique standing alone, looking over the place. When Monique reached her, she didn't complain as Emma had thought she would. "This is actually kinda cool."

Emma admired the view with her. Patches of a variety of

colors jumped from one field to another, like those on a quilt. The sun shone brightly, and a cool breeze kept them refreshed. She hadn't let herself miss this place, but now, Emma felt the emotions gurgle up through her throat. She was home, and it was almost perfect.

Mamm went by and they followed her into the *haus*. "Why don't I get you two some lunch." *Mamm* smiled at Monique as she put on her cooking apron. "Does anyone have a hankering for something?"

"I'll eat anything." Monique sat down at the table, and the girls followed suit. They seemed enamored by her to the point that Emma could see a battle for attention coming to a head.

"I'd love some cooked oats." Emma had been craving the dish since she left.

"Coming right up." *Mamm* started gathering the ingredients, and Emma stepped in to help. She noticed Monique watching while she talked to the girls. It was customary to help in the kitchen, and that was one of many things Monique would have to learn. Emma combined the cooked oats, brown sugar, cinnamon, eggs, butter, and milk with some spices, and then started to mix them together.

Martha brought over some berries and lifted them up for Emma to take. "These make it the besteth." Her excitement made Emma smile.

"*Danke*, they are the best."

Martha's strawberry-blonde hair had more waves or maybe it was just longer. She looked at least an inch taller when she walked by Emma, and she carried herself a little more like a young lady even though she still enjoyed rolling in the mud with the pigs.

How could I have missed so much in that short amount of time?

When they sat down to eat, Monique kept a close eye on everyone. She didn't copy what they did, just studied everyone as if deciding what she might do, once she got more comfortable. The prayer was silent, which she seemed relieved about, but she wasn't intimidated, either. *Daed* was quietly analyzing the dynamics with a newcomer in their home, but he kept his eye on Emma, as well.

For whatever reason Martha loved Monique. She followed her around the kitchen and led her outside after they'd finished washing the dishes.

"You use a pump for water?" Monique gave her a quizzical glance as she pumped the handle.

"*Jah*." She tilted her head in thought. "Where does yours come from?"

"The faucet." Monique didn't seem to understand that Martha didn't know what she meant, but neither of them seemed to mind. Soon Martha ran off to play, leaving Emma and Monique sitting by the pump. Maria came out and brought each of them a slice of banana bread, and they sat in the green grass together in silence. Emma knew it wouldn't last but drank in every moment.

"So, tell me everything." Maria broke the silence. She'd waited longer than Emma thought she would. Her curiosity had to have been building with each minute since they arrived home. Maria rolled over onto her side and chewed on a blade of grass as they filled her in on what they'd been through and she quietly listened. Emma left some out, but for the most part, Maria had a good idea of the hardships and special time Emma had while she was away.

Maria rolled over on her back and rested her hands on her chest. "I'd never want to go there. I'm glad you're home."

"Hey, that's my beat," Monique reminded her, but not with words Maria completely understood.

"Well it's no place for an Amish person to be," Maria said boldly.

"I agree with that. But I don't know what I would have done without Emma." Monique paused for a moment. "It was almost like Abe knew he had to fight harder with you and Caleb there."

Maria's face brightened. "I wouldn't be able to leave Caleb if I were you, Emma."

Monique grinned. "I don't think she has."

Emma felt a rush of sadness and anger mixed together. It was as if just the sound of his name created a sensation she couldn't discern. She jumped up and made her way to the barn, the place that gave her privacy and intimacy with *Gott*. Emma hoped she would also find peace without Caleb in her life.

Chapter Thirty-Five

Zeb hit his forehead against the side of one of the Holsteins, and the heifer mooed at him with irritation. He slapped her hide. She kicked the air, and he spat when she smacked him with her manure-coated tail. As Zeb stood then walked outside to the water trough, the heels of his boots hit the ground hard. He cupped his hands and wiped off the dung from his cheek and neck.

It shouldn't be this way. He'd waited for two months, and now that he'd finally gotten Emma home, he still didn't get much time with her. Not alone, anyway. With Monique staying with the Miller family, it was more difficult than ever.

He walked out of the corral, leaving the machines going. Just over the next farm was the Millers' place. He couldn't see it clearly with the trees in full bloom, but he knew exactly where the large, red barn sat. Mark was probably milking their cows, and Emma would be teaching Monique some chore. It took Emma twice as long to get things done now. Had he known, he wouldn't have agreed to bring Monique. She had lived in that godforsaken place long enough to make her own way.

Merv went over and stuck his nose in the air. He came closer. "Is that you that smells?"

"Heifer gave me a smack of her tail." Zeb rubbed his neck again, but the smell wouldn't go away until he took a bar of soap to it.

"So, are you and Emma still together?" Merv set down the

two milk containers he'd cleaned, seeming oblivious to how the question angered Zeb.

"Why would you ask that? Of course we are." He dragged his hand against his homespun pants, knowing he'd have to get them washed now that he'd spread the smell on to them.

"You're never together. It's like she didn't come home." Merv didn't realize how big his mouth was. He'd never been able to figure out when to open it and when to keep it shut. "And after all that time with Caleb…" He looked up at Zeb. "You just never know."

Zeb let out a breath so he wouldn't smack him. "Monique takes up her time now. She won't be around forever." He shouldn't have said the last sentence out loud. Merv would end up letting it fly the next time he was around Emma or Monique, and that would be even worse.

Monique had a way of looking at him like she wanted to whip up on him. Her need to protect Emma was not only irritating but unnecessary. The dangers here weren't like Philadelphia. He thought back in disgust, angry that he'd ever let Emma go there.

At least Caleb is out of the picture. That's what matters most.

Zeb was sure Emma and Caleb would get together again while she was gone, but to his pleasant surprise, they hadn't. He hoped Emma chose him because she cared more for him, but even if she didn't, he'd get what he wanted. The sooner he married Emma, the sooner he could have a working produce farm as well as the dairy.

"Zeb!" Merv yelled at him louder than necessary.

"Lower your voice. I'm standing right here."

"You wouldn't answer." He shook his head. "I don't know what's going on with you, but you're acting strange." He turned to get another canister.

Zeb almost stopped him to find out what he meant, but then decided he didn't care. His mission today would be to find Emma and talk with her in private. He'd ask her to make time for him and make plans for Monique to leave. He would help get her home again, to show his good side—that should smooth things over—and their lives together could finally begin. Courting was in full force with summer half over—wasted time that he couldn't get back.

A ruckus from the barn got his attention. He'd left the cows too long. "Merv!"

He was out of earshot.

Zeb's boot skidded as he bore down to make the corner of the barn. Merv rushed through the side doors. A kick by a cow to Merv's gut bent him over and left him gasping for air.

Zeb reached for the heifer's lead rope and yanked her close to calm her down. If one did, they would all fall into place.

Merv went down the stalls to calm them, but moved too quickly, and got a quick hit in the side as he walked by. A cow can see what's beside her, but not what's directly behind.

"Darn cow."

"You know better." As Zeb grinned, he realized he hadn't had reason to smile for too long. Merv helped him clean the cows, led them out to pasture, and cleaned up the barn. "I'm going over to Emma's. Don't count on me for the noon meal."

"*Gut*. I'll hold things down here." Merv began the tedious work of washing the equipment. With as many Holstein as they now had, it would take a good part of the afternoon.

Oh his way to Emma's, Zeb thought of a number of different ways he could draw Monique away. He'd have to think of something that would warrant her full attention. He pondered a few scenarios, but nothing came that would work to the extent he needed. Then he stopped cold. What better way to take away her biggest distraction than to bring Abe into the picture? Even the threat of him being remotely close would send her packing.

A smile spread across his lips as he hatched his plan. An anonymous letter giving Abe information as to where Monique could be found would be simple enough, but he didn't know Abe's location, only the church where they'd stayed.

I'll just have to make it work somehow. Sending the letter to Alex and asking him to give the letter to Abe would be absurd—unless there was some sort of information that he would need to know.

Deep in his thoughts, he'd reached Emma's farm in no time. When he considered his plan he shamed himself, until he looked up to see Monique walk out on to the porch. Then he started scheming again.

"What are you doing here?" She crossed her arms over her chest. He didn't know how she meant it, but he'd give her the benefit of the doubt. He didn't want to tangle with her.

"Came to see Emma." He stretched out his hand. "And you." The lie would only go so far. They had a mutual animosity toward each other. Zeb's was because she seemed to see right through him, and he hated her need for Emma to babysit her. Monique's seemed to be that he just existed. It didn't matter much. They agreed to disagree, tolerating each other for Emma's sake.

"She's busy." She ignored his hand and kept her arms crossed.

"So am I. So if you could find her for me, I'd appreciate it."

Martha came to the screen door and stared. "*Hallo*, there." Since she was willing to acknowledge him, Zeb took advantage of the opportunity and asked her to get Emma.

She turned her head back toward the mudroom and shouted, "Emma, Zeb's here!"

He could see Monique's face flush with irritation.

"*Danke*, Martha." He held out his hand to her. She came out and accepted his handshake, tucking her small hand into his.

"We don't have the time that you do," Monique said. "This family has to work for what they have, unlike you with that fancy cow farm." She waved her hand in the direction from which he came, clueless as to what she was talking about, in his opinion.

"Sounds like someone's put a bug in your ear." He tried to smile but was sure it looked as fake as it felt.

"I hear things," Monique said.

He speculated as to who it would be, but then decided he didn't care. If his plan worked, she'd be gone soon enough. "We run a dairy farm." He came across condescending, but he felt too strongly to hide it. He did wonder where she'd heard the line. She hadn't been here long enough to know he had a flourishing dairy farm. "Everyone here owns livestock of one kind or another, and some are more lucrative than others. We've been blessed."

She took her steps quickly and walked over to him. "You're blessed to have *Emma*." She stuck a finger in his face and continued her attack.

He saw Martha jump and seized the moment. "Martha, are you afraid?"

Monique grunted and bent down. "Let's go inside and eat one of those sugar cookies Emma and your mamma were making."

Zeb squeezed Martha's hand a bit too hard.

"Ouch!"

He instinctively let go, and she went running into the house. Without Martha there, Monique could continue her banter, so Zeb moved to the side and went toward the door. "It's always good to see you, Monique," he said in a loud voice. The timing was perfect—Emma came to the door.

"Zeb, I was just thinking I should make a call over your way." She led him to the kitchen and offered him a cookie. He took it, making sure their hands touched as he did.

"*Danke*. Why didn't you? I haven't seen enough of you." He was tense, waiting for Monique to come in and say something he didn't want to hear.

"Monique's been learning her way around. It's nice to have company while I work." Emma and Monique shared a smile as she came in and sat right next to Zeb.

Emma's eyebrows pinched together as she watched them interact. She was too observant not to notice the tension between them, so Zeb would make sure he brought out Monique's bad side, which wasn't difficult.

"Why don't you show me some of these chores you've learned, Monique?" He stood to show her he meant it.

She frowned and glanced at Emma. "You coming?"

"Go on ahead. I'll be out after this last batch of cookies is done." Emma watched them go, her brows still knitted.

The minute they were out the door, Monique started in. "What you stirring up?"

"What do you have against me?" As soon as they were in the barn, he stopped.

She put her hands on her hips and gave him a sideways stare. "You want Emma for all the wrong reasons. Not like Caleb, who wants her for all the right reasons."

Zeb's chest burned when he heard the name. "Caleb's not here. If he cared about Emma, he would be."

Monique frowned. "He does care about her. They just want two different things."

"They had time to reckon with that, and they did. It's over, Monique." When he noticed her brows wrinkle and then release, he knew she'd considered what he said to be truth. He widened his stance and analyzed her. Emma was all she had now, and he was the only obstacle in the way. "We've been courting for some time now. Come fall, we'll be married."

Monique met his eyes and squinted. "That's not what Emma wants."

"You'll be gone by then. This is none of your concern." With that he went by her and started tidying up the barn. Everything was pretty much in its place, but he wanted the diversion to give Monique time to think. He wasn't done with her—she had a tough spirit—but he would break her down. His plans depended on it.

She started to walk out of the barn and then stopped short. "If you don't think I know what you're doing, think again." She turned to leave right as he called her name.

"Monique. It's interesting you think you know more than anyone else does, and you just got here."

"I know people. I been around all kinds. And I know what people are. Emma, Caleb, Abe. And I know you." Her dark eyes shone flecks of gold, mesmerizing him.

"Don't be so mysterious. If you have something to say, say it."

"I don't know what you're after. But it ain't Emma you really want."

Zeb chuckled with unease. "Of course it is. What else would there be?"

"I don't know. But I'm gonna find out." She waited a beat and then turned away with the appearance of rejection, but she'd had the last word and gotten him worked up while she remained cool and calm.

Zeb threw the tool he held, letting it hit the back of the workbench. If he didn't know better, he'd think for sure she knew his plans for the land they stood on.

Chapter Thirty-Six

"It's too early." Monique rolled over and pulled the quilt tighter over her shoulder. She had no interest in chores, and now that the curiosity was gone, she was stubbornly difficult to get out the door. Emma worried that she was unhappy, that she wanted to go back to Philly. As much as Emma would hate to see her go, keeping her there against her will for Emma's sake wasn't right.

"I'll be down in a minute." Monique's eyes still hadn't opened.

Emma looked over at Martha's empty bed, a sign of how late they were getting started. She pulled off the quilt and stood with her hands on her hips. "Up and at 'em."

Monique lifted herself up onto her elbows and frowned. "Does that really mean something?" She rubbed her face, turned and put her feet on the wood floor. "What are you gonna make me do today?" Emma started to speak, but Monique held up her hands in protest. "No, don't tell me. I might not get up."

She dragged herself to the closet where her dress and shoes were. It had taken a while to get her into a dress, but they'd compromised, and let her trade off days when she could wear her city clothes.

"You haven't been here long enough to be tired of the chores," Emma teased, but knew she spoke the truth.

They'd done the bare minimum of what was usually a much more vigorous day of work, and it would only grow more difficult as time went on. Emma wondered how long she would stay. She wanted her to for as long as Monique felt comfortable, but she didn't know whether Monique would ever feel this was her home.

"Stop thinking," Monique ordered as she let the dress fall down over her arms and to her knees. It was difficult to find one long enough for her. Emma planned to get some material in town to add on to the bottom.

"Why... what do you mean?"

"That brain of yours is in overdrive." She went over to the dresser and took a brush to her long, dark locks. Emma had never been envious of someone's hair before—everyone wore theirs up in a bun—but Monique wore hers in a long ponytail. The dark strands shimmered in the morning sun that was just beginning to peek up over the fields.

Emma sat at the end of her bed, picking at a piece of thread. "Are you happy here, Monique?"

She shrugged. "Better than being on the run from Abe."

Emma's worry lightened a bit. Maybe she *would* consider staying for a while, maybe longer.

Monique's hair flipped down across her chest. "But it's not where I belong."

Emma's heart sank just a little. She was realistic enough to know this was about as opposite as it could be for Monique. But she still, in her selfish way, wanted her friend to like it here enough not to leave any time soon. Monique's tension and rude behavior were slowly melting away, making her a much better person to spend time with. Before, it was an obligation Emma felt *Gott* was calling her to. Now, they seemed to be more like friends, able to enjoy each other's company instead of the constant worry they'd had before.

Emma's thoughts went to Caleb, as they did every day. Many moments were taken up with the time she had with him, although she knew she would be with Zeb, and she had to come to terms with that and let Caleb go.

They made their way to the kitchen in thoughtful silence.

"Morning." *Mamm* gave them a tight smile, cautioning their tardiness.

"Sorry we're behind. What can we do to help?" Emma scanned the kitchen and beelined to the potatoes Maria was cutting up. "I'll do this."

"*Gut*. I'll check in on Martha." Maria wiped her hands on a towel and turned to Monique. "Morning."

Maria had become Martha's sole babysitter since Emma had been spending so much time teaching Monique the daily routine. She didn't seem to mind, but then Maria wasn't one to complain.

After a fine breakfast of eggs, fried potatoes, bacon, toast, milk, and fresh-squeezed orange juice, they were finally out of the kitchen and on to the first chore of the day.

They went to check on the garden first. The rains had come down steadily throughout the night, so they would have to wait for the soil to dry before they could work in it.

"What will you plant?" Monique reached down to feel the moist dirt.

"Cabbage and broccoli for now and maybe some peas in a few weeks. *Daed* loves cabbage. I think he'd eat it every day if we let him."

"So get some at the store," Monique scoffed, and then looked at Emma's confused expression. "Guess you probably don't buy stuff you can grow."

"*Nee*, that would be silly." Emma tucked some wisps of hair under her *kapp* and headed for the barn. A wringer washer and baskets of clothes sat waiting for them. She knew

Monique didn't like to use the washer, so she started gathering the clothes, submerging them into the sudsy water.

Once they got into the rhythm, Emma ran the clothes through the wringer and placed them in the basket for Monique to hang on the line. By the time they'd finished, it was time to start lunch.

"That's a lot of clothes." Monique shook her head like she did every time after they finished. "There are too many people in this family." She chuckled.

"What's your family like?" Emma hadn't heard her talk about them, but didn't want to pry. If Monique didn't want to tell her something, Emma had learned, she wouldn't tell her.

She didn't respond right away, so Emma dismissed the question. They were almost to the *haus* when she finally answered. "You know how Abe is?"

"*Jah*."

"It's like that."

Monique hadn't lifted her head during the long walk from the barn to the *haus*. Emma's question must have taken Monique to a place she didn't want to revisit, and Emma was sorry she'd said anything. That might explain why she kept going back to Abe. If she'd grown up with such upheaval, it may appear to be more acceptable. It made Emma sad to think Monique felt she couldn't leave that kind of environment.

They had a light lunch of ham sandwiches with some of the leftovers from breakfast. Then they made rhubarb custard pie for dessert after dinner. While they swept and mopped the floors, *Daed* and Mark trimmed the yard and shrubs around the *haus*. Then they started training Stormy, a two-year-old miniature pony.

"Can I try, *Daed*?" Martha tugged on *Daed*'s shirt. He lifted her up as gently as if she were made of glass. Emma watched

Monique. Her large eyes followed their every movement as he placed her over the little horse but didn't set her down on the animal's back. Martha didn't seem to mind, giggling as if she were on a carnival ride.

Daed glanced over, smiling, and then kept a steady eye on Monique. She was never one to hide her feelings. Her expression alone told a story of its own, not to mention the body language, and all of that was before she opened her mouth.

"Are you all right, Monique?" Emma couldn't keep from asking. Maybe it wasn't her concern, but she knew what it was like now, being away from home or from people who loved you. After her visit to Philly, she felt even more fortunate to have such a family.

"Being here makes me think of home. You're lucky, Emma." Monique shrugged, as if wasn't an issue. But Emma could tell by the look in her eyes that she was hurting, missing her own home, maybe one she couldn't return to.

"Where's your *mamm* and *daed*?" Emma guided her away from her family and sat on a swinging bench under a large cottonwood tree.

"Not far from where Abe lives." She glanced over to see Emma's face, but Emma had seen enough not to be too surprised.

"It would be hard to stay away from him with him so close." It seemed like an obvious thing to say. But Monique shook her head.

"My dad lived farther away, but he drank too much, and he was a mean drunk." She crossed her arms over her stomach and squeezed so hard, Emma thought she'd squeal with pain.

"I'm sorry, Monique." She put a hand on hers, and Monique jumped. "I didn't mean to bring things up that hurt you. I just want to help."

She scoffed. "How? You have a perfect world." She spread out one hand, leaving the other on her stomach. "You don't know what it's like."

Emma kicked herself, but then thought back to her time in the city and discovered she did know. She'd learned a lot while she was gone, enough to know to some extent how things were for her. "*Jah*, in a way."

Monique turned to her and studied her face, staring at her long enough to make Emma uncomfortable. "Yeah, I guess you did."

Daed and Mark started cutting the grass, bringing Emma's mind back to the laundry they needed to get off the line. "I'm glad you're here."

She stood, not expecting a reply, and none was given.

"Emma." *Daed* waved her over and started walking to the barn. She followed and found him leaning against his workbench. "We need to talk about what your plans are now that you're home."

"The same as they were before, I guess."

He slapped the top of the workbench. "There's no guessing. You have two men who you might end up with from what I can tell. Do you know what you're getting into?"

This conversation was awkward. *Daed*s didn't usually have this discussion, but he obviously had a reason.

"Zeb is the only one."

He scoffed and rolled his head. "Caleb. It was always Caleb until he pulled that stunt moving to the city."

"So why consider him in this conversation, *Daed*?" She almost resented his pulling Caleb into this. She was at an age when she needed to settle down, not continue to wait for someone who wasn't there for her.

"Because I won't give you my blessing to marry Zeb." He

kept his eyes on her, waiting for her to digest the shocking words he'd just said.

"But Zeb came to you and asked your permission...you agreed." She stumbled over her thoughts, not knowing what to say to fix this. Would she be an old hen who never married or had children of her own?

"When he talked to me about his plans, I had some doubts. Since then I've found out some things he's done that the deacons are looking into. I have my own suspicions about his reason for marrying into our family. I don't trust him, Emma. And neither should you." He'd made his decision, without giving her a say, but she had to know why without making him mad.

"A lot happened while I was gone." As soon as she said it, she started thinking about her own concerns about Zeb and where her heart was. But Emma didn't see that she had a choice like her *daed* did.

He let out a long breath. "He's not an honest man. I'm leery of him. And I won't be giving anyone any of my land unless I know they have my daughter's best interest in mind. I'll be telling him as much the next time I see him. And that's the end of it." He walked out without another word.

So that's it? No other explanation? What am I supposed to say to Zeb? He's on his way.

She went to the *haus* in a daze.

"Who's that?" Monique pointed to a buggy coming down the dirt road to their *haus*. "You always have somebody coming over. I can't keep track."

Emma groaned, not wanting to sort this out with relatives around. "It's some of my aunts and uncles."

Emma started to walk over, but Monique hadn't moved. Emma turned around. "You coming?"

Monique shook her head.

Emma didn't blame her. They were strangers to her, and she wasn't very hospitable to start with, let alone to people she didn't know. Emma only looked back once to see her slowly swaying in the swing. Emma sat on the porch with the extended family and had a nice chat. Then her *mamm* and two aunts went to the kitchen to start dinner.

The men stayed outside making chicken on the grill. Emma heard *Daed* introducing Monique to her uncles and knew it was uncomfortable. She eventually wandered in while the women finished with the side dishes—potato salad, corn, cheese, and rhubarb pie for dessert. Emma set out the utensils. Monique was placing the napkins when she suddenly stopped, her body stiff and eyes peeled out the screen door.

"What is it?" Emma looked around the room and then followed to where her eyes were set and heard Zeb's voice. "It's just Zeb." For the first time Emma understood her stiff disposition as she mechanically moved to the side of the long oak table. Her stare was so hypnotizing, Emma took her by the arm and moved her away. When he came in, Monique's face changed from tense to angry—the same expression as when Abe was near.

"*Hallo*, Emma." Zeb slowly turned toward Monique, eyes set directly in hers, as if looking for something. "And...Monique."

Monique didn't respond, just stared until he looked back at Emma. Then Monique walked out of the room and kept going until she got to the cottonwood tree, leaning against it with her back to the house.

Emma wiped off her hands with a towel, looking from Zeb to Monique, with a new understanding of what was happening between them—something she needed to know so she could put the pieces together. She knew they could both have sharp tongues and had obviously tangled over something, and now she had a good idea why. "We need to talk," she told Zeb, but kept her eyes on Monique.

Zeb's boots hit the wooden porch, crunching bits of dirt that rang in her ears. "Maybe she doesn't like company."

"I don't think that's what's bothering her." She moved her head over his way. This wasn't the time to make a scene, but she had a lot to say when they were alone. "She was doing fine until you came."

"I simply said *hallo*." He put his arm around her and urged her forward to join the group who were gathering in the kitchen to eat. She moved away, letting his arm drop beside him.

"Do you want to fetch her or should I?" Emma asked.

He paused as if sensing something was wrong. When he didn't answer, Emma started to leave, but felt him pull on her hand.

"I'll go get her." He tried to tap her under the chin, but she stepped back. His confident smile disappeared as he descended the wooden stairs, taking great strides to reach Monique. Monique leaned forward, almost into his face, before turning to walk to the *haus*.

Emma was beginning to realize that a lot had happened while she was gone. It was all *Gott*'s plan. Zeb's character may not have been exposed had she stayed. Judging from Monique's behavior and her *daed*'s words, it seemed Zeb had taken advantage of her time away to make plans that would benefit him by using her.

As Monique stomped by Emma, Zeb shook his head and made his way back to the *haus*. "She'll be fine, Emma."

Back in the house Emma watched her *mamm* introduce Monique to the rest of the family and take a seat next to her.

"I finally understand why you two can't get along," Emma said.

Zeb crossed his arms over his chest. "Have you thought about her being homesick?" He sat down against the arm of a chair. "Her home isn't something we'd miss, but it would be to her." He peered into the room as they handed around the food. "She isn't happy here."

He took Emma's hand. "I'll take her back when she's ready to go." He pulled her into his chest as if expecting her to need to be comforted. But Emma now knew what was going on.

When Emma pulled away from Zeb, she saw Monique grinning and talking to one of her uncles. Emma moved closer and stood in the doorway with Zeb close behind her. She wished he wasn't there, that he'd disappear. But she'd hold her tongue until their guests left. She prayed for strength.

Monique looked up with a smile. "Emma, good news."

"*Ach.*" She took a seat across from her, and Zeb pulled out a chair to sit next to her. "What's that?"

Monique smiled so wide, Emma's curiosity piqued. "Caleb is back."

Chapter Thirty-Seven

A quiet buzz stirred as Emma and Monique walked into the room. The Hostetlers were hosting church this Sunday, and even though most knew about Monique, there was talk. She was hard to overlook, especially for those who weren't informed. But Emma's mind was somewhere else.

She hadn't slept, wondering if Caleb was really there. She didn't want to believe it. It would be too disappointing if it was just talk, and she didn't have the courage to ask anyone. There was enough going around about her time in Philly, as it wasn't a normal trip. Only Zeb, his family, and her own family knew about their quick departure, but no one really knew why. Emma was glad the deacons hadn't asked anything out of the ordinary—at least not yet.

Emma watched Monique observe the bench wagon pull up and the men clear the kitchen where the women would sit and set up the great room for the men. They brought in benches, lining them up close together, as they were a large community. Not long ago they had separated into two groups, meeting opposite Sundays so they could share the benches.

Monique watched the trail of people walk into the room that had transformed into something with a completely new purpose. "When they gonna stop coming?"

"There are over a hundred of us, but most are already here." Emma had tried to get Monique to go to the last service, but she'd declined, saying she was uncomfortable. This time Emma didn't ask. She'd just told her to get ready and given her a simple idea of what to expect. It was a lot different than the Stock Pot, where a short sermon was given before the meal and no songs were sung.

"How long does this last?" Monique's usual tough exterior was slowly melting away with her pride. Services were a sincere and consuming time to spend with the Lord and to fellowship with others. Emma thought Monique might be starting to understand what that looked like after being there for a while.

"Three hours, maybe more." Emma left Monique to digest the information and gathered the girls together, placing Martha by Maria, *Mamm,* and herself. Then Monique sat at the end.

The boys came in from the barn, and the women who were gathered in the *haus* came in to find a seat. The bishop, deacons, and preachers sat down next to one another, deciding which two would be preaching while the congregation sang from the *Ausbund*.

Emma kept tabs on Monique, watching her smile at a tiny girl's starched church bonnet that was too big and slid down her forehead. The girl stared right back at Monique. A number of the children did. *Mamms* redirected their children's attention and reminded them of their manners.

Emma knew Monique was overwhelmed with questions, but it could wait. A lot of what they did at service eventually explained itself.

The first pastor gave a message, "Judge not, that ye be not judged," creating an emotional response. Tears and soft cries could be heard throughout the room. After being away, Emma was more appreciative of the way these untrained clergymen could preach the Word with such knowledge and passion. She wished Monique could understand what they were saying.

Monique laughed once when old Roy started snoring, and Emma couldn't help but smile and suppress laughter. Monique grinned watching a zealous young man nod his head throughout the sermon.

The martyr's tunes drew out Emma's love for song and made her feel closer to her Savior. Her people's shared faith brought up the hope she'd missed while being away. Monique listened quietly, unable to understand their Pennsylvania dialect, when a second pastor gave a sermon.

Once it was over, Monique started in with questions. "Why are there so many pastors? And where are the instruments? That was just weird, not havin' some music."

A little one ran in between them. "Well, it's about time one of these kids moved. How do those mamas keep 'em quiet all that time?"

Her mouth dropped when she noticed the lunch spread the women were gathering together on a long table. The men took the benches outside along with some tables.

"I never seen so much food. But that's not saying much." She shrugged. Emma understood. Monique had to fight for whatever she had growing up—even food. *Especially* food.

The bits and pieces of information she'd told Emma was all she'd managed to get. Monique would share sparingly, rarely answering any questions Emma asked her. It was probably too painful to go to certain places in her mind.

As they filled their plates, Emma scanned the room for the umpteenth time, but no Caleb, only Zeb, who was walking her way. The deacons were having a difficult time proving his unethical plans. But Emma had made up her mind.

He tipped his hat. "Emma, Monique, I've been looking for you." His smile stretched into a straight line. He was obviously irritated, and Emma knew why. Monique had told her everything.

Monique grunted and went over to where Emma's family sat together. She'd had her fill of controlling men, and she felt that way about Zeb. Monique had said as much in so many words. But the men were head of the household in Emma's world, even if they didn't deserve to be.

Zeb watched her go. "What are Monique's plans?" His eyes darted over to Emma.

"That's up to her." Emma wasn't sure what Zeb's motive was, but she thought she'd said enough for the moment.

He put on a smile. "How are you? I see you almost as little as when you were gone."

I have no obligation to him. What is being said about him? I don't know what is true. Until I do I can't be around him. I still haven't got Caleb out of my head.

She'd had moments when she thought she would stay to make a life in the city so she could be with him, but she couldn't leave her home, friends, and family. Caleb couldn't fill in all of those gaps. It would be a miserable thing to expect of him.

"Emma?" Zeb was talking to her.

"*Jah*?" She looked away, wishing he would leave. Emma meant that in more ways than he knew, even though Zeb didn't know what she was thinking.

He took her by the arms. "I'm sorry if I upset you."

Tears filled her eyes. This secret she kept bottled inside was tearing her apart. Her love for one man verses the convenience of another would make her a hypocrite.

A touch to her shoulder made Emma startle and turn to see the bishop's wife standing behind her. "Emma, I didn't mean to alarm you." When she smiled, numerous wrinkles rippled across her forehead.

Emma couldn't guess why she'd come over to talk to her. She never gave her much attention. So it must be about Caleb, or now that she gave it some thought, maybe it was Monique. Then again, it could be her and Zeb. She froze, thinking of all the possibilities, and suddenly felt sick. Everything seemed very complicated all at once.

"*Nee*, I'm fine."

At that moment a mockingbird chirped a raspy note. She'd never liked that type of bird because of its annoying mimicking of other birds. The harsh *chewk* came again, and she tried to ignore the unpleasant sound.

"You don't look so *gut*." Zeb was being overly chivalrous, as expected.

It irritated her, and Emma worried she might throw up.

He looked over to the bishop's wife. "Please fetch her *mamm*."

"I don't feel *gut,* either." She put a hand to her cheek.

Zeb led her to a nearby bench. "I'll get you a drink." She closed her eyes and tried to distract herself so she wouldn't lose her breakfast.

Someone gave her a glass of water, and she took long gulps. Emma didn't know whether it was the water or embarrassment that gave her the strength to stand up. Another call from the mockingbird rang in her ears as she slowly took a step, and then another to show that she could walk. To be honest, she did feel a tad better physically, but her emotions were all over the place.

Maria came over with *Mamm* close behind, furrowed brows etched across their faces. *Mamm* crouched down and rubbed her forehead. "When you have the strength, I'm taking you home."

Emma stared into her eyes. A rush of emotion filled her upon hearing what she needed most, right at that moment—to go home. It was more of a refuge than she'd realized before she'd left it for a season. There Emma didn't have to cover up how she felt or what she wanted to say. Emma could hide and be alone or be with her large family so she wasn't lonely. *There is one way I can find out where I should be and with whom. I'm tired of waiting. I'll find him and confront him. It's the only way I'll know for sure what my destiny is.*

She nodded, still looking at her *mamm*, finding strength through her. Her quiet, solitary personality was comforting, and she had the faith and determination Emma admired.

"I'm ready."

The next thing she knew, her *daed* was next to her. His crooked smile and slow stride reminded her she wasn't in a hurry. It was a bright Sunday afternoon, surrounded with family, and she felt *gut* all around. Then she stopped short. "Monique, can you tell the bishop's wife to come by the *haus* for me?"

She specifically wanted Monique to ask so they could have a chance to meet. Emma was also too curious to wait and see what the bishop's wife wanted to talk about. If it was about Monique, this would be a good time for her to make an impression.

The mockingbird jeered at her again. Emma turned around to find the persistent nuisance, most likely a male.

"You never did like those birds," a voice said behind her.

Emma's head started to swim again, as if she'd moved too fast. Spots danced across her eyes.

Caleb moved toward her.

All went black.

Chapter Thirty-Eight

Emma's eyelids fluttered as she opened them, coming out of a sleepy fog. Caleb sat in a chair by the bed, looming over her as she blinked to focus. Her eyes cleared, and she looked around the room, then stopped, her gaze pinned on him.

He peered down at her with concern. "Hey, you okay?"

"Caleb?" It took her a minute to orient herself staring and blinking at him.

"Hello, sleeping beauty. You've been asleep for a couple hours." It was nice to see her big brown eyes. He smiled and brushed his hand across her forehead. "Do you know what happened?"

She raised a hand and placed it on his arm as if to see if he was real. The sensation it created made him pause.

"The last thing I remember was the mockingbird mocking me." She shook her head as if disgusted at the bird.

Her bright smile warmed him inside. He didn't move or talk. All he wanted was to take her in, bit by bit. Her big, chocolate eyes twinkled at him, and his arm warmed under her touch.

"I can't believe you're here," she said in a breathy voice.

He kept his eyes on her. "Neither can I." Caleb sat back in his chair. "Pretty good timing, wouldn't you say?"

He treasured the way she was looking at him right now, so vulnerable, with obvious gladness that he was there. He'd always had doubts about how she felt about him. But if he could judge just on what he was seeing and feeling right at this moment, he knew for sure that she cared for him.

"When did you get here?" She rolled to her side and tucked her hands together under her cheek. She hadn't taken her eyes off him.

"Yesterday."

He took in everything about her. It was as if he'd been away from her for a very long time. Three weeks, a day, a year... any of it was too much time away.

"What are you doing here?"

He paused and tried to read her face again to make sure he saw what he thought he did. "Came to see you."

Emma smiled. "Are you always this kind to damsels in distress?"

He thought of a lot of answers—things he wanted to say but couldn't yet. His one and only reason for being here was her. But until he knew how she felt, he wouldn't put any kind of a burden on her. He'd had his chance with her once, so she could easily turn him away. Caleb had needed to go out into the world, do what he felt his calling was, but his time with Emma had made him realize he didn't want to be alone anymore. Being around people all day wasn't the same as having that one special person.

"What in the world are you thinking about?" She grinned. "The question wasn't that hard to answer."

Their banter kept things light, which he appreciated. But he had a lot to talk to her about, before it was too late. "You... us."

"Caleb." Zeb's voice made him wince. When he opened his eyes, Emma was staring right at him. Her face held no expression, but he was sure she had an opinion about his response to Zeb.

"Zeb, I didn't hear you come in." Caleb had no intention

of hiding his reason for being there. He knew the plans Zeb had for Emma, but he would do whatever he could to sway her toward him, recognizing that the ultimate decision was Emma's and hers alone.

"I didn't want to interrupt." Zeb bent over and touched Emma on the forehead, but Emma looked at Caleb, not Zeb, after he'd made the obvious gesture. He glanced at Caleb. "What brings you back?"

"Emma."

That's all he said or wanted to say. That was all Zeb needed to know, so he waited for Zeb's reaction. The man's face reddened just a little, but it was enough to show he didn't like Caleb's answer. Caleb was tired of being polite to Zeb, tired of a lot of things in his life.

"Is there something I should know?" Zeb's beady eyes bored into his and then flickered over at Emma. He let out a breath and sat back farther in his chair. His retreat reminded Caleb not to look like the bad guy. He was here to fight for what he wanted. Emma was no pawn to be fought over, but he did want to say his piece.

If she doesn't accept, I don't know what I'll do. Settle in on my family's farm? Go back to the Stock Pot or get a real job?

None sounded desirable, but he needed to prepare himself if things didn't go his way.

He wanted Zeb to know what his purpose was here, but not until Emma knew. "I don't know yet. But as soon as I do, we'll let you know."

Zeb's head jerked back when he heard "we."

"So you're asking me to leave?" Zeb's overreaction got Emma's attention, which was exactly what he was trying to do.

The irritation it brought almost made Caleb want to fight

dirty, but he wouldn't stoop to that level. He wanted the truth and what was best for Emma.

Zeb kept his hand on his chest for effect, annoying Caleb, who was analyzing everything. Maybe that was okay. It might save him time in knowing what move to take. Or it could make him crazy in trying to decide where he stood in this three-ring circus.

"Could you give Emma and me a few more minutes?"

Emma sat up. Her curiosity must be piquing. Her face grew serious. She dropped her feet to the floor and placed her hands in her lap. "We'll be just a minute, Zeb."

Zeb didn't move.

"It's all right, Zeb." When Emma turned back to Caleb, Zeb scowled at him, as if warning him, but Caleb wasn't intimidated. Emma was the only person he cared about right at that moment.

As soon as Zeb walked out, Emma started in. "How is Adrian?"

The question took him off guard, but he found that he wanted to answer. "He's much better. He'll have some permanent scars and he had some lung damage, but he and his family are doing well. The police wanted to do an investigation, but Adrian said no."

Emma frowned. "Why? Maybe they could finally catch Abe in the act."

"I thought the same thing, but Adrian said that he'd learned from his Amish friend about the vow of no resistance, and he wanted to follow that."

Emma's eyes watered. "Mark?"

"Yeah, because of Mark. Adrian said if Mark was there, he would forgive them."

The tears spilled over, sprinkling down her dress, but Emma didn't try to hold them back.

Caleb couldn't stop talking. He heard himself going on about a matter completely different than he meant to talk to her about, but he didn't quit.

"He actually listened to Mark when he told him not to do drugs, that it was hurting his body, and he wanted his friend to live a long time. Adrian asked how he could be held accountable after Mark left, and he asked Adrian to think of it like what if Jesus walked in the room."

"He didn't say anything to me about this." Emma wiped her cheeks and nose. "Thank you for telling me."

Caleb nodded and handed her his handkerchief. "Mark did a lot more than we knew."

"And he was the one we worried about." She shook her head. "No wonder he wanted to stay. I wish I'd known."

"You couldn't have. Mark didn't communicate with you. That's not your fault."

She gave him a meek smile. "You're so good with those teenagers. I can see why you've stayed there as long as you have, and the *rumspringers* respect you."

He looked away, not wanting the accolades or any regret about his decision. "I won't be going back."

Emma put a hand to her chest. "What do you mean?"

When he looked up, she moved closer to the end of the bed, sitting up straight, and her forehead tight. He struggled with what to say and blurted out the first thing he thought of. "I'm staying at my folks' farm."

She shook her head. "What do you mean? For a visit?"

He lowered his head to meet her eyes. "I want to make things work here."

She stood, walked slowly to him, and then knelt on the floor. "You're coming home?"

He nodded, keeping the emotions at bay.

Her face lit up, and she closed her eyes for a brief second.

"Only if you're a part of it, Emma."

A knock at the door made her startle. Zeb opened the door to see her down on her knees at Caleb's side. He pursed his lips tightly and crossed his arms over his chest. "Caleb, we need to talk."

Caleb was just plain irritated now. He couldn't get a minute long enough to do what he'd set out to do. He stood, brushing Zeb's shoulder as he passed by him, and stopped at the door. "Emma, come see me when you're up to it."

The last thing he heard as he walked down the stairs was Zeb calling his name.

Chapter Thirty-Nine

Caleb decided to take a stroll after he finished helping with the morning chores. The fields were starting to turn green with crop, and the light-yellow tobacco made for a nice balance of color.

It was turning into a nice afternoon that made for some much-needed solitary time to think. He probably hadn't handled the situation with Zeb as well as he should have, but he was tired of walking circles around him. Zeb had Emma on such a tight leash he couldn't get near her, let alone have a conversation with her for more than a minute. But then she wasn't making much of an effort either.

He hadn't made it to the end of the dirt lane leading from their house when Mark came riding up. "Mornin', Caleb."

"What are you up to?" Caleb put his hand against the buggy's side and then he noticed it wasn't his *daed*'s. "Is this yours?"

"*Jah*, you like it?" Mark was busting with pride, but tried to hide it like a good Amish young man.

"Clean it up, and it'll be like new." Caleb grinned as he examined the scratches on the black paint.

Mark scratched behind his ear. "How about now?"

Caleb chuckled. "You got plans?"

"*Jah*. If I don't get to Rylie before Andy does, I'm sunk." Mark gestured to the other seat, and Caleb jogged around the front of the horse and climbed in. "Do you think I'm *narrish*?"

Caleb shrugged. "Not any crazier than any guy your age. Rylie's a sweet girl."

"*Jah*, I'm sorta late, trying to court with fall harvest around the corner." Mark looked at him intensely. He seemed to have grown up a lot over the last couple of months.

Caleb was glad Mark was taking this seriously. "There's always next spring. You don't have to rush things." Caleb chuckled at his own advice. He'd done nothing but wait, and look where it had gotten him. He envied Mark, going after the girl he was smitten with. If he'd done the same with Emma, maybe he'd be better off than he was now.

"Something wrong?" Mark glanced over at him and pulled the buggy around to the barn.

"Nah, I'm happy for you. Maybe a little jealous." He winked at him and walked over to the water pump. He'd had to get used to all of the inconveniences of his childhood, one of which was not having faucets.

"Then why don't you do something about it?" Mark jumped out of the buggy, waiting for an answer, but Caleb didn't have one. That was why he was there—to find his place, a permanent place he could call home.

"I'm trying. It's more complicated than I thought."

But only because of the way Zeb suffocates Emma. With him out of the picture, I could read her better to find out where we stand with each other.

They gathered some rags and soap to clean the old buggy up inside and out. They reminisced about their time in Philly and talked about the future. Mark's seemed a little brighter than Caleb felt about his.

Mark wiped down the roof for the third time as if he were in a trance.

"You're gonna rub the paint off," Caleb teased.

Mark finally stopped and leaned against the buggy. "I guess I'm sort of nervous."

"Well, that's perfectly normal. If you weren't, I'd be worried about you." Caleb's hands were worn out from rubbing down the buggy, so he leaned back against it and took a rest.

Mark took a drink from the pump and went back over to Caleb. "I'd like to see Adrian again some time."

Caleb smiled inside and out. "I'd like a reason to go back, crazy as it sounds, I just got home." But old habits die hard. If he decided to stay, it would be a tough adjustment. "I'm sure we could make that work."

"What do you think happened to Abe?"

Caleb didn't answer, didn't know whether he wanted to, but there wasn't much to say, and Mark deserved to know what little he knew. "Probably nothing legally. He's chosen the road he wants to take—one that will probably get him killed sooner or later."

"Why did he do that to you, when he…?" Mark tried to finish the sentence, but seemed unable to.

"Smacked me around?" Caleb took in a long breath, not wanting to share what he was about to say but knowing it was the only way for Mark to understand.

"When Zeb showed up, I knew Emma was going to leave. I didn't handle it well, couldn't stand the thought of her gone. I had falsely hoped she might stay. I didn't want Monique to be there without Emma. Things were too out of hand."

"I thought she might stay too." Mark was keeping a sharp eye on him as he talked, as if he were in Caleb's shoes, understanding how he felt.

"It's not always as intense as when you were there, but it still wasn't the place for her." He shook his head. "If we wanted to take Monique away, Abe would want a sacrificial lamb, so to speak."

Mark's breath increased, and his brow tightened. "That's

not right—you taking the hits for Monique. Did she know about this?" Mark was heating up, hearing about the violent ways of the street.

"I went for her, but it was between him and me, also. There was no better person Abe would want to take down than his *righteous* brother. In his eyes, anyway." The Bible's account of Absalom and his brothers resonated what their lives signified. Caleb's being true to the biblical description staying faithful to God, and Absalom's self-serving, manipulative ways, resolved with violence.

Mark's fists turned white with anger. "You shouldn't have done it, Caleb. Violence only leads to more violence."

Caleb paused. Hearing Mark speak that Amish way of thinking told him Mark was right where he belonged. Caleb envied that solid comfort.

Then Mark's hands loosened, and he tilted his head. "You did it so he'd leave the rest of us alone and Monique would be free from him."

"Pretty much."

Mark didn't need to know the history of who they were or why. The differences between the two brothers breached decades. Mark had latched on to the part that would make sense to him, and that was enough.

He smacked him on the arm. "You've come a long way, Mark."

"I'm glad I went to Philly. It made me realize how much I don't want to be there and how much I want to be here." He shook his head. "I admire you for doing what you did there, but I don't know how you lived that way for so long."

Caleb had to wonder the same thing. Living in the city, he'd had to become one of them to a certain extent—the opposite of what was ingrained in them growing up Amish. He'd tried to get Abe to go back to that way of thinking, but his brother had kept going the other direction.

"I prayed for God's timing, and the verse that kept coming into my mind was this: '*Do not suppose that I have come to bring peace to the earth. I did not come to bring peace, but a sword. For I have come to turn a man against his father, a daughter against her mother, a daughter-in-law against her mother-in-law—a man's enemies will be the members of his own household.*' So I hung on, but when Emma left, the verse changed."

Mark hung on to his every word, leaning against his buggy with his arms folded across his chest. "To what?"

"In Genesis, when God talks of 'not being alone.' I was around people every day, but something changed." The void left by Emma being gone had impacted him more than he'd ever thought it could. "It was as if God wasn't waiting around for me to do what He wanted me to do this time. So I packed up everything and bought a one-way bus ticket to Lititz."

Mark kicked the dirt beneath his boot. "You got big plans for Emma?"

Caleb thought for a moment and then turned back to Mark. "I don't think I need to do anything."

Mark frowned. "How's that gonna work?"

Caleb figured Zeb was anxious, in a hurry to speed things up with him there. So he could create a wedge between them or he could let Zeb do that all by himself. "Patience is a virtue."

Mark pushed off the buggy. "Another Bible verse?"

"A proverb, they all seem to work well for me." Caleb grinned while Mark nodded and then looked over his head. He turned around to see a buggy coming down the road. "Is that who I think it is?"

Mark took one look and scrambled to his buggy. "*Jah*, and

this is when I leave." He climbed into his shiny buggy. "I'll be praying for ya." He clucked at the horse and waved at Emma as she passed him.

Caleb's stomach tightened as he watched her step down from the buggy. He tried to read her face but couldn't. "To what do I owe the pleasure?"

She turned around abruptly to face him. "You told me to come by when I felt well enough." She put one fist on her hip. "So, here I am."

Caleb moved back, not used to Emma being so feisty. What had he done between the time he left her until now? "Why are you upset?"

She tightened her lips together and looked away. "*Jah*, I am, and you should know why."

He wasn't sure what to say. If he confessed he didn't know, she'd be mad, and if he took a guess, it could be fatal. So he just stood there and waited for a clue.

A minute clicked by and he couldn't stand the silence. "I'm sorry."

She stepped closer. "For what?" Her big, brown eyes held more hope than anger. Whatever it was he was supposed to know about must be very important to her.

"Leaving so abruptly yesterday."

She tilted her head to the side and kept her eyes on him.

When she didn't respond, he continued. "And not fetching you today?"

She stood straight, the tension gone. Her defenses dropped, and she let out a breath. "What are you doing here, Caleb?"

He frowned. "I've told you."

"Tell me again, because I'm confused." Her eyes watered as she gazed at him, waiting.

"What do you want me to say or do? I wouldn't be here if

it weren't for you, no other reason. Just you." Right at that moment, he questioned why he'd come too. "I'll do whatever it takes to prove that to you. Just tell me how."

No matter what he said, Emma looked miserable. "Never mind. I shouldn't have to ask." The next thing he knew, her back was to him, and she was in the buggy, going home.

Chapter Forty

Now that she'd had time to think about it, Emma was embarrassed she'd talked to Caleb that way. He was trying to settle into the community and find his place here. That was hard enough, and then there was Abe, who probably came to mind often, as well as everyone else he'd left behind. Not to mention she was already in a sour mood after dealing with Zeb.

"You people do everything the hard way," Monique said to Emma and Martha, as they lit gas lamps around the *haus*.

Monique seemed to be coming around a little more, but Emma didn't know whether she would ever get used to the work ethic of the Amish. Emma had noticed that when she was in the city. People would work at desks but wanted food made for them and someone to wash their clothes, among other things the Amish did themselves.

"Did you know some people sent the hymns we sing and a picture of a barn-raising into space?" Martha informed Monique as she handed her a smaller lamp that went on the kitchen table.

"Is that true?" Monique seemed interested, but didn't sound like she believed what she was hearing.

"That's what my teacher said." Martha glanced up at the porch where her *dawdi* and *mammi* nodded off to sleep. Emma went up the stairs the same time as Monique, watching *dawdi* snore.

Monique looked at them. "They make you feel better about getting old."

"And that relationships can endure." The elderly couple, so relaxed and serene, didn't even know they were there.

"Wasn't like this when I was growing up. My granddad was never around, and when he was, he was ornery. I can't imagine living all together like you do." She looked toward the *dawdihaus* where Emma's grandparents lived. "I couldn't let a man be the boss of me."

Emma understood her position completely. Monique had every right to feel the way she did, but Emma came from a different way of thinking. "The way we say it is the man is the head and the woman is the neck."

"I don't get it." Monique squinted her eyes.

"The man may decide, but the woman can turn his head to change the way he's thinking." Maria answered this time, and Monique smiled as she soaked in the meaning.

"How do you make a living? It can't just be from the goodies you sell and quilts you make." Monique gathered the lighters and followed Emma to the rockers on the porch. They sat and looked across the fields that burst with vibrant color, prime for harvesting soon.

Maria leaned against the white banister that ran the length of the porch. "The mainstay of our economy is cash crop, but we also do other things to make ends meet. Land is getting harder to find and afford."

Emma rolled her head over to Monique, too lazy to lift her head to look at her. "You seem to have settled in a little."

Monique shrugged. "Somewhat. I don't worry so much here, and I'm getting used to the quiet. Drove me crazy when I first got here, but now I sort of like it."

"Can I ask you something without you getting mad?" Emma asked.

"Am I that bad?"

Maria grinned. "Sometimes, *jah*."

Emma waited for the nod from Monique and took a chance she'd get an honest answer from her. "I see Merv look your way during church, and sometimes you look back."

Monique lurched back as if shocked. "He may be looking at me, but I am *not* looking at him." She wagged her finger for emphasis.

Maria giggled, and Emma smiled to herself. Monique's response confirmed what she'd seen. "If you say so. But I do wonder what keeps you here."

Monique slowly looked over their farm. "I stick out, but people here haven't made a big deal about it."

"What about the chores?" Emma teased. That was the worst part for Monique, and she knew it. Once she got the routine down, Monique had stopped complaining, but Emma still heard her grumble from time to time.

A shrill scream came from the barnyard. They all stood.

"I'll get *Mamm*." Maria hurried into the *haus*.

Emma and Monique ran toward the sound that came again. Emma knew it was Martha's screech they'd heard. Monique passed Emma at an alarming rate, but when she turned the corner, she stopped cold. Caleb was kneeling, holding Martha in his arms.

Emma rushed over and squatted next to them. "Is she all right?"

"Mule kicked her pretty good." He showed her the red mark on her thigh that was growing brighter as they spoke.

"Let's get some ice on it." Emma caught Caleb's eye and

tipped one side of her lips to show him she was grateful he was there. "You must have caught her right away."

"That mule is a crotchety old thing." Caleb looked down at her. "But then, Martha shouldn't have been teasing him, either."

Martha frowned and nestled into his chest.

Monique went to the *haus* ahead of them and had a bag of ice in the works when they walked in. *Mamm* placed a towel on Martha's leg and put the ice on it. "How's that?"

"Too cold." Martha's tiny voice could barely be heard. "Sorry, Caleb."

She'd always had a crush on Caleb, which is the only reason Emma could rationalize why she was apologizing to him.

"For what?" He brushed a curl away from her eyes and listened. Emma admired his strong jaw and attentive ear. It wasn't possible to stay angry with him. But it was more than that. It was this whole mess they'd had for years, from the time he'd left leading up to this very moment. Emma needed things to settle into whatever it was meant to be; they both did.

"Walking on the fence." Martha shied away, holding her hands up over her face with only her blue eyes showing.

"You were on the fence by the mule's pasture?" His head tilted and his brows lifted. "You were asking for trouble."

"I didn't think Festus would kick me." Her bottom lip stuck out, taking the kick personally.

"His name doesn't fit him. He's not one bit joyous. He's always given me a hard time when I've hitched him to the wagon." He smiled, making her smile, and Emma couldn't help but join in.

"You come sit over here with me, and we'll eat some of this bread." Maria got out the milk and cut up the friendship bread they'd made that morning—Martha's favorite.

Emma turned her attention to Caleb. "*Danke*. I'm glad you were there when it happened."

"Me, too." He moved his head toward the door. "Wanna take a walk?"

"*Jah*, I'd like that." She glanced at Martha. "Are you all right?" Emma didn't need to ask. Martha seemed perfectly content with her fresh milk and bread sprinkled with cinnamon.

Martha nodded up and down more than once, and Monique covered her mouth so she could eat and answer at the same time. "Go. We're good."

He led them out the door, and they strolled in silence to the nearby pond. The old willow tree's leaves swayed in the wind and frogs leaped into the water as they approached. Emma waited for him to say something, but he remained quiet.

"Why did you come over?" She crossed her arms over her chest, feeling the need to protect herself. She felt something was going on in his mind that she didn't want to hear. She'd rather get it over with and stop wondering.

"When I finished the chores, I set out walking. I was deep in thought, and before I knew it, I was at your farm." It was quiet again—somewhat awkward, but not enough to break the silence, so she waited.

"It seemed like a long two years."

She didn't know what he meant at first, and then she decided that he had been gone a long time. She started wondering where this was going.

"The last one was harder." She knew what he meant. It was a difficult but enlightening time for both of them. She had felt before that it had been harder for her, but after being in his world, she could see it was probably harder for him. She'd had family and a predictable way of life, whereas he had many needs to meet, especially concerning his brother.

"I never did evangelize like I wanted to." She was thinking it. It didn't need to be said. He knew that already.

Caleb looked over at her with a stern expression. "You mean with Monique?" He shook his head. "You've done more for her than you ever could have in Philly." He turned toward her. "God had me put you with her, you answered the call, and now she's here with you. Don't you see how amazing that is?"

A wave of incredible redemption flowed through her mind and soul. Emma had been so hard on herself when she left, but Caleb was right. She had been evangelizing from the time she met Monique.

The spiritual high plummeted at the sight of Zeb's buggy coming down the road to her *haus*.

"I missed you." She hadn't meant to say what she felt, at least not yet, but an overwhelming need to tell him had taken over when she saw that buggy.

He didn't look at her or answer, just kept looking at the prairie grass bending in the wind. "If you ever change your mind—"

"About what?" Emma bit her tongue to stop the urge to tell him how much she wanted to make this happen between them. *But if I've read his signals wrong...*

"Zeb." His sad eyes pierced hers.

Emma decided not to tell him the truth about Zeb. He didn't need to know everything—no one did. Zeb's own conscience would guilt him into submitting to God. Nothing she could do or say would hold the same significance. And it would mean more to Caleb knowing she wanted him over Zeb even if she hadn't discovered his true motives for courting her.

"What would happen if I did change my mind?"

"You would have no other choice"—his eyes glistened into the morning sun, taking her all in—"but to marry me."

Zeb pulled up, and Caleb started walking down the dirt path away from her farm, away from her. The best friend she'd ever had. She would never know if they could have had more between them. No choice had been made.

"Caleb!" She put up a hand up to block the sun so she could see him. She squinted, making out his silhouette, unsure whether he was moving away or walking back to her.

She started walking, then running, her shoes hitting the soft dirt leaving puffs of dust kicking up behind her, until she reached him.

Caleb turned when she got closer and waited, watching her with wide eyes. Emma stared at him, thinking about what he'd said. She stopped and caught her breath. "That's all I've ever wanted. You always have been, and I'll make sure you will always be, no matter where you are or what you're doing, as long as it's with me."

He closed his eyes and enveloped her in his arms.

Caleb was home at last.

GLOSSARY

ach — oh
Ausbund — hymnal
bruder — brother
daed — father
danke — thank you
dawdi — grandfather
dawdihaus — addition to the house for grandparents
Englisher — non-Amish person
Gott — God
gut — good
hallo — hello
haus — house
jah — yes
kapp — hat
mamm — mother
mammi — grandmother
nee — no
rumspringa — teenagers running around
shunned — disregarded

Coming From Beth Shriver Fall 2014

Clara's Wish

Chapter One

Come home. Clara needs you.

That's all the letter said.

Home was the last place Zack Schrock wanted to be, but it was about his sister, Clara, so he'd made plans to leave straightaway. Questions flew through his mind. It had to be something bad for Lizzy to be the one to write to him. He didn't particularly like Lizzy, but she was friends with Clara, so he tolerated her.

Clara was the only one in the community who kept in touch with him, and that was only by letters. Guilt washed over him now that he thought of how few times he had written back. He'd lived in the city long enough now to pick up a phone, something the community frowned on.

Her community, not his; he'd washed his hands of that place years ago, and he had no plans to go back. Not that they'd let him.

Dried prairie grass bent in the breeze as the cold Pennsylvania wind whistled through the window of his beat down rental car. He looked over his shoulder as he neared the town of Lititz, and patted the duffel bag by his side. If the sheriff didn't get to him before he made it to the community, he'd be in good shape. The police wouldn't look for him there. He didn't have to avoid any cops leaving Philadelphia either, one advantage of living in a big city.

One question plagued him: Why would Lizzy write instead of Clara? Something was very wrong, and it made the drive seem twice as long as it was. His mind raced, but all that came through loud and clear was that she was ill. She'd fought off illness when she was young.

Lord, please don't let it be that again.

That would make all of his troubles seem small, although he did have some bad choices catching up with him. If something happened to Clara, he'd make a vow to God he'd change his ways. He was in a bad place, but God understood, didn't He? Surely He wouldn't let Clara die.

The light of the small town lighting up the gray sky like a beacon did little to keep the foreboding from creeping up inside him. He couldn't remember the last time he was home, but he did remember the last conversation he'd had with his father, confirming his decision to leave. His two younger brothers might not even recognize him. If it wasn't for Clara, he wouldn't be there at all.

Clara had told him she wanted to make a visit, travel to the city and spend some time there with him for a short while, but her true intentions were revealed when she told him she really wanted him to come home to stay. He wondered now whether she'd known something back then about what Lizzy was telling him.

"It's been long enough you were away from your own flesh and blood, Zack Schrock." Clara's voice was sharp, like their mother's, impossible to ignore, and easily swayed him. She had tried to get him to agree to come home for Christmas. He'd had no intention to go, but it was weeks before Christmas, so why the hurry?

Yet, he'd come as far as his car would take him.

Well, now he was on empty, and he would have to go in and pay cash at a gas station. A strange noise in the engine had started up a few miles back, so for once in a very long time, he was glad he was back in this small town of Lititz, Pennsylvania. But Zack had to be cautious and take situations into his own hands. Because of his past he couldn't do things the easy or legal way, but Clara must need help so Zack would do what he had to.

He filled up and put some oil in the car, and scanned the area once he was behind the driver's seat. He was close, and the last few miles created anxiety as he thought of entering a place that didn't want him. The horse and buggy trotting along going the other direction told him how close he was. The exhaust from his car and constant bouncing irritated him, and he wished for the shiny black Mercedes he drove in the city.

A cough from the exhaust forced him forward, encouraging him to pick up the pace, but the way his car was sputtering, he couldn't.

"Won't be too long now," he muttered.

There would be no comfort for him once he got there.

EXPERIENCE THE

Beauty of the Amish Community With a Touch of Grace

After learning she was adopted, Annie sets out on a journey to find out who she really is, but she may lose the only family she has ever known.

Elsie Yoder can't forgive her sister for leaving the Amish community. Can she humble herself enough to give and receive the grace that is needed?

When Abigail's abusive father becomes violent, an Amish community is the only place she can turn to. Can she overcome her pain and find love and acceptance there?

AVAILABLE AT YOUR LOCAL BOOKSTORE
AND IN E-BOOK

WWW.CHARISMAHOUSE.COM
WWW.BETHSHRIVERWRITER.COM

12504

Why subscribe today?

- ❑ **DELIVERED DIRECTLY TO YOU.** All you have to do is open your inbox and read.
- ❑ **EXCLUSIVE CONTENT.** We cover the news overlooked by the mainstream press.
- ❑ **STAY CURRENT.** Find the latest court rulings, revivals, and cultural trends.
- ❑ **UPDATE OTHERS.** Easy to forward to friends and family with the click of your mouse.

CHOOSE THE E-NEWSLETTER THAT INTERESTS YOU MOST:

- Christian news
- Daily devotionals
- Spiritual empowerment
- And much, much more

SIGN UP AT: **http://freenewsletters.charismamag.com**

8178